DEATH

Although best known for her children's series of 'Jill' pony books, Ruby Ferguson wrote in a wide range of genres; detective, romantic and supernatural novels, as well as children's books. She was born Ruby Constance Ashby in 1899 in West Yorkshire, the daughter of a Wesleyan minister. Her English degree from Oxford and her experience as a publisher's reader and book reviewer provided good grounding for her literary career. She began writing detective stories as serials in the *Manchester Guardian's* weekly subsidiary, the *City News*, on which she was a reporter. Her first book. *Moorland Man*, appeared in 1926. and several more 'R. C. Ashby' detective stories followed, many having a supernatural element to them (*Out Went the Taper, He Arrived at Dusk*). She married Samuel Ferguson in 1934, and turned to writing romantic novels under her married name, Ruby Ferguson. The best known of these is probably *Lady Rose and Mrs Memmary* (1937), apparently a favourite of the late Queen Elizabeth, the Queen Mother. Another great favourite is *Apricot Sky*, a charming comedy of manners set in the Western Highlands. Her last book was her fictionalised autobiography, *Children at the Shop*, and she died in 1966.

Also by R. C. Ashby

Moorland Man
The Tale of Rowan Christie
Beauty Bewitched
Plot Against a Widow
He Arrived at Dusk
One Way Traffic
Out Went the Taper

DEATH ON TIPTOE

R. C. ASHBY

Greyladies

Published by
Greyladies
an imprint of The Old Children's Bookshelf
175 Canongate, Edinburgh EH8 8BN

© R.C.Ashby 1931

This edition first published 2009
Design and layout © Shirley Neilson 2009
Preface © Kirstie Taylor 2009

ISBN 978-0-9559413-5-1

All rights reserved. No part of this publication may be reproduced, stored in or introduced into a retrieval system, or transmitted, in any form or by any means (electronic, mechanical, photocopying, recording or otherwise) without the prior written permission of the above copyright owners and the above publisher of this book.

Set in Sylfaen / Perpetua
Printed in Great Britain by the
MPG Books Group, Bodmin and King's Lynn

Preface

From its first sentence *Death on Tiptoe* sets the tone for a Gothic literary mystery. " 'Childe Roland to the Dark Tower came!' said Lionel West and, glancing at his companion, laughed at the aptness of the quotation." Rather than finding it funny, those of Miss Ashby's readers who knew their Robert Browning would consider that such a comparison augured ill for Mr. West's visit to Cleys Castle. While the poem's outcome might be so shrouded in obscurity that in *Falconer's Lure* [Antonia Forest], Peter Marlow and his friend could produce quotations to support either victory *or* defeat for Childe Roland, the most a jaded Mr. West has to look forward to is winning the fight to the death. And yes, Cleys – "Backed by the mountains of the Welsh border, the twin towers of the keep commanded a widening plain," does correspond rather too closely for comfort to the ominous Dark Tower.

The idea that fairy stories are cautionary tales guiding one through life (what to do if you meet a good-looking wolf in the forest, for instance,) seems to have passed the characters by. Lionel West, like others in the story, recognises the similarities but doesn't heed the warning. Using well-known poetic versions of folk tales such as 'Childe Roland' or 'The Mistletoe Bough' [Thomas Haynes Bayly] heightens the suspense; a character treads blindly to her doom while the alert reader is shrieking "Don't do it!"

Continuing the helpful hints to readers, some of the characters' names are highly suggestive: Pandora Hyde, for example, (*not* Pandora Jekyll!), who undergoes a sudden change. However, the most flagrant signalling of a person's character is reserved for the castle's châtelaine, who is called – " 'Undine?' 'Yes. It . . . kind of suits her'." And that's her *husband* speaking! One can only assume that this jovial chap had missed out on one of the most famous literary fairy tales. Baron Friedrich de la Motte Fouqué's *Undine* is a water-sprite who has to marry a human to gain a soul (hardly an altruistic basis for marriage), she contrives to be rescued by a knight (does being stranded on an island *sound* like a problem for a water-sprite?) and she waits until she's safely married before revealing that she's not actually a mortal. (Lady Undine Stacey's secret is a little bit different) Just to emphasize the point, Lady Stacey has "rippling" auburn hair, exactly like the 1909 edition of *Undine* illustrated by Arthur Rackham. Any husband of such an Undine has serious cause to be worried for no, the fairy story doesn't end Happily Ever After. But Harry Stacey optimistically believes in his wife.

Gullible or sinister, the characters are all potentially dangerous; animal comparisons abound - "inwardly we are all ravening wolves" – after all, one them is capable of murder. Then there are the children.

As befits a future children's author, Miss Ashby gives a delightfully realistic portrait of a pair of brats. It is noticeable that despite describing his children as "topping", Sir Harry manages to see very little of them - that is the poor governess's privilege, and *she* describes the girl as "a perfect little fiend." Both the children are attracted to immorality and nastiness; Lionel West "had thought that the minds of nice children would gravitate naturally to the heroic characters of the history book. But had his own? He remembered Deadwood Dick" No false Victorian sentimentality here.

No, it's a darker past that is evoked, and one that has passed its sell-by-date. The builders of Cleys, the Sabelle Marcher Lords, originally held power of life or death, now the current, dispossessed, heir describes himself as the "Court Jester". Decayed past grandeur runs throughout the story; the banquet hall is structurally unsound; the Sabelles have been replaced - modest Sir Harry considers that he is "the wrong sort of fellow to own Cleys . . . I hope the household gods don't despise a tame fellow like me!" Maybe, maybe not, but just to highlight that things ain't what they used to be, when a guest dresses up in Tudor finery from the castle, at first glance she presents a brilliant picture, but "to one who scrutinised, the gold and silver were tarnished, the velvet was moth-eaten, the brocade slit in its folds and the gay colours sadly piebald."

Such characters look on the past as a Technicolor backdrop; they regard costumes, tapestries or oubliettes as Romantic props for their games with no relevance to the twentieth century. But on the Welsh Marches one century is very like another. Lionel West realises this when looking at his fellow guests: "In what way does this company differ from the folk of what we call the Dark Ages? . . . Has love changed, or greed, or passion, or loyalty, or jealousy or hate?' " Immediately a guest says they are "safe in a place like this so long as we keep the lights of the twentieth century burning." Then Undine switches off the lights for Hide-and-Seek. Playing games with history is dangerous.

The physical connection to that history, Cleys Castle, is almost a character in its own right, eliciting reactions as diverse as "a priceless treasure preserved from the past" to "a mouldy old ruin". Its sinister grandeur is painted with a lavish hand: light is lurid, ivy hangs like a pall, walls are hoary, and rafters ring with the shrieks of death. Naturally there are rooks uttering harsh cries from the castle walls. Apart from providing a Gothic setting for the action, Cleys' layout mirrors the murder mystery in a maze of confusing stone. On her way to the garret, Undine pursues a "circuitous" route and Mr. West, searching for the dining-room, "blundered helplessly in a maze of ancient by-ways."

Lionel West also struggles through the intellectual maze of the murder, worrying about motive, distrusting friends, being deceived, and following blind alleys until he reaches the point of confusion where "in this atmosphere of strange happenings, death and suspicion, he could not help wondering whether such trivial events as the disappearance of an heiress and twenty-two silver pepper-pots had a deeper and more sinister meaning." Maybe, maybe not.

The policeman might determinedly state: "We're not in a melodrama here . . . " but he's wrong. This is a Gothic melodrama with an heroic finale, an Agatha Christie-esque summing up, and a reward for Lionel West including "three new books from his favourite bookseller." Let us hope that they were as atmospheric and intriguing as *Death on Tiptoe*

Kirstie Taylor, Edinburgh, 2009.

DEATH ON TIPTOE

Chapter I
THE DARK TOWER

" 'CHILDE ROLAND to the Dark Tower came!' " said Lionel West, and glancing at his companion laughed at the aptness of the quotation.

Cleys Castle flung its swart shoulders back against a wet, saffron sky where tattered rags of cloud fluttered like banners above the Norman keep, and the waves of the moat, reflecting that evil light, fretted in yellow flood the downward plunging of the tremendous walls.

Cleys stood heavy and uncompromising upon the mound which had held it for a thousand years; the drawbridge down, the portcullis lifted, waiting for a troop of cavalry; a king; a shrieking prisoner; or a Rolls-Royce car bringing the master and a friend home from town. Restored through the centuries by successive owners, the old pile had never lost its air of brooding majesty. It held its secrets well. Backed by the mountains of the Welsh border, the twin towers of the keep commanded a widening plain, in summer thinly wooded, but now desolate and haunted under the October wind by poor ghosts of thickets, lost and shivering along the edges of the high road. It was impossible to imagine this grim giantess of a castle with her battlements and arrow-slits as a twentieth century home; a fortress, a prison, a fantasy out of the past, perhaps. . . What was the meaning of her challenge?

"Dark deeds have been done here," said Lionel West, in what Harry called his "Old Bailey voice."

A ragged flight of rooks tore out of the yellow heaven and circled the massive walls; the black shadow seemed to creep closer into the shelter of the mountains; across the miles of the wild Welsh country went the soughing October wind. Nothing else stirred but the ancient water and the chains of the drawbridge.

Harry Stacey laughed.

"You always were romantic, West. So the place gives you the creeps? We'll soon put that right with a drink and a few gramophone records. All twentieth century comforts when we get beyond the keep."

The Rolls plunged over the drawbridge and entered the frowning gates of antiquity. Both men were silent.

Lionel West, K.C., tired of the South, tired of the East, sated with sunshine, bored and neuralgic and over-strung, longing for the work he was strictly forbidden to do, had prowled day after day in the wet streets of London and spent muggy evenings with a book over his bachelor fire. His friends, lucky fellows, were all busy. It maddened him to hear them talk about their work. He followed their cases in the papers, forecasted their line of defence, prepared appropriate speeches, bit on his pipe and cursed when they went astray.

It was October, a depressing month. After Christmas he would drag himself to Cannes, but meanwhile – what?

He went out in search of tobacco, and in the shop met Harry Stacey.

Such things do happen. Harry! With whom he had rolled, a muddied oaf on the Rugger field, who had lived on his staircase at Oriel, and littered his rooms, and shared his last fiver, and whom he had lost for sixteen years.

The recognition was mutual.

"Stacey?" Rather hesitant, uncertain.

"West? . . . West!"

"My good fellow, what are you doing here?"

"Buying tobacco, old thing; what else? Look here, come and have something to eat! I've got to catch a train."

They sat opposite one another at a small table. After an excited exchange of news and reminiscences West said, "Didn't I read in the paper a few months ago that you'd bought Cleys Castle?"

Stacey smiled. He was forty and had the frank, ingenuous face of a schoolboy. He had been popular at Oxford, having a tremendous gift for friendship and simple, unassuming ways, in spite of being the grandson of Sir Digby Stacey, the shipowner and the richest man in England.

"Yes. I bought Cleys from the Sabelles. I was sorry to see an old family like that go under, but the last three generations have – well, mismanaged to say the least of it. Degenerate . . . it's a pity. We have young Cecil Sabelle staying with us now; the last of the line, and they've owned Cleys since the twelfth century. He's a pleasant young fool. You see, my grandfather died and Edward and I were his heirs."

He said it modestly and with a slight blush, as though he felt he ought to apologise for inheriting practically a half-share of old Sir Digby's eleven millions, to say nothing of the baronetcy.

West thought, "Dear old Harry! He hasn't altered a bit. He'd be far happier with five hundred a year and a bungalow and a Baby Austin."

He said aloud, "What has happened to Edward?"

"Edward? Oh, he's staying with us, too. He's just back from twelve years on the Afghan frontier; Major in a Sikh regiment. Just the same lad . . . good old Edward."

The brothers had always been devoted to one another. It had been a mean trick on the part of old Sir Digby to send them to different schools, then one to Oxford and one to Sandhurst.

In appearance they were utterly unlike. Edward the soldier took after his mother's people, the handsome Meads of Gloucestershire, and was in his youth the finest figure of a man West had ever seen; Harry was a throwback to some honest strain of industrial Lancashire; but they had always thought the world of one another and done their best to disguise the fact, scorning any suspicion of demonstrativeness.

"You must come down to Cleys," said Stacey; "What are you doing? Can you come at once?"

"Yes, I'm not working – unluckily. Doctor's orders."

"Good! Then why not travel down with me to-morrow? I'm going to Guildford now, but I shall be back in town and could meet you at Paddington to-morrow for the 2.7. Would that suit you? My wife has a few friends, quite a nice crowd. Helps to brighten up this foul October weather."

West welcomed the invitation; it promised a relief from boredom, and the blowing airs of the country instead of London smoke.

"So you're married, Harry?" He smiled. "Do you

remember at Oriel, we were going to be bachelors and share a flat in town? I've got that bachelor flat, alone. It looks as though I owed your wife a grudge."

Stacey's youthful face softened into yet more boyish lines.

"Wait till you meet Undine! It was a bit of a romance, you know."

"Undine?"

"Yes. It . . . kind of suits her. I'll tell you."

He pushed his cup away.

"It was twelve years ago. I was having a wandering holiday, alone in France. I got to a little village, Gosière, ten miles from Avignon, and at the inn I found a beautiful girl, alone and in mourning. That was Undine. Poor child, it was a pathetic story. Her father was an American artist and they'd lived a jolly, vagabond life, the pair of them, all over France and England and Austria. He had died two months before, and there she was, utterly alone and bewildered, still wandering without a friend to protect her."

"A young girl?"

"She was twenty-six, but that's young enough to be stranded. She had about two hundred pounds. I simply had to do something for her – ("That's like Harry!" thought West; "Homeless animals, homeless girls, he has to do something for them!") – and to tell you the truth, West, it was easy to fall for a girl like that. I'd have married her on the spot, but I was afraid she'd be frightened. I got her to come to England to Lady Mead. And the end of it was we were married in six months."

Lady Mead was their mother's cousin who had brought

Harry and Edward up.

Stacey's face glowed with the remembered romance and delight. West, more cynical, thought it sagacious of Miss Undine to have got herself stranded in the same village inn as the soft-hearted heir to half of eleven millions.

"So you've been married twelve years! Time swoops by, Harry."

"Rather!" Stacey beamed. "We've got two topping children. You'll see them tomorrow. And the castle is simply magnificent. You've never seen it? Well, I'm the wrong sort of fellow to own it. It suits Edward better. I've stood in the courtyard and pictured Edward, riding out in black armour at the head of his troop of halberdiers. Or hurling back an army from the battlements; or entertaining the king in the banqueting hall, with minstrels and men-at-arms. I hope the household gods don't despise a tame fellow like me . . . but then I'm as good-looking a man as young Sabelle, if he has got the blood!" He chuckled boyishly . . . "I must send a wire down to say that you're coming. Now don't forget! 2.7 at Paddington."

The nearest station to Cleys Castle was Cwm Dyffod, ten miles away. Driving through a rainstorm which obliterated the view of the spreading country and open hills, West said: "I want long talks with you and Edward. Are there many people down?"

He was thinking that a large house party might prove a terrible nuisance, for he disliked 'society' in its accepted sense and was not tempted by a prospect of bridge, dress, gossip, and flirtation. Young women with their unmodulated voices, long legs, uniform garb, and flat metallic hair, he abhorred.

He cast an anxious eye upon Stacey, who replied with admirable understanding: "Well, the castle's big enough, if you want peace. Enid is down, and her husband. You remember my cousin Enid?"

"Lady Mead's daughter? Whom did she marry?"

"Oh, Willoughby – Jack Willoughby. Rather a rabbit . . . Poor Enid! I mean, he's supposed to be in the Diplomatic, but he has been quietly removed from two embassies already and is at present 'out of a job.' You know what that means . . . sheer inefficiency. Galling for a capable girl like Enid. I never could understand why she took the fellow."

"Has she been married long?"

"They were married about two years after Undine and myself. We often have them to stay, for Enid's sake. Being brought up together she was practically a sister to Edward and me. There's nothing mean about Enid." He lighted a cigarette, and frowned over it for a moment; then added, "But you want to know what social horrors await you. There's young Sabelle – I told you about him. It seems only decent to keep him on the premises where his ancestors have lived and died for the last thousand years. He's amusing and the children like him; so do the dogs, and that's supposed to be a recommendation according to the old wives' tale. And there's Basil Crown — "

"*The* Basil Crown?"

Stacey grinned.

"If by *the* Basil Crown you mean the five-foot-nothing of pretty male arrogance who draws pastel sketches of duchesses and gives interviews to women's papers on Why

Women Lose Charm, we have the identical article at Cleys."

"But, my good Harry, why?"

"Because he's doing pastels of the children. Undine likes his work, and he's fashionable. Unfortunately, he's one of those people who can't stand success. Two years ago he was a decent young fellow, quite unknown, living in a bed-sitting-room at Battersea and selling black-and-white sketches to provincial papers. By a stroke of luck he was 'discovered' by Monty Richmile, and now he spends his mornings deciding which to accept out of six luncheon invitations. Bah, says I; pish tush! That's all the party, except for a couple of girls. Do you know Rene Fullerton?"

"I knew her father, if you mean Fullerton the builder."

"Good fellow. Of course she's an heiress now and they've given her a season in town. I think it's a pity. I liked her better with her attractive Lancashire bluntness before she acquired her social graces. She won't trouble you, West; she's rather occupied with young Crown. The other girl is Pandora Hyde, vicar's daughter. She doesn't get much fun and Undine asked her down for a treat. Now you talk as much as you like to Edward if I'm not available. We shan't call you unsociable . . . This is wild country, isn't it?"

West looked out across a tangled waste of fen and woodland glistening with rain under the passing storm.

"I suppose I'm seeing it at its worst. Why did this storm spring up so suddenly?"

"Our weather's treacherous," said Stacey; "we're so near the mountains. But the rain is stopping. In five minutes you'll see Cleys in all her grandeur."

The clouds parted sullenly, and great gaps of sky became splashed with the colour of a washed-out sun; and there out of the fenland sprang Cleys Castle, flaunting its menacing frontage, threatening the stranger as it had threatened through the ages the approaching foe.

"There she is, West."

" 'Childe Roland to the Dark Tower came!' " quoted Lionel West.

Chapter II
UNDINE

"Rita! If you don't put that whip down and learn your verbs I shall ask your mother not to let you ride tomorrow!"

"That won't make any difference. She's keener that I should ride well than know French verbs."

"Shut up, Rita!" shouted Nicholas suddenly. "You've flicked my leg, you beast!"

He snatched the switch from his sister and threw it on the fire. Rita screamed and struck at him with her French grammar. The ink was overturned and a thick black stream flowed over Nicholas's neat copy. He was proud of his work and this infuriated him. Plunging his hands into Rita's long hair he tugged until his sister was hysterical with rage and pain.

Amy Farbell tried to separate them, and received an accidental blow on the cheek which made her feel faint. In the midst of the hubbub a little French clock struck three with its sweet chime. The fighting children fell apart; it was the signal for their release.

"Put the books away," commanded Amy sharply.

With more haste than precision they bundled the lesson books on the shelf and into the cupboard.

"Hurrah, it's still fine!" yelled Nicholas. "Don't let's bother with tea; I want to show you where that rat was yesterday."

When they were gone, Amy Farbell flopped down in the

deep window seat with a sigh. Her head ached to-day, and Rita's punch on the cheek had not improved her feelings. It was no joke being governess to the young Staceys at Cleys Castle.

The castle itself was romantic enough, and she loved living there and exploring the old, dim rooms and ruins; but the children were spoilt and difficult to manage, and she was often lonely and longed for company.

Amy Farbell was twenty-two, but she looked eighteen; slim and fair, and with large grey eyes, at once wistful and wary as though they wanted desperately to laugh and sparkle but dared not for fear of a rebuff. She had no home. Her parents were dead, and she was fortunate to have such a splendid post with the Staceys; but sometimes she wished that she had a home to visit in the holidays, instead of dragging about some French *plage* with Rita and Nicholas, while Sir Harry and Lady Stacey sought more sophisticated pleasures elsewhere.

It was three o'clock, and beyond preparing the raffia designs for the children's handwork to-morrow, her duty was over for the day. She drew her knees up to her little pointed chin, and gazed out of her casement window in the thickness of the great castle wall.

The regular schoolroom was being decorated, and the children were having lessons in Amy's own little room in the East Turret. Below her window was a red shale tennis court where three people stood swinging rackets, apparently waiting for a fourth.

Amy recognised them with interest: Mrs. Willoughby, in her perfectly fitting white wool sweater and white pleated skirt; Mr. Sabelle; and – yes, it was! The hero, Major Stacey.

Amy's grey eyes grew larger. This handsome man, this military Adonis, who faced savage tribes, won battles, wore a breastful of decorations and piloted his own plane, was lately home from the performance of these wonderful deeds on the Indian frontier. He was to Amy Farbell a reincarnation of all the gods and heroes – Achilles, Hannibal, Charlemagne, Prince Charlie. Breathlessly she admired as he tightened the net. How fine were his hands, his shoulders, the powerful lift of his bronze head!

For whom were the three waiting? Miss Hyde, or the heiress, Miss Fullerton?

A wave of self-pity swept over her. Why should those girls have everything and she nothing? Why should they be able to play tennis, and laugh down there with Major Stacey in their beautiful white clothes, while she, Amy Farbell, the governess, might only watch from a casement window? She was pretty too; she was just as fond of beautiful things as those privileged creatures, but oh! the gulf between them! Miss Fullerton's frocks . . . that severe little green moire she wore the other night with the chiffon coat must have cost more than Amy could spend on clothes in a whole year. Lady Stacey had let her come down that night to the billiard-room, and they had danced. She had danced twice – with Sir Harry, who was always kind, and with Mr. Willoughby; both dull, married men. Major Stacey had danced with Mrs. Willoughby, and Mr. Crown with Miss Fullerton, and Mr. Sabelle with Miss Hyde, who was one of those sulky, Spanish-looking beauties.

Amy hadn't enjoyed it very much, though Lady Stacey

had meant kindly in asking her down. It had only emphasised her loneliness, and the strange "difference" which society exacted between herself and these people.

It was twenty past three. The people on the tennis court were getting impatient.

"This won't do!" thought Amy. "Sitting here only makes me drearier and drearier, like the young nun of Siberia."

With an effort she got to her feet, rubbed an impatient hand over her tired brow, and began to search for her sewing basket.

In the oldest part of the castle, the original Norman keep, bare and grim, was the boudoir of Undine, Lady Stacey; and there at her desk she sat, writing letters. She wore a green silk dress patterned with violet flowers, the same colour as the wide eyes which had bewitched Harry Stacey at Gosière; and under the softened light of the high windows her auburn hair, rippling from its central parting, was dimmed to the gold of a saint's head painted in a missal.

This room Undine had chosen out of the whole castle, for it was high and cool, stonewalled and chastely dignified as the bower of a great lady should be; and upon the smooth wall hung a wonderful tapestry twelve feet square, depicting the return of Yves de Sabelle from the first crusade.

Pondering over a tricky sentence, Undine's violet eyes leapt to the drooping flag on the north turret, and found the gap in the crumbled battlement through which she could see the wild blue mountains of Wales. She was conscious of a peculiar sense of exaltation. Her heart shouted. She had been mistress of Cleys Castle for six months, and already she felt as though it were her ancestral home. She was fiercely proud of every stone of it; far prouder, far more possessive than the Sabelles, who had allowed the place to go to ruin, gambled away all its treasure, and gladly sold to strangers their thousand-year-old inheritance.

Undine thought, "My son Nicholas will grow up here. His son will be born here, a real Stacey of Cleys. In a hundred years Harry and I will have founded a great line to live in a great house!" She turned to the long mirror on the stone wall and confirmed her own beauty. Thirty-eight, and still most beautiful, because so happy . . . the happiest woman in the world, for she had everything she had ever wanted. She would talk to Nicholas; make him realise his responsibility. He was only eight, but old enough to love the place and treasure jealously every stone of it.

The room darkened as a few clouds climbed the high, limitless sky. She switched on her electric lamp and, sitting to her desk, wrote:

My dear Sharlie,
It was good of you to ask me to act in your Orphans' Home Pageant. At the time I said I thought I could do so, and was looking forward to it, but now things have become awkward. Harry and I have to go to Scotland on the 17th, the day before the pageant, and I very much fear that —

Bang!
Somebody had hurled one terrific, thudding blow upon the door.

Undine started, and said angrily: "Who is that? Come in – quietly, please!"

"I say! I'm frightfully sorry! A bogy grabbed my leg, and I fell against your door."

The young man pushed in his head and giggled. She might have known it was Cecil Sabelle! No one else in the house could be quite such a prize idiot.

A lanky, flannelled figure sidled in.

"What is it, Cecil? I'm in the middle of a letter."

She felt like adding that her men guests did not usually come blundering into her boudoir, but one had to excuse a lot in this young scion of a noble house.

He held a tennis racket before his face, and gave an abandoned imitation of a monkey in a cage.

"I say, Lady Stacey, would you mind having a look for Miss Hyde? Is she dead, or – or blotto, or anything? We said tennis at three and it's now twenty-past, and we're a bit fed up with waiting. If she's dead, shove the corpse down the *oubliette* – first to the right past the chapel – and come yourself; but the light goes so quickly, and Mrs. Willoughby —"

"Miss Hyde is probably in her room," said Undine; "I'll go and see. Go back to the others, Cecil; I'll send her down."

"Thanks, most awfully. Forgive my foul intrusion!"

The young man held open the door with exaggerated politeness and, bowing low, his long lock of hair tumbled across his impudent face until he caught it in his teeth and wagged it at Undine.

She burst out laughing. "You are ridiculous!"

"Court Jester," he replied with a sigh.

"I always understood that court jesters were funny!"

"Then Court Ape."

"We'll let that pass. Who is waiting to play?"

"The Marchioness of Willoughby, Major-General Lord Stacey, K.C.B., A.B.C., R.S.V.P., and my Infernal Apeness."

"I should advise you to begin a game; Edward can play you and Enid. It may take me a few minutes to find Miss Hyde."

"Ri' chuar, mum!"

The sudden Cecil leapt a flight of eleven stone steps, and instead of smashing his head landed miraculously on his feet; pretended to put his foot through his racket, swore a round oath, and dashed away shouting a music-hall song, turning at the bend of the dark, flagged passage to wave to Undine who stood, grey and gold and violet, a soft shadow against the harsh stone wall.

Visitors' rooms were in the new west wing, added by Roderick Sabelle in 1794. This building was typically Georgian, and the rooms high, square, and unimaginative.

In a basket-chair drawn up to the deep window of one of these rooms, a dark-haired girl crouched, a sodden rag of lace handkerchief pressed to her lips, watching every movement of two persons on the terrace below.

These were a small, dapper young man sketching at an easel, and a tall, splendid, rosy girl who occasionally leant over his shoulder to make remarks which had the effect of sending the artist into fits of laughter.

The girl above them in the Georgian room had a riotous mop of black hair and a warm, ivory skin which suggested Spanish beauty but it was difficult to tell whether she was good-looking, for her face was swollen with crying, and from time to time her shoulders shook with furious sobs. She wore a pretty white knitted skirt and jumper with a scarlet monogram on the pocket, and a tennis racket lay on the floor beside her chair; but her thoughts were far from the game she ought to be playing and the people who were waiting for her on the court.

Pandora Hyde was having a bad half-hour. She had had several lately; the luck was all going against her. She had spent twenty-seven dull, blameless, cramping years as the daughter of a country vicar in one of those villages where a stranger never appears, and there's nothing to do but take the dog for a walk, and the vicarage has twelve bedrooms and a bad roof, and no maid will stay, and the increment is three hundred a year.

Now Pandora had a rich, eccentric aunt who lived in London, and was always taking a violent fancy for people, usually followed by an even more violent dislike when the novelty wore away.

This Lady Chuff, suddenly carried away by an inexplicable attachment to Pandora, had invited her to visit London on a six months' visit, bought her a trunkful of clothes, and pushed her into a social whirl which drove the girl wild with excitement and delight. Five happy months sped away, and the blow which might have been expected fell. Lady Chuff, just as suddenly and inexplicably, grew tired of Pandora. She must be rid of the girl. Pandora must go home. Back to Little Mattleton and oblivion for the rest of her young, ardent life! Having soared in the sunshine, to be pushed back into that dreadful cage!

If she had only guessed what was coming she might have made hay while the sun shone, might have married someone, any one of the scores of men she had met. She hadn't tried. Like a fool, from the first month she had chucked her heart on to the knees of one man, and he had been the only man in London for her. Oh, what a fool! Too late now to remedy this crazy infatuation.

Her dark eyes dilated with the intensity of her gaze directed at the companionable pair upon the terrace, and she caught a long, shuddering breath. She was invited to Cleys for another six days; then – doom! Everything must be done in another six days . . . impossible! Hopeless! If she only had some money, enough to share a flat in London with another girl. This time next week she would be back at the vicarage, doing the housework, with an allowance of ten pounds a year.

She sprang to her feet and began to pace the room like a young wild animal, her cheeks flushed crimson. Money! Money! Undine Stacey had thousands and thousands a year, while her own life was to be spoiled for want of a few hundreds.

There was a light tap at the door, and Pandora's hostess entered and confronted her.

Undine was taken back at the sight of the girl's flushed, tear-stained face, wild hair and furious eyes, but she pretended she had noticed nothing, and said: "They're waiting for you for tennis, Pan. Cecil asked me to find you."

"I'm not coming!" the girl flung out, and added defiantly: "I forgot all about it."

"But you're dressed?" Undine closed the door, and added anxiously: "What's the matter, Pan? You've had no bad news, have you?"

The girl sobbed, set her teeth, and flung over to the window.

"Come here . . . look!"

Undine glanced out, and said quietly: "I see Mr. Crown and Rene Fullerton. Well?"

Pandora Hyde suddenly lost all self-control. With clenched fists and blazing eyes, the words tumbled from her lips: "Yes – and it's all your doing! You've done it on purpose! You know I've loved him for four months, and he was just beginning to care about me. You've called yourself my friend, and I've told you everything. You promised you'd invite me and Basil down here together. When he knew a fortnight ago that I was going to be here too he said: 'We'll have some topping times together, Pan.' I loved him! I loved him! My whole future life depended on him. And now I've lost him. Oh, yes, I have! And you've worked it, Undine — "

"Pandora! Stop shrieking!"

"You asked that girl Fullerton to be here too. You put them together at dinner the first night. You knew what would happen! She's amusing to talk to, and so rich. And she could have had hundreds of men, and Basil was the only one I ever wanted. Look at them now! Undine, you beast! I hate you! I'll get even with you! You wanted to humiliate me — "

The girl choked with her own hysterical passion and, flinging herself into a chair, her whole body writhed.

Undine said coolly: "I'll get you a drink."

She brought a glass of water from the adjacent bath-room, and Pandora gulped it down, her teeth chattering against the rim.

"You don't know what you're saying," said Undine. "You ought to control yourself in these absurd rages. Supposing I were to fly into a passion now and demand your blood for insulting me? Shouldn't we look absurd? I'm sorry you're upset about Basil — "

"Upset!" The girl laughed shrilly.

"Yes. It's a nasty experience for you, and I sympathise; but really, Pan, am I to have no right to invite any girl but yourself to the house— "

"You knew — "

"Be quiet, please. There are three unmarried men in the party already, and Harry is bringing another to-night. Surely there is room for both yourself and Miss Fullerton!"

"Rene Fullerton appropriates every man in sight. It's her mission in life."

"You're deliberately misjudging her."

"You mean, you'd make any excuse for her. I wish I'd never come!"

Undine lost her patience.

"There's always the morning train, if you feel like that," she said.

Pandora twisted her fingers together and rose to her feet.

"All right," she said in a smothered voice. "Forget it!"

Undine gave a sigh of relief. She said in a confidential tone: "I'm no more anxious than you are for anything to develop between Basil and Rene. I didn't think he was her type at all. Now Edward— "

Pandora turned desperately. "Do go, please. I can't stand any more. I shall be saying something I'm sorry for."

"Poor kid!"

"Undine! If you pity me, I'll kill you!"

"Go and have a game of tennis. It'll do you good."

"With a face like this? No. Tell them I'm not well. I'll be down to dinner."

Undine went quickly back to her boudoir and rang the bell. A maid appeared.

"Tell Miss Farbell to come here to me."

"Yes, m'lady."

In two minutes Amy tapped at the door.

"You sent for me, Lady Stacey?"

"Is that you, Amy? They're wanting a fourth at tennis, and Miss Hyde is not well. Dress quickly and go out; they're tired of waiting already. Draw that curtain as you go."

"Oh, thank you, Lady Stacey!"

She closed the door softly and sped like an arrow to her turret, pulling off her house frock as she ran. She reflected ruefully that she had no white sweater and pleated skirt like Mrs. Willoughby's. She had so few chances of a game in winter that it was not worth while straining her slender purse to obtain these luxuries. She unearthed a clean, if crumpled, white pique frock, leapt into it, slipped a bandeau over her hair, seized her racket, press and all, and raced down the winding stair.

Alas, poor Amy's luck was out. The gathering clouds gave their signal of attack, and down came the rain at the very moment when Major Stacey had drawn her for his partner.

"Oh!" she could not resist saying. "I did so long for a game!"

He was touched by the miserable disappointment in her face. Lighting a cigarette, he said with a laugh, "What about an orgy of ping-pong in the billiard room? Will you fight a duel with me?"

Her face broke into incredulous smiles.

"I'd simply love it!"

"Come on, then, or you'll be soaked."

Chapter III
THE SECRETS OF THE HEART

ENID WILLOUGHBY left the others and ran towards the castle, and when she reached the shelter of Mervyn's Gate she stopped to look at her wrist-watch. It was twenty to four. There was just time before tea for that interview with Undine – if she could screw up her courage.

Enid did not like the castle; its grimness depressed her, and she could never traverse the cold, hollow-ringing passages without an unpleasant feeling that ghostly eyes of the past were watching her. She shuddered as she made her way to Undine's room, thinking of the wretched prisoners whom the cruelty of past ages had immured within those walls. She was a sensitive woman and suffered frequently from nervous depression, and a light, bright, modern house was essential to her comfort. Cleys had a definitely bad effect on her, physically and mentally, and she realised it.

Undine had just settled down to her letter-writing when Enid entered. She glanced over her shoulder and said: "Oh, do find a seat, Enid. There's *Country Life*, on that chair. I shan't be two minutes, but I must finish this letter. I've had it lying about all this afternoon."

"It's all right. I can wait. Don't hurry."

Enid sank into a well-cushioned lounge chair and let her head droop back. She was just forty, and still retained something of the delicate prettiness which Lionel West had remembered, but there were far too many lines about her eyes and mouth, and sometimes her expression was that of a middle-aged woman who had seen more than her share of anxiety and suffering.

She closed her eyes and her brows wrinkled painfully. She hated the task to which she was being driven. How cruelly unfair life had been to her! To think that she, the pretty, popular Enid Mead of ten years ago, should be so humiliated! Just an accident . . . just a trick of Fate . . . or she would have been sitting where Undine sat, rich and sheltered and honoured and secure, as Harry Stacey's wife. If only they had insisted on his going yachting with them that summer twelve years ago instead of wandering off alone to France, to that wretched inn at Gosière! But for that, he would never have met Undine; he would have married her – Enid – as everyone in their circle expected. Life would have been so different . . . oh! She clenched her thin fingers. Useless, this taunting it-might-have-been. She had gone over it all a hundred times before, lying awake at nights, crying into her pillow, beating hot hands against her breast.

She opened her eyes wearily upon the back of Undine's auburn head. Her resentment against Harry's wife had grown with the years and her own misfortunes. After the first shock of disappointment, when Harry brought Undine home to Lady Mead's twelve years before, Enid, whose nature then was by no means grudging, had been friendly towards the strange girl, acting the part of Harry's "sister" to perfection. It was only in the last few years, since Undine had prospered and she, Enid, had been dragged down with Jack Willoughby, that the contrast had made her bitter.

Meanwhile Undine took up the unfinished letter and carefully read over what she had already written. She had filled the sheet, and taking a fresh one, she wrote in continuation of the broken sentence:

I shall have to stay away for several days. I can't explain here but will do so as soon as I see you. Don't let this make any difference to your plans. You can manage perfectly well without me. Have you ever thought of Irene Fullerton?
With love from
Undine.

She addressed an envelope to Lady Charlotte Wright and was about to insert the letter when a sudden scream from outside brought her to her feet in time to see Rene Fullerton, the North Country heiress, race across the outer bailey with Basil Crown in hot pursuit.

Undine turned to Enid. "That girl is a dreadful hoyden; and Basil Crown is acting in rather a ridiculous manner nowadays. I shall speak to him about it."

"Isn't it their own business?" drawled Enid. "Don't overdo the châtelaine rôle, darling. It doesn't suit you."

"I thought you were playing tennis?"

"It's raining."

"So I see now."

Undine came over to the cavernous hearth and rested one white hand on the heavy, stained stones.

"You're looking fagged, Enid. Why not take a proper rest? Will you stay on here for a few weeks – over Christmas, if you like? The place is big enough, and you can have your own rooms."

Enid shook her head.

"No, thanks. I don't like all this antiquity It's too terribly depressing."

"I love it!"

Enid thought, "You've everything to make you love it!"

She sat up suddenly, and fixing her eyes on the toe of her shoe, said: "I want to see you about something important, Undine; and it's dreadfully hard to begin."

"Then don't try to break it gently; blurt it out."

"Very well." The older woman turned a shade paler. "Jack and I are broke."

"Enid!"

"Yes. It's come to that. You know he's been out of a diplomatic job for two years and they wouldn't offer him another if he paid them for it. They've hushed things up most kindly, but you and I and Harry know that Jack is the world's worst blunderer. He nearly brought about a European war that time in Bukarest! Well, he and I have been living from hand to mouth for two years, and we've got to the end. I shouldn't tell you this if it wasn't quite definitely the end."

Undine slid down into a chair beside her friend.

"Does Lady Mead know?"

"Mother?" Enid shrugged her shoulders. "She hasn't got to know. She's over seventy, and she only has eight hundred a year and the place to keep up. Undine, you don't know how I've been through it! I've lain awake at nights planning until I thought my head would split. You know what Jack is – he never worries! He'd go and beg pennies on the Strand if the worst came to the worst, and expect me cheerfully to do the same."

Undine knew that Jack Willoughby had about as much sense of responsibility as a guinea pig.

"And there's worse to come," went on Enid, her face set in a mask of disgust. "Some idiot asked Jack to be treasurer of the Banner Club's charity fund, and he took it on. This was eight months ago, and he's supposed to have had all the subscriptions in, over three hundred pounds. He's sent the individual receipts, but kept no accounts, and now he can't imagine where all that money has gone to. All he can lay hands on is ninety-two pounds. I presume we've been living on the other; he never told me. And yesterday he had a demand from the club for the balance of two hundred and twenty-seven pounds. I've got to breaking point, Undine. Perhaps you can imagine what I've gone through before I could bring myself to tell you this."

"My poor old Enid!"

Enid made a gesture of impatience.

"I haven't finished yet. I might as well get down as low as I can. Jack's broken my pride and made a beggar of me. Yes, I'm begging. I'm asking you for five hundred pounds, to pay our debts and keep us going until Jack . . . gets something."

"Enid, of course! Please don't feel so bad about it." Undine took one of the cold, clenched hands in hers. "Don't take it so hardly. Of course you shall have the money. Your mother was good to me when Harry brought me from France; I owe you far more than five hundred pounds. But, Enid, why not go to Harry? He's like your brother. He could help you better than I — "

"No, no!" Enid shuddered and snatched her hand away. "If you so much as tell him, I'll never forgive you. That's why I came to you."

"But why? He'd be very understanding."

"I should hate him even to know."

Enid, distracted, overwrought, could not explain to Undine that she loved Harry, had always loved him, and had married Jack Willoughby to find escape from her disappointment. Harry to know that Jack had brought her to this – never!

She twisted her one ring, hoping that Undine would perform the necessary act without further discussion. A sudden wave of jealous misery nearly choked her. She wanted Harry as she had never wanted him before, and not for his fortune, either. She would have seen the whole earth submerged if she and Harry might be left alive together, even in a wilderness.

She pushed her hair behind her ears and rose.

"It's very good of you, Undine," she said with forced casualness. "I wouldn't have asked if I hadn't been desperate. I dare say Jack will be able to get something in the spring."

"That's all right, Enid. I'll write you a cheque, and please don't think about it any more."

Undine opened the drawer of her escritoire.

"Oh, I've finished the book! I forgot. And I forgot to ask Harry to bring me another from town! I'll tell you what I can do. Edward has Midland Bank cheques; I'll go and get one from him. He'll think it's for myself. By the way, have you any idea where he is?"

"I heard him say something to the governess about a game of ping-pong in the billiard-room."

"Ping-pong! Miss Farbell!"

Undine hesitated, and then said, "Wait here, Enid. I shan't be long."

Ping-pong is a strenuous game and a little goes a long way. After a hot and exciting set, Amy, scarlet and breathless, had tumbled into a big leather chair.

"Help! My head's going round. I can see three bats and about nine balls!"

Major Stacey paused sympathetically.

"I feel like that too. Here's something drinkable – swish – fizz. Isn't that good?"

He offered his cigarette case.

"Oh, but I ought to be going back," said Amy.

"Surely you've done with those kids for to-day?"

"Yes, but — "

"Then sit tight. It isn't what I'd call a picnic teaching Rita and Nicholas. That boy ought to be at a strict prep. school."

"He's only eight. Lady Stacey says he isn't to go to school until he's twelve."

"By the time he's twelve you'll be a nervous wreck!"

"Oh, no, Major Stacey!" She laughed, showing very pretty teeth. "Nicholas isn't nearly so bad as Rita. Rita is a perfect little fiend. There! It's done me good to say that to one of Rita's relations."

" Bravo! Carried unanimously!"

The Major spread himself comfortably against the stone mantelpiece.

"Now, what part of England do you come from, Miss Farbell?"

She thrilled deliciously. She was actually having a *tête-à-tête* conversation with her hero. If only he might not think her too young and unsophisticated!

"From Devon." She lowered her eyelashes and her cheeks grew carnation pink.

"You lucky person. Think of having a home in Devon!"

"But I haven't." She added with exquisite plaintiveness: "I have no home now. I'm an orphan."

"Oh!" he said awkwardly. "You poor little thing – you must feel very lonely sometimes."

"I do," she whispered. Her heart thumped madly.

"I've a sin to confess," he said with an air of friendly confidence. "I stood outside a door the other evening and overheard someone playing the violin very beautifully. Will you forgive me for eavesdropping?"

"If I was practising I should think that to listen was enough punishment!"

"You were playing the 'Londonderry Air.' "

She twisted her fingers. "I love the melody."

"I could tell you did. So do I. Am I forgiven?"

She smiled. Her grey eyes were starry.

"It's a mutual crime, Major Stacey. On Friday night when you were talking to Mrs. Willoughby I was in the window seat mending a dress for her. She knew I was there, but you didn't. You told her all your wonderful adventures in the Indian hill station, and how you and the four Sikhs followed the robber tribe over the snow-covered pass. Do you remember? I couldn't sew. I just clasped my hands and lived it all as you told it. Oh, you must have had glorious adventures – such a marvellous life!"

He was flattered. His handsome face grew sombre.

"A man grows tired. Everything palls."

"But to feel you've done something really worth while, for your country – for any cause!"

He lifted his gaze from his shoes and looked straight into her shining eyes.

"You don't understand, child. There's the tea gong!" In fact, it was rather an anticlimax.

He put out a hand to help her from her chair; and as she lifted her glowing face in a shy smile the inevitable happened, and he stooped and brushed her lips softly with his.

"Happy days to you – Amy."

The kiss ran through her veins like wine of the gods. It was not surprising that the Major should repeat the experiment, this time with a certain lingering pleasure, but it was a pity that Undine should have chosen that moment to enter.

She hesitated for only a second, and then said briskly: "Can you give me one of your cheques, please, Edward? My book is empty. Miss Farbell, you may go. Come to my room in half an hour."

When Amy had fled, gently closing the door, Undine said, "I have only had that happen once before in my house. I hardly expected it from you, Edward."

"Expected what?" he asked lightly.

"You know what I mean!"

"Who was the other fellow?"

"The other fellow?"

"Who kissed Miss Farbell?"

"It was not Miss Farbell. It was one of the maids."

He laughed. "I see. Well, forget it! You ought to have been scarce at that moment. You're surely not going to say anything to Miss Farbell, are you?"

"I'm certainly going to warn her. She's an orphan. I'm responsible for her while she's in my house." Major Stacey gave a short, contemptuous laugh which sounded strangely in Undine's ears.

"You – responsible! I like that!"

"What do you mean?" she demanded.

"Look here, Undine!" The Major straightened his shoulders and faced her squarely, his face the severe mask of a man who has ruled soldiers in a dangerous country. His eyes were definitely unfriendly. She was at a loss.

"Well?"

"I've known my brother's wife for a week," he began slowly. "When I came down here a week ago, I came – to expose you!"

He hurled the last three words at her. She flung up her auburn head.

"That's a peculiar thing to say!"

"It was a peculiar situation. You see, I happened to meet Corbett, the one who lives at Marseilles."

Slowly the life ebbed away from her face, the vitality from her body. Her very lips grew grey. She stared – and stared – and felt the stern probing of his steady eyes.

Major Stacey went on. "You thought me stiff and uncordial, for your husband's brother. Now you know why.

I say, I came here on purpose to expose you. I would have exposed you – but I found that my brother was still in love with you. That you had been his wife for twelve years, and made him happy!"

A long, pent-up breath shuddered from her lips.

"I decided, for my brother's sake, to give you a chance, Undine. He's the one person on earth I care about, and I care about him a lot. I don't care a damn about you! I'm a man without mercy; the hardest type of a soldier. If it weren't that to do so would break Harry, I'd kick your lying body into the gutter where it belongs. I'm sparing you for his sake, do you hear?"

"Yes — " She fought for self-possession.

"Why didn't you tell him? Were you really so rottenly unscrupulous?"

"I fell in love with him," she faltered.

"In love! At that inn at Gosière! I wish to God he'd drowned before he went there! Yes, I'm shaking you a bit, Undine. It's doing you good. I mean to shake you. So long as you can make Harry happy, for his sake I'll leave you alone. What about the other Corbett?"

"Life," she whispered. "The penal settlement."

"Was he your lover?"

"No!" she broke out fiercely.

"And the one I saw at Marseilles, is he safe? My God, if Harry should hear through a stranger! I'd shoot you first and myself too."

"He never troubles me. He never will."

"He said you had sent him money."

"He lent me two hundred pounds after – after . . . I only

returned it, and a little for interest."

"Are you under any other obligation?"

"Oh, no!"

"Who is this cheque for that you're wanting?"

"For myself."

He took from his trousers pocket a purse and from the purse a key, and fitting it to the drawer of a small knee-hole table took out a cheque book and tore off a cheque.

Undine watched him in an agony. She had just had the shock of her life. After twelve years! Her hands were numb and her lips felt stiff and strained.

He held out the cheque.

"Take it! I shan't trouble you with my company for many days longer. When I invite Harry to my house in town you will please be too busy or too unwell to accompany him."

"Edward – you'll have to be – more friendly to me. Harry already notices."

"Oh, I'll act the part, now we know where we stand!"

"But — " Her violet eyes were black with dismay. "You're not going to keep up for ever that awful – animosity towards me?"

He took a step away from her.

"I think you're utterly despicable – rotten. It takes a lot to make a man say that to a woman, so you can judge my feelings."

"You admit I've made Harry a good wife. Don't I deserve any credit for that?"

"Certainly not. You've only been serving your own ends."

Suddenly she felt sick and faint. The room reeled about her. She kept her balance with a great effort and managed to reach the door. He did not offer to open it for her. She found the handle blindly, and staggered out.

Once out of his presence, she realised that the scene was over and that the awful impending disaster was averted. She had made a compact with Edward. She was virtually safe. She drew long breaths of the wet October air as she crossed the grass-grown stones of the courtyard. By the time she reached her room she was herself again.

Enid lay with closed eyes in the lounge-chair, a cigarette drooping from her long, nervous fingers.

"Sorry to have kept you waiting," said Undine.

"It doesn't matter," Enid drawled.

Undine hastily wrote the cheque for five hundred pounds, signed it, and put it into an envelope.

"There, Enid! You can put that safely into your bag. And I hope the luck will turn."

When Enid was gone she turned to her mirror. The hue of life was coming back to her cheeks, but her eyes were the colour of drenched irises. She decided that she would not go down for tea; by dinner she would be completely controlled.

A light tap at the door startled her. She had forgotten Amy Farbell until the governess entered and stood just inside the door-arch, with drooping eyes; drooping, be it confessed, not so much from shame as to hide the dancing of the elves of delight which the Major's kisses had awakened in their wistful depths.

"Oh – Amy!"

"Yes, Lady Stacey?"

"Amy, I want to give you a very brief word of warning.

When a man in a house party kisses a girl in your position, he does so because he is bored and wants to be amused. He knows too that it is a very questionable form of amusement. When a girl in your position allows a guest to kiss her, she makes herself not only cheap but dangerous. As my children's governess, I will not allow you to become either cheap or dangerous. I think that will do. You may go."

"Major Stacey isn't like that!" the girl flashed.

"What do you mean?"

"Major Stacey isn't the kind of man to play at underhand flirtations. He kissed me because – we're friends!"

Undine drew herself up haughtily.

"You had better keep to your own room in future, Miss Farbell. You are evidently not able to mix with my guests without forgetting yourself."

The girl's breast rose and fell quickly. Those kisses had given her a kind of feverish daring.

"You mean," she said in her clear, level young voice, "that a man who's noble and rich and clever, like Major Stacey, couldn't find any legitimate pleasure in the company of a governess. He could be quite properly interested in Miss Hyde or Miss Fullerton, but not in a governess. If you had seen him kiss Miss Hyde or Miss Fullerton you would have thought it such a pretty romance! You saw him kiss the governess, and you thought, 'How vulgar! How nasty! Of all the men who have stayed here, Major Stacey is the only one who was ever kind to me. I think he's the most wonderful man in he world! Do you think I'd let anyone kiss me? Indeed I wouldn't! That conceited little rabbit, Mr.

Crown, or that Sabelle lunatic who's always hanging round the schoolroom, do you suppose — "

"Have you quite finished, Miss Farbell?" Undine's voice was dangerously cold.

"Yes – except it isn't fair to send me to my room in disgrace. I haven't done anything I'm ashamed of."

Undine was angry. She had never made any attempt to understand the girl's position, or the loneliness of the life she spent shut off from the gaiety in which others joined. She saw only impertinence and presumption in Amy's outburst.

There came the distant note of a klaxon; Sir Harry was returning from town.

Undine said finally: "I sometimes think you have been with us too long, Amy. The children are not so well behaved as they used to be. Perhaps a change would be advisable."

The girl's colour left her. Was she being dismissed? But she would never find another post, and she had nowhere to go. So few people wanted governesses, and there were queues of girls waiting at the agency in town!

She stood dumbly, not knowing what to say.

"Well? Don't you think so?"

"I don't want . . . to leave," she faltered.

"Then behave yourself!" said Undine curtly. The scarlet rushed to Amy's cheeks. She suddenly fled from the room, afraid to stay for fear dreadful things would come tumbling from her lips; determined she would not stay another day to be insulted and misunderstood; realising that she must stay because she had nowhere else to go; furious that a smear of ugliness had already been drawn across the memory of her delicious moment.

As she fled along the passage that led to her turret, the car containing Sir Harry and Lionel West rolled into the courtyard of Cleys Castle.

Chapter IV
THE SETTING OF A STAGE

"THIS is the outer bailey," said Sir Harry. "My wife's rooms are above us in the keep. She prefers the bower of a Norman lady. On your right the chapel; on your left the banquet hall. Sorry I can't 'banquet' you there, West, but the architect condemns it as structurally unsound. That queer exterior stair to the second story is called the Jew's Stair. I don't know why. One feels there ought to be a legend, and that young Sabelle would be the proper person to ask, but he knows nothing! He takes no interest in the history of the place; says his ancestors never did anything for him, and why should he keep their memory green? . . Oh, and there he is, with my son and daughter in admiring attendance."

Long-legged Cecil Sabelle, his dun-coloured hair on end, was sprawling on the mounting-block, with Nicholas squatting beside him and Rita draped over his shoulder.

"Come and be introduced," said Sir Harry.

The children dutifully extended paws and said, "How do you do?" and Rita spoiled the effect by adding, "You interrupted! Cecil's telling us a yarn."

"Shut up, Rita!" said young Sabelle; and to West agreeably, "So you've come down to join the party! I don't know what you'll think of this mouldy old ruin after the decent country houses you've probably stayed in."

"I think it's a priceless treasure preserved from the past," said West gravely.

Sabelle grimaced.

"They all say that, sir. Well, thank goodness, some people like it or I should still have it on my hands!"

"Oh, do go away, daddy!" said Nicholas impatiently. "Cecil! What did Guido want the rope for? Hurry up and tell us!"

Sir Harry laughed and passed on. West lingered for a moment or two to watch the group on the mounting-block, now happily oblivious of his presence, and then followed his host.

When the gong sounded for dinner, West set out from his distant room in the direction of the cheerful strains, and soon became completely lost. He blundered helplessly in a maze of ancient by-ways, and finally came upon a long, dark, pompous man who approached him cordially and said, "You must be Lionel West. I expect you've heard of me – Willoughby of the Diplomatic. I've seen a good bit of service in various parts of the world. Very keen on my job. I helped to bring that South Europe Amalgamated Canals scheme about, you'll remember. I'm on extended leave just at present. Should like to go to Canada next. I've already mentioned it in the right circles, so I expect I shall leave Cleys for Ottawa."

Enid Mead's husband . . . h'mph!

"How do you do?" said West. " 'Fraid I'm lost. I was trying to follow the sound of the dinner gong."

"Oh, dinner. I'll take you along. Have you only just arrived? Feel I know you; old friend of Enid's, aren't you?"

"I came down with Sir Harry."

"Oh, yes? Good fellow, Harry, but a trifle bourgeois. Not

my idea of the king of the castle. Now Undine – have you met her, by the way?"

"Not yet," snapped West. What a detestable fellow this was!

"As I was implyin', Undine goes with the place. The haughty chatelaine, you know. She's a beautiful woman. Can't bear her myself; *mais chacun à son goût.* She's one of these perfect women; always right, you know, and laid on ice. Have you seen Enid yet?"

"I haven't seen anyone."

"Enid's a bit under the weather. The Mead women never had much spirit . . . See where you are? Turn to the right here and you'll smell the soup."

To West's relief Sir Harry appeared and presented the newly arrived guest to Lady Stacey.

Undine gave a cordial greeting to her husband's old friend. He thought her both charming and intelligent. Something in her face recalled a memory which he could not capture. A few minutes later he was gripping hands delightedly with Major Stacey.

"We'll have a tremendous talk after dinner," declared Edward; "Harry and you and I."

"I don't know whether we can spare you," said Undine with mock severity. "We've planned a tango evening to-night, and we women can't do without partners."

"I'm afraid I don't tango in any case," said West.

"You can learn," said Undine, with a merry glance of her lovely eyes, "and I'm particularly anxious for Harry to learn. Basil and Pandora are the exponents."

"Harry and West and I are spending the evening in the

library," broke in Major Stacey curtly.

The apparent rudeness to his sister-in-law puzzled West, coming from a man of such exquisite courtesy as Edward Stacey; and he was even more puzzled that Lady Stacey should turn meekly away as though in acceptance of the enforced situation.

They sat down to dinner; a perfect riot of people, thought West. He was introduced by Sir Harry in wholesale fashion: "Good people, this is Lionel West. As I say your names you get up and bob. Enid – Cecil – Rene – Basil – Jack – Pandora. Now you know everybody. That's Pandora next to you, Lionel. She'll tell you all the news."

The girl next to West was dark and pale and wore a rose-coloured Spanish shawl round her shoulders. He found her silent and uninteresting, and wished his place had been beside the other young woman, Rene Fullerton, who was keeping young Crown in roars of laughter with her somewhat broad jokes.

To the dark girl West essayed, "I hear you're going to teach all these people the tango tonight. You're a public benefactor. I hope you'll survive the fray."

She did not smile.

"Some of them know it already," she said languidly. "But we have something arranged for every night. To-morrow it's hide and seek, and Thursday we are dressing up."

"Both good fun."

"Quite."

With a sigh of relief West turned to Enid on his other side and was soon absorbed in conversation.

After dinner, to his great satisfaction he heard nothing

more of the tango party, and spent a glorious three hours with Harry and Edward talking about the past, old friends, old times, in the newly-captured intimacy of a great friendship of youth.

He went to his room at one. It was then for the first time that the weird majesty of the castle overawed him. The walls of his room were lofty and Georgian; he was occupying a comparatively new guest wing. The silence was heavy and down-pressing. Nothing stirred. He might have been alone with the spirits of dead warriors and rotting prisoners in the old black fortress under the wild mountains of Wales. The sky was tremendously lofty beyond his window, and a wet, stained moon lay on its back in a couch of ragged cloud. The howling waste of the marches swept into the darkness of night from the foot of the wall below his window, and the eternal seeping of the moat was broken only by the louder complaint of the wind in crumbling window niches.

"I bet there are owls," thought West. "If they begin hooting, heaven help my slumbers!"

But no owls hooted. He slept deeply, but with rather nightmarish dreams, and woke to the unhappy drone of pouring rain, with all the view from his window a swirl of grey mist drowning even the tops of the castle turrets.

At breakfast there was a great deal of moaning about the weather, especially since the barometer had fallen so low that there was every prospect of the deluge continuing throughout the day.

"And it's Harry's birthday, isn't it?" said Enid Willoughby. "I seem to remember the eighteenth of

October."

The modest owner of the castle blushed, while everybody jumped up to pat him on the back and make appropriate noises.

"Isn't there some ancient ceremony at Cleys for the birthday of the head of the house?" asked Undine. "I'm sure I've read or heard of it. Cecil, you ought to know."

"Dunno, I'm sure," grunted Cecil Sabelle, helping himself slyly to kidneys before anyone else could reach the dish.

"Oh, rack your brains – just this once! Didn't your father keep it up?"

"My old man?" Sabelle thumped his forehead obligingly. "Ah, I've got it. Lot of silly rot, you know!"

"Spill it," ordered Rene Fullerton.

"Well, it's the most frightful nonsense; but on the birthday of the head of the house the eldest son is supposed to smite the hearthstone three times and say 'Milk-o!' "

"Idiot! What does he really say?"

"But it's such frightful piffle!"

"We may not think so."

"Well, he sort of gawks at his pater, y'know, and sings out, 'Lord of the Marches, waes hael!' That means, 'Can you lend me a fiver until next week?' And the pater replies, 'Drink hael!' which means, 'Not on your life, son; I'm broke myself!' "

Undine's eyes shone.

"What a glorious little ceremony," she cried. "I think it's wonderful, and it must never be allowed to die out. We'll do it! Miss Farbell shall bring Nicholas."

"It would be more to the point," said the incorrigible

Cecil with a wide grin, "if you asked the retainer to bring some more eggs."

"Oh, you're hopeless! You haven't a bit of romance in you!"

Amy Farbell brought in Rita and Nicholas. The little boy was excited and important when told what he had to do. His mother took his hand and led him to the hearth, repeating softly the words he was to address to his father.

"Clump it a good wallop, Nicky," shouted Cecil Sabelle, his mouth full of egg and toast. "I'll give you five bob if you make a dent in it."

"What shall I hit it with?" asked Nicholas.

His mother lifted a slender lance from the wall where it hung among other old trophies. The stone-walled chamber had been in use for hundreds of years. Nicholas looked round excitedly at the vaulted roof, the high, pointed windows, the carved and painted arms above the door, the double row of modern faces at the board where fierce knights had sat.

Everyone was watching him. He smote the hearthstone three times with all the exuberance of eight years old. At the third blow the lance splintered in his hand. He threw away the pieces, and facing his father cried, "Lord of the Marches, waes hael!"

Harry Stacey, very self-conscious, mumbled "Drink hael!" and the whole company rounded off the ceremony by clapping, while Cecil Sabelle with the aid of two fingers and a blown out cheek made a noise like the popping of corks, to the delight of the two children.

In the confusion Amy Farbell stole a glance at Major

Stacey, but it seemed to her that he deliberately avoided it. Her spirits sank. Had Lady Stacey been reprimanding him? She looked at him again as she left the room with the children, but he was talking to Miss Fullerton now. She went away disappointed and resentful.

"What are we going to do all the morning?" asked Rene Fullerton. "Is anybody game for a scamper in the rain with me?"

"Yes, I am," replied Basil Crown promptly.

Undine looked surprised. Crown the young exquisite, who chose his dressing-gowns to match his morning tea-sets, and had a different one for every day in the week, was the last person on earth one would expect to see "scampering" in the rain over the Welsh marches on a raw October morning, especially in the company of a rosy-faced broth of a girl from Lancashire, utterly unlike the languid beauties with whom he dined and danced in town.

"Some of you might be interested," said Undine, "to see the Isabella Tapestry come down."

"What's that?" asked Jack Willoughby.

"The big tapestry on the wall opposite the guard-room. It's wasted there in the dark, and I'm having it taken up to my room to be hung on the north wall, to correspond with the Crusader tapestry on the other side. Don't you think it's a good idea?"

"Will it stand the removal?" asked Enid. "Supposing it falls to pieces?"

"Oh, but I had an expert down from Harrods to examine it, and he says it's marvellously preserved. There won't be the slightest danger in moving it."

The door opened and a late-comer slipped in – Pandora Hyde. She looked even more pale and sullen than on the previous night, as though she had slept badly. Even before saying good morning to her hostess her glance flew to Basil Crown, who was making quite a business of dropping sugar into Rene Fullerton's third cup of coffee.

Lionel West, who was trained to read faces, surprised her secret. This Spanish-looking girl was in love with the artist, who had fickly transferred his affections to the north country heiress. He watched her sit down listlessly next to Enid Willoughby and receive a cup of coffee from Undine, and he could find no reason for the fact that in so doing she should favour her hostess with a decidedly unfriendly glance.

Enid Willoughby, too, looked pale and distrait this morning; her hands were restless and she seemed disinclined for talk. West could see that she was in a highly nervous condition. One other thing which surprised him, and for which he could not account, was the obviously strained relationship between Lady Stacey and her husband's brother. He avoided contact or direct conversation with her, and at times it seemed as though she were even making appealing efforts at easy friendliness with him, only to be rebuffed. Altogether there was a queerness, a lack of harmonious jollity about this house-party, which to a man so sensitive to atmosphere as Lionel West, was disquieting.

"But why," said Rene Fullerton, "do they call it the Isabella Tapestry?"

"I know that one," said Cecil Sabelle. "Because it was

worked by twelve of my female relations in the Dark Ages, all called Isabella. Can you think of anything worse? Time and time again has the poor old mater tried to pawn the thing — "

"To pawn it! . . . That beautiful old thing! . . . What a shame! . . . " cried all the ladies.

Cecil Sabelle, enjoying their consternation, cocked a light eyebrow.

"Meat bills and so on, you know. We tried it on all the rich Americans, but they wouldn't bite. There's a funny little place behind it in the wall; a Priest's Hole."

"A Priest's Hole! How thrilling! Cecil, why didn't you tell us before?"

"I say," broke in Major Stacey, "Hadn't we better switch on the light? It's like the end of the world."

While they were talking and laughing a strange, thick darkness had crept out of the lowering sky and plunged the company into gloom. The contours of the room were slowly blotted out; a hush fell. It was a purplish, sullen darkness, very different from the soft falling of night.

"How hideous," cried Enid. "There's going to be a storm." In a moment they could hardly see each other's faces. The silence grew oppressive; the windows frowned into blackened slits.

Major Stacey switched on the lights and everyone sighed with relief, but the thunderous atmosphere still held.

Rene Fullerton pressed her face against the thick glass of the central window.

"My stars! Isn't it weird and awful-looking? I'd love to be out in it. See the colour of the sky over there in the east!"

All the horizon was painted a filthy and lurid scarlet which merged into the purple wrath of the swooping clouds.

Pandora Hyde pressed her hands to her temples with a frown of pain.

"Is it giving you a headache?" cried the kind-hearted Lancashire girl. "How beastly! I'll fly up and get you some aspirins."

"I don't want them," said Pandora, biting her lips.

And as suddenly as the blackness had descended out of the morning sky it lifted and passed on, and the clear, grey rain was falling once more.

After breakfast Lionel West contrived to have a few moments alone with Sir Harry and Lady Stacey. He had brought Undine a present, or rather she was to choose one of two very lovely antique rings, an emerald and a sapphire. She found it very difficult to choose; in fact she was fascinated by the contrasting novelty and beauty of the rings, and she wanted them both! She wondered if by some means she could find out where they came from and get her husband to buy her the one which she now rejected, for West said he was going to return it to the shop.

"They are so very lovely," said Undine, setting one upon the first finger of each hand and holding them alternately to the light. "I don't know which to choose. Wherever did you find such charming things, Mr. West?"

"I got them from an old antique dealer called Mallaby, at Stratford-on-Avon. I've had some fine pieces from his place."

Ah, she knew now! Harry should buy her the other ring.

She said, "Please may I choose the sapphire?"

"Certainly." He touched her fingers and bowed. "May you have many happy occasions on which to wear it!"

He replaced the emerald ring in its case and put it into his pocket.

During the morning, with the assistance, or rather hindrance, of the whole party except Basil Crown and Rene Fullerton, the Isabella Tapestry was taken down. The passage where it had hung for five hundred years was certainly a dark and dismal one, and the work would show to far better advantage upon the wall of Undine's room.

"Please be very careful how you touch it, people!" she cried.

"Rats!" said Cecil Sabelle. "It's as tough as mutton, that old thing. You could use it for covering a football."

"Vandal!" cried Enid, admiring the needlework.

Major Stacey, teasing Pandora Hyde about ghosts, was the first to enter the newly discovered Priest's Hole.

The door had once been a secret one, indistinguishable from the rest of the wall, but now it was broken and gaped open. There was revealed a small, musty chamber about ten feet square, containing a worm-eaten bench and table and a few rusted iron pots.

"Ugh!" shuddered Undine. "What a horrible smell!"

"There's probably a priest or two left here under the dirt," suggested Jack Willoughby.

"I shall send some maids up and have it thoroughly cleaned out," said Undine.

"But, Undine, it's so gorgeously mediaeval!"

"I won't have filth in my house just because it's

mediaeval! What have you got there, Cecil?"

"It looks like the remains of a fourteenth century blanket."

Undine shuddered, and taking the rag at arm's length, dropped it out into the passage.

"That," she declared, "will find its last resting-place in a twentieth century furnace."

"It's still raining," said Enid, when everything was cleared up and the party was assembled in the billiard-room, with still an hour to go to lunch. "Won't you show us the costumes we're to dress up in to-morrow night, Undine?"

Undine shook her head.

"No. We must keep to the programme. Hide-and-seek to-night; dressing up to-morrow. Nobody is to have his or her costume until after to-morrow – that is except Rene Fullerton. I'm lending her an Elizabethan costume for a fancy dress ball at the Savoy next week, and she's going to try it on in my room this afternoon."

"Costumes?" said Lionel West. "Who is going to be dressed up?"

"Everybody," said Jack Willoughby. "I'm goin' to be the Duke of Plaza Toro."

"It's my idea to amuse them," explained Undine. "You see, one day when I was exploring the castle I found in a garret some old chests full of the most wonderful period costumes, real clothes that were once worn by real people; petticoats and farthingales and ruffs, and jerkins and breeches and satin coats, and even wigs – oh, a treasure! I went through them all most carefully and packed them into a large wicker hamper so that they could be more easily carried about. And I thought wouldn't it be fun to-morrow night to dress all my guests in these things and have an old-world dinner."

"We shall look like the inmates of a mediaeval workhouse!" shouted Cecil Sabelle. "I shall be a Spanish corsair in a red sash, and Pandora shall be my bride. Eh, my bonny leman?"

Pandora slipped impatiently out of his reach.

"You'll wait until *I* tell you what you're to wear," said Undine. "I've got it all planned. To-morrow after tea I shall give out the costumes."

Her delight in the costumes was genuine. How glad she was that the Sabelles had been only too willing to sell all such treasures along with the castle, provided they got their price; and they had got it! Harry Stacey had paid a quarter of a million for Cleys.

The door opened and there entered two panting figures in macintoshes and sou'westers; Basil Crown and Rene Fullerton had returned from an hour's "scamper" in the rain.

Rene's eyes were sparkling and she seemed to be bursting with high spirits, and even the languid Basil displayed an unusually healthy exuberance.

"Go on, Basil!" cried the attractive tomboy, with an infectious giggle. "Spill it, son!"

Basil Crown threw his arm across her wet shoulders.

"Rene and I have just become engaged," he declared.

"We'm tokened," giggled Rene, "and us'll soon be gettin' wed."

"How delicious!" laughed Enid Willoughby.

"Oh, I say; congratulations!" cried genial Sir Harry.

Pandora Hyde, past all shame at the fact that she was making herself conspicuous, slipped off the end of the billiard table where she had been perched, and rushed from the room.

Undine, frowning, followed her less obtrusively, and found the girl in violent hysterics at the end of the open passage which led to the outer bailey.

Pandora turned upon her hostess with a flood of bitter recrimination, which at last by sheer force Undine checked, dragging the girl into the open air where the rain on her face seemed to bring her to her senses.

"I'm all right now," she gasped. "I knew it was coming, only I didn't expect it just then. I'm all right, I tell you! I'll go back now and no one will notice there's anything wrong; only – it's your fault, Undine, and I shall never forget it or forgive you!"

"You'll think differently in a few days, Pan. You're too shocked to see things reasonably."

The girl shook her head, and with a proud, set face marched back to the billiard-room.

After lunch Undine drew Basil Crown aside. "Please come to my room for a few minutes. I want to speak to you."

"Oh? . . . Er – certainly," he replied carelessly.

He followed her, hands in immaculate pockets, to the keep; through the frowning arch and up the worn and winding stair to the lady's bower on the second floor overhanging the drawbridge and the moat.

"I say! What a topping room! Jolly fine tapestries, too,

what?"

"The Crusader and the Isabella," said Undine proudly. "But those aren't what I wanted to talk to you about. I won't waste time. It's serious. I'm not a bit pleased with you, Mr. Crown!"

His eyes flickered into surprised annoyance, but he veiled them and drawled, "Really?"

"I've known you for a considerable time, Mr. Crown. I've got you several commissions from my friends. I've introduced you to people. I've asked you down here to draw my children and join my party; and I think you might have mentioned it to me before proposing to a girl you met in my house for the first time a week ago!"

He passed a hand over his crisp black hair, and flicked an imaginary speck off the well-fitting blue coat which sat so nicely on his drooping shoulders.

"Honestly, Lady Stacey, one doesn't prepare these things! I'd no notion of proposing to Rene when we started out this morning. Circumstances just – er – brought it about. Sorry if I've been discourteous!"

"It isn't that. It's simply that the engagement is unsuitable, and Rene's mother will be furious, and I won't have it said that it all started in my house. I'm being straight with you, Mr. Crown."

"Indeed, you are," he murmured frostily.

"Now please don't be cross." She smiled at him enchantingly with her violet eyes. "I like you, Mr. Crown. You're young and you've got a future, and that's partly why I don't want you to spoil a good career by marrying an heiress; and I like Rene too, far too much to allow her to be married for her money — "

"Thank you, Lady Stacey!" The blood rushed to his usually pale face. "You do express yourself with the utmost clarity!"

She faced him, still smiling.

"But you are marrying her for her money, aren't you, Mr. Crown?"

"I refuse to answer such an insolent question!"

He suddenly realised that rage made him look ridiculous, and he cooled down and assumed a man-of-the-world air.

"I think you've got a nerve to suggest that, Lady Stacey. It isn't true."

"But you wouldn't marry her if she hadn't eighty thousand pounds? I've seen you wince at her Lancashire accent and tomboy ways."

"Rene's a very charming girl, and I intend to marry her." He spoke very deliberately. "If Rene has money, I have my talent, and the success I've already made for myself. There aren't many young men in London who are fashionable portrait-drawers at twenty-four. She gets quite as much out of it as I do."

Undine shrugged her shoulders.

"I could marry an earl's daughter if I wanted to!" said Basil Crown, with the *naïveté* of complete egoism.

"A man doesn't usually tell these things!" said Undine curtly. "Well, you'd better go, but I still insist on having this engagement remain in abeyance while you're in my house. If you persist in it, I shall have to ask both you and Rene to leave. I won't have her mother say I encouraged it."

"In that case," replied Crown coldly, "you may be assured that Rene and I will leave to-morrow morning. Is that all?"

"Since you take it like that."

He bowed and turned towards the door, but with his hand on the latch he looked back and said: "Let me tell you, Lady Stacey, that you'd be a great deal more popular among your guests, and with society in general, if you learned to mind your own business and interfere less with other people's!"

He was very rude, was Basil Crown, but he was also very furious.

So was Undine. She had never been so insulted in all her indulged, luxurious married life, and had half a mind to order the car and send this impudent upstart of a portrait-drawer headlong to town. But soon she controlled herself. He was going to-morrow, in any case, and Rene Fullerton with him. She hoped that in her present frame of mind Pandora Hyde would go too, and she would be glad to see the back of Jack Willoughby and Major Stacey. What a house party!

A few minutes later Rene Fullerton presented herself to try on the Elizabethan dress. Undine liked the girl, and decided that she would not precipitate another stormy interview.

In the billiard-room everyone had settled down to a boring afternoon when a laughing apparition appeared, skipping between the arches of the ruined cloister, and finally landing with a hop and a jump under the lintel of a little oaken door which opened from the billiard-room upon a flooded parterre.

"I hope I haven't torn anything!" gasped Rene Fullerton. "Gee, I had to skip between the rain-drops! No wonder those Elizabethan dames were prim and proper with five tons of petticoats slung round their waists."

The girl made a splash of glorious colour against the grey background of the open door. Her rose-pink farthingale was stiff with gold and silver embroidery; above it she wore a tight little pale green stomacher laced with silver cord, and a dress of myrtle green velvet slashed with lavender and scarlet. Her ruff was yellow with age but bravely stiffened, and her bright chestnut head bore a square lace cap as dainty as a snowflake.

To one who scrutinised, the gold and silver were tarnished, the velvet was moth-eaten, the brocade slit in its folds, and the gay colours sadly piebald where the sun had robbed them; but Rene, flaunting herself in this bygone finery, made a brilliant picture as she curtsied and skipped and giggled in the dark corner of the billiard-room on that wet October day.

Basil Crown applauded languidly.

"Bravo, Rene! You look like a suburban amateur dramatic society's conception of a Tudor lady. Where did you get the things?"

"Ha-ha, Mr. Clever!" sang back his fiancée. "That's where you're wrong. It's a real Tudor dress, and it belongs to one of the portraits in the hall. Lady Stacey compared it."

"I recognise you," said Cecil Sabelle. "One of my good old has-beens. *Dear* grandma!"

Rene turned to Enid. "Isn't Lady Stacey kind? She's lending me this for the Operatic Ball next week. Of course,

I shall let everybody know it's a *real* sixteenth century costume."

She swung round delightedly to watch the swirl of her petticoats; and – a merciful interruption – tea arrived.

Darkness closed in early. The rain had stopped falling, but it was too late now to go out, and the sucking of streams in the wide old gutters of the roof made a dismal accompaniment to half-hearted attempts at conversation among Undine Stacey's guests.

"I feel horribly depressed," said Enid Willoughby to Pandora. "I suppose one can't suggest going to bed at six o'clock in the afternoon, but I shall go directly after dinner."

"There's hide-and-seek," said Pandora. "It might amuse you."

Lionel West overheard the remark.

"Hide-and-seek? What's all this talk about hide-and-seek? Won't someone explain to me?"

Undine laughed. "It's nothing but an old-fashioned, childish romp. We're going to put out all the lights. Then one person will be drawn for seeker, and he has to wait in the hall while everyone else scuttles away and hides. At the end of fifteen minutes, Seeker sounds the gong to show he is coming. Then he begins to hunt, and each person as he or she is found joins in the hunt until the last person is found. You can go anywhere in the castle you like, so there's a chance for brave, bold people to find all sorts of romantic hideyholes."

"And what does the last person get?" asked Lionel West.

"How do you mean?"

"Well, he's the winner, isn't he? He ought to have a prize."

"I suppose he ought," said Undine. "We must find something."

"Let me give the prize." West's fingers flew to the velvet box in his pocket, and he brought it out and disclosed the lovely setting and deep brilliance of the emerald ring.

"This shall be the prize for the last man found."

"Oh, Mr. West!" cried all the ladies together. They flocked round in admiration. The game of hide-and-seek had acquired a new attraction.

Undine frowned. She had set her heart on that ring.

"It's too beautiful," she said. "Far too good for a prize. I can find something more suitable."

"But I want to give this," said West. "You'd like to win it, wouldn't you, Mrs. Willoughby?"

"Wouldn't I!" Enid laughed rather cynically. "I never win anything. I never got a prize in my life."

The banal Jack Willoughby made a large gesture.

"You forget me, my dear! First prize in the matrimonial sweep!"

Enid's lip curled, and a look of annoyance passed over Harry Stacey's face.

"Oh, I must win it! I must!" cried Pandora Hyde.

"Emeralds would suit you," said Rene Fullerton generously.

Pandora said nothing. She had not pictured the wearing of the ring. She was thinking that it might be worth a hundred pounds.

"Supposing a man wins it?" said Edward Stacey.

"Then he hands it to his lady."

"Oh, win it for me, Basil!" cried Rene. "I'm no good at hiding. I always sneeze or wriggle, or something."

The door softly opened, and Amy Farbell entered with Rita and Nicholas. The group round the ring broke up, and West replaced the case in his pocket.

"Hallo, here come the kids!" cried Cecil Sabelle. "Are they going to be in at the death, Undine?"

Undine hesitated. She was in a curious frame of mind. She was unreasonably annoyed at this public disposal of the emerald ring which she had regarded as her own. Her mental process was a curious and petty one. She thought: "If I let Rita and Nicholas play, I shall have to let Amy Farbell play. If she plays, I'm certain she'll win the ring; that's just the kind of exasperating thing that does happen, and it would be *too* much! I shan't risk it".

She said: "No. I have something else for Miss Farbell and the children to do tonight."

"What, mummy?" asked Rita.

"I'll tell you later."

"Something nice?"

"Yes," she said hurriedly. She would have to invent a treat for them.

Amy Farbell's face turned blank with disappointment. She knew all about the hide-and-seek, and had been certain that she would be allowed to play.

"Come and tell me a good hiding-place, Miss Farbell," said Enid Willoughby, strolling up. "Or are you going to keep the best for yourself?"

"I'm not going to play," faltered Amy.

Major Stacey overheard her. "Oh, but you are going to play! Why not?"

"Lady Stacey wants me to be with the children."

"Oh, nonsense! Undine, Miss Farbell thinks you don't want her to play hide-and-seek tonight."

"Neither do I," said Undine quietly. "I want her to be with the children."

There was a sudden, thunderous pause; a pause ominous out of all proportion to the subject under discussion.

"Amy," said Lady Stacey, "you may take the children upstairs."

"Oh, but, mummy, we've only just come!" Undine turned her back to prevent further discussion.

Amy grabbed the children and managed to hustle them to the door, her cheeks flaming; and there she found Major Stacey holding it open. She dared not look at him.

He followed her out, and closed the door. The children raced away. They were alone in the passage.

"Amy!" he said in his deep, commanding voice.

She suddenly found control of herself, and smiled at him.

"It doesn't matter, Major Stacey. I don't mind, really."

"Amy, you shall play! I promise you. I shall speak to my sister-in-law, and then come up and fetch you, at eight o'clock."

The twin stars leapt to life in the eyes which had already intrigued him.

"Oh, thank you! You are good to me, Major Stacey!"

"Oh, frightfully good!" he laughed. "Are you coming down to dinner?"

"No."

"I shall fetch you directly after dinner."

He put his fingers under her soft little pointed chin, tilted up her blushing, willing face, and rewarded himself with the thrill of a long kiss from those bloomy, virginal lips.

Life for Amy after a long and wretched day had suddenly become an anthem of bliss . . . the thoughts of future moments, future kisses. She went to her turret-room in an ecstasy of anticipation, and changed into her prettiest dress which she only wore on the most special occasions, a soft green georgette with a dipping hem, clasping round her neck a little link of real pearls which Lady Stacey had once given her for Christmas. After her hasty dinner she sat down to wait until her hero should come to fetch her; and there, let it now be added, she waited in vain until a sick dismay replaced the ecstasy, and it was too late to expect him any longer.

Major Stacey had forgotten his lightly made promise!

Chapter V
A GAME OF HIDE-AND-SEEK

DINNER was eaten hastily at Cleys Castle that night. The possibility of winning the emerald ring had given new zest to bored, and in some cases resentful guests.

The dining-room which they used was like a refectory; a long, narrow, austere apartment, the walls half panelled in grey, unpolished oak, and the upper half of rough-cast stone under the lowering beams of the high roof. The long table was six hundred years old, of pale old wood to correspond with the benches upon which the guests sat. Electric lights were cunningly hidden in the iron sconces on the walls; but Lady Stacey disliked such imitations, and had caused a single line of yellow wax candles in brass candlesticks to be placed the length of the table for its illumination.

The pointed windows of the room were inaccessible, twelve feet from the ground, and there was a stone hearth and chimney big enough to roast an ox whole.

They ate in silence. Lionel West in a moment of curious insight thought: "In what way does this company differ from the folk of what we call the Dark Ages, who sat in this room, at this table, on many a similar night while the wind howled across the unchanging marches? Our dress is altered, but perhaps in our hearts we are the same . . . in the secret impulses of our hearts. Has love changed, or greed, or passion, or loyalty, or jealousy, or hate?"

They rose from the table, and Enid Willoughby began to

blow out the candles. Soon they would be in the dark.

"Don't!" cried Pandora sharply.

"Why not? We can't play with the candles burning."

"I don't know – but somehow it seems dreadful to be in this place in the dark. It's so old – so haunted. The spirits might come into their own, in the dark."

"Rats!" said Rene Fullerton. "I say, people, Miss Hyde has got the heeby-jeebies!"

"I haven't! I was only joking!" she cried indignantly; but her bare arm brushed the hand of Lionel West as the last candle went out, and it was trembling violently.

He caught her wrist. "You are frightened! Why?"

"Don't you feel it too?" she whispered. "As though we were safe in a place like this so long as we keep the lights of the twentieth century burning – but if once we let them go out . . ."

Lionel West felt a tremor of apprehension, as though the girl's suggestive words found some ominous echo in his subconsciousness; but before he had time to reply he was swept away with the crowd to the hall, where Rene and Cecil Sabelle were doing a dervish dance round the gong, and Lady Stacey was handing out slips of paper for the lots.

"My luck!" drawled Basil Crown. "You can't have anything much shorter than that, can you?"

He had drawn a slip about an inch and a half long; but Major Stacey's was even shorter, and it was upon him finally that the post of Seeker was conferred.

"Oh, I am thankful it isn't Basil or me!" sighed Rene. "I should be too mad if I hadn't a chance of that lovely ring."

"Now, final instructions," said Lady Stacey.

"You know what you have to do. You can hide absolutely anywhere in the castle, but no one is to go out of doors, or into any of the places that are boarded up, because they aren't safe. And no two people are to hide together! Edward, you sit on that chair for fifteen minutes by your watch – has it a luminous dial? Good! And then bang the gong to warn us you're coming. As you find people, they join in the search. Good hunting, everybody!"

"I don't have to play, do I?" exclaimed West.

"Why, of course!"

"Oh, I say, Harry!" He turned to his host: "I thought you and I were going to have a good talk over the fire."

Harry Stacey made a rueful face.

"No luck, old man. We're all in this."

"Now!" cried Undine; and switched off the hall lights.

"Help!" someone groaned.

"I can't find the stairs!"

"Who's this I've got hold of?"

"Well, so long, everybody!"

"Oh, wait for me, people! I'm scared stiff!"

Undine Stacey was absolutely determined to win the emerald ring, by remaining hidden longer than anyone else, and when Undine made up her mind to anything, she seldom failed to achieve her object.

After switching off the lights, she withdrew quietly to the recess by the stairs, and stood waiting for the others to disperse. There was plenty of time for her to hide when this confusion was over. She listened to thuds, shufflings, scrambles, giggles, and snatches of facetious conversation. Gradually the hubbub subsided; people were getting away.

Still she stood, listening to departing sounds, until the last footfall had died away and the hall was silent.

She could dimly see the dark patch of Edward's figure as he sat motionless in the great Stuart chair. She stole to the stairs, and he moved as though surprised at the unexpected sound in the stillness, but he did not rise or speak.

Undine ran lightly up the first flight and turned left along a wide gallery which connected that part of the house with the Keep. Half-way along that gallery she turned again, under an open arch, crossed a small chamber, opened a low door, and discovered an ascending flight of stone steps. Upwards she ran to a higher floor, left the stair, and traversed a couple of rooms to find another smaller, spiral stairway set in the thickness of an angle of the outer wall. This stair led to a small landing from which sprang another flight, wooden this time and worm-eaten, which was little better than a ladder.

Through arrow-slits in the wall a little light penetrated from the sky. Up went Undine fearlessly, thrust aside a grating, drew herself through, and stood in an ancient garret under the very roof of the castle.

Even here she was not quite safe. Some of those enterprising searchers might stumble on the garret stair.

Mouldering, broken furniture was stacked round the walls where it had been left for centuries, and in the farthest corner stood a chest, surely the grandfather of all ancient chests. It was fastened by a hasp through which a bolt was thrust, very easy to open.

Undine flung up the lid. Inside was a pile of thick cloth, which felt like old hangings or arras, but it was soft and smelt fairly clean. Undine stepped into the chest. It was so large that she could lie comfortably. She lowered herself gently, and with uplifted arm let the lid close silently down above her. Then with a little sigh of relief she nestled snugly in her retreat and waited for whatever might happen.

It must be a quarter of an hour by now, she thought. She had not heard the gong, but that was understandable. She was so far away and the walls were thick. She knew from experience that you might yell yourself hoarse in any room in the castle and be inaudible a dozen yards away. The search must have begun. Had anybody been found already? How many were there to be found besides herself? Harry, Mr. West, Enid, Jack, Basil, Cecil, Rene, Pandora – eight. That would take some time. Undine realised that if, as she intended, she was to be the last found, she must be prepared for a long wait, perhaps an hour or more. She wished she had a novel and a flash-lamp! She would be bored, but the ring was worth it.

What was that? . . . A footstep? . . . Undoubtedly! . . . Edward had discovered the garret already? Impossible . . . and yet . . . someone was in the room! She could hear soft footsteps coming nearer! She crouched without breathing, absolutely motionless. Probably someone was looking for a place to hide and one of the servants had told them the way to the garret. And she had particularly warned the servants they were not to leave their own wing. What a nuisance!

Suddenly to her dismay she felt the brushing of fingers across the surface of the chest, and then fumbling at the fastening as though to raise the lid. Should she warn them off? It couldn't be Edward so soon!

She whispered, "Go away! This is my den!"

There was a second's hesitation, and then the footsteps obediently began to retreat.

Undine lay quietly for several moments. This wasn't such a good place after all, and she had given herself away. That wretched person when found would lead the searchers to her. Had she time to go somewhere else? She could think of no other place, and it was too late now.

The waiting was very tedious and the chest was becoming unpleasantly hot and airless. She would lift the lid for a moment while there was no one about.

She raised her right hand, and pushed. She encountered resistance. Both hands. What was the matter? Why wouldn't the lid open? She thrust with all her strength. She heaved with her shoulders. Had it caught? Had it stuck? She must get it open! She was so hot . . . she couldn't breathe . . . oh!

Could it be that the unknown who had tiptoed in was playing a practical joke on her? Had fastened the chest, and was now standing silent in the dark garret waiting until she had received sufficient fright to deserve release?

Forgetting caution she called, "I say! Undo this thing. I'm stifling! Honestly – I'm not joking!"

Silence. The dead, thick silence which means that no living creature is there.

She had forgotten everything now except her desperate plight. A sweat of terror broke out on her body. She beat on the chest with her fists, and they fell back against her panting breast, bruised from the hopeless onslaught.

Someone must come! Someone must come soon!

"Harry! Enid! Help! Help!"

She screamed, but the agonised shouts were smothered almost before they left her throat. Perhaps the stars breaking through the cloud-wrack above the castle roof heard them, but that great stretch of wild sky had heard so often the shrieks of death ring from the rafters of Cleys Castle, and one century was very like another on the Welsh marches.

Another sound was more clearly heard: the booming of the castle gong.

Down in the hall Edward Stacey accompanied his lusty tattoo with a warning shout:

"Look out, everybody! I'm coming!"

Now where would these idiots be likely to hide? Whither should a good sleuth-hound proceed? Ah, that vile-smelling Priest's Hole, discovered this morning behind the Isabella Tapestry! It would be sure to appeal to someone without much imagination. Bruising his knees in the dark against projecting stones, and cursing this outlandish sport, Edward found the gaping doorway and stepped into the tiny chamber.

He paused; easier than going down on hands and knees to hunt. Ha! The beggars had to come up to breathe . . .

"Come on out, Jack!" sang the Major. "I can hear you snorting. The game's up!"

Jack Willoughby stumbled out, not unwillingly.

"I'm not sorry to be found. You don't really appreciate that atmosphere until you've had a quarter of a hour alone with it."

The next person to be found was Pandora Hyde. She had climbed up and fitted herself neatly into the embrasure of a window, and it was only by a stroke of bad luck for her that she was found at all. Jack Willoughby's clumsy, groping hand came into contact with the toe of her shoe.

She hopped down obediently to join her captor and the Major. All chance of winning the emerald ring was lost, but she never did have any luck!

A quarter of an hour later, passing through the Long Gallery, Pandora gave a sharp yell.

"Oooh! Something grabbed my hair!"

There was a delighted chuckle from above, and looking up they beheld the recognisable shape of Cecil Sabelle astride a rafter and grinning down at them.

"Couldn't resist playing the ghost, Pan. What a shame I gave myself away!"

"How on earth did you get up there?"

"Oh, they taught us all such things at Borstal."

He neatly swung himself over and dropped to the floor.

"How many more to find?"

"Nearly all of them."

"Then I'll bet there's somebody in the powder closet off the State bedroom. Let's go and see."

Enid Willoughby was in the powder closet.

They searched other bedrooms and cupboards very thoroughly, but found no one. They searched the guardroom and the arms-rooms of the keep, but found no one. At the end of an hour's search Sir Harry was run to earth in the butler's pantry, and Rene Fullerton in the servants' hall, where she had disguised herself in cap and apron and might have remained unrecognised had not the maids betrayed her by laughing.

Very hot and tired, they all returned to the hall for drinks; and there reclined Lionel West, napping luxuriously on the settle before the hearth.

"I've been here all the time," he yawned. "Edward never looked for me!"

"Who is there left to find?" asked Sir Harry.

"Only Crown and Undine," said Edward.

Enid Willoughby sank into a chair.

"I'm frightfully tired. This game goes on too long; it's past eleven o'clock. Does anybody mind if I go to bed?"

"Run along," said her husband. "Only I'm rather interested in this hunt. I want to see it through."

"I do believe," cried Rene Fullerton, "that Basil is going to win that ring for me."

"To save him the expense of an engagement ring," said Cecil Sabelle. "Very canny of him, I'm sure."

"Beast!"

"Oh, come on!" said Pandora impatiently. "I want to get this thing over. I'm bored with it too."

And it was she who eventually discovered Basil Crown, wedged inside the organ box in the chapel and dirtier than he had ever been in his life.

"Have I won?" he asked, when he saw the crowd of searchers.

"No, you haven't. Undine has won," said Rene, rather crossly.

"But where in the name of goodness is Undine?" asked Jack Willoughby.

"She's had an unfair advantage," said Pandora sulkily; "she knows the place so well."

"We can easily find her now," said Lionel West. "We'll all go in different directions and call to her that she can come out, she's won."

Some time later, in the hall, Edward Stacey said, "Do you know if anybody has found Undine?"

"I don't know," said Jack Willoughby. "I gave up huntin' long ago. Not my idea of sport."

"Somebody is sure to have found her," said Rene Fullerton, yawning. "I expect she has gone to bed. I'm going too. Good night, people!"

"Probably she withdrew from the game," said West. "She may never have hidden at all. In that case Crown gets the ring; we'll decide to-morrow."

"Funny we never found her," said Jack. "I shouted all over the place. But you can't go rowsting her out of her boudoir."

"No . . . good night," said Edward Stacey. West was alone by the sinking fire in the billiard-room when Sir Harry entered.

"All alone, West? Where are the others?"

"I think everybody has gone to bed."

"Has anybody seen Undine? Who saw her last?"

"I fancy the last that anyone saw of her was when she switched off the lights in the hall, before we began to hide."

Sir Harry took out a sheet of note-paper.

"I found this on my pillow. Rather extraordinary."

West took the sheet – a small, blue, single sheet torn from

a block of note-paper – and read in a firm, flowing hand:

I shall have to stay away for several days. I can't explain here but will do so as soon as I see you. Don't let this make any difference to your plans. You can manage perfectly well without me. Have you ever thought of Irene Fullerton?
With love from
Undine.

"What a queer note!" said West. "What do you make of it?"

"I'm just mystified! But Undine apparently expected me to be mystified. 'I can't explain here,' she says. A few days? She must have taken her sports car."

"And driven to Cwm Dyffod? What a peculiar time to go!"

"She may have gone the other way. There's a village three miles from here, Abertefn . . . What the Hamlet does she mean? Have I ever thought what about Rene Fullerton? What's Rene got to do with it, anyway?"

"You mean, you haven't the least idea where she can have gone, or why?"

"Not the least idea! She was quite normal at dinner. You were there and saw her. And afterwards she seemed to be full of this hide-and-seek game . . ."

He paused, and then with sudden reserve said, "Never mind. She's gone, and there's some good reason. Undine's all right. Do you want to sit up, or shall I put the lights out?"

West went to his room, and truth to tell the mysterious departure of Lady Stacey did not cause him to lose any sleep. He had only known her for twenty-four hours and possibly she was given to outbursts of eccentric behaviour. As for the note she left behind, that was Sir Harry's business, and by now he had probably thought of an explanation.

Chapter VI
THE PARTING GUESTS

NEXT morning the clouds were all gone, and a pure, pale sunlight sparkled in the lofty sky and brightened the old grey walls of the castle. There was a touch of frost in the air, and the mountain slopes were clear and purple, their misty shadows driven away by the morning light.

All the members of the house party seemed to have overslept themselves, for Lionel West descended ten minutes after the gong to find Rene Fullerton eating her breakfast alone in the sombre room where last night's blown-out candles still stood forlorn in their brass holders. Patines of sunlight from the high arched windows flickered on the rough-cast wall, but the table was in shadow, and looked gloomy and bare.

Rene wore a tweed travelling suit and a tiny scarlet suede hat.

"Hallo!" she cried. "Isn't everybody late? Do you know, the servants are saying that Lady Stacey went away last night on some sudden business, and left a note explaining to Sir Harry? No wonder we couldn't find her! Not my idea of good sport, by any means!"

West helped himself to coffee.

"I think the business that called her away must have been urgent. Sir Harry showed me the note."

He was thinking of the curious introduction of Rene's name into that mysterious note. Did she know something? Was she acting ignorance for his benefit?

"Basil and I are leaving after breakfast," said Rene.

"I didn't know that. Isn't it rather sudden?"

"Basil told Undine yesterday. As a matter of fact, Mr. West, there were slight ructions over our engagement, and Basil was horribly touchy, and decided to leave on the spot. It isn't my doing" – she shrugged her shoulders – "I don't want to go."

West smiled. "What exactly are 'slight ructions'?"

"Oh, first cousin to a jolly old row! I'm awfully fond of Lady Stacey, but she does like to do things all by herself, if you know what I mean. Basil said she was thoroughly peeved that we'd fixed our affair up without consulting her . . . Oh, here is Basil!"

Crown came in with a rush, wearing his overcoat.

He ignored the ceremony of saying good morning, and exclaimed:

"Ready, Rene? That's good. I've told them to have my car round in ten minutes. No, I won't bother with breakfast. We can stop at some place on the way. Just a cup of coffee." He poured himself a cup.

"By the way," said West, "you're the official winner of the emerald ring, Crown."

"I am?" He ceased for a moment from gulping his coffee. "By Jove! Thanks awfully!"

"Oh, Basil, how clever of you!" cried Rene. West looked puzzled.

"I don't remember exactly where the thing is. I haven't seen it since last night. I wonder if I put it down on the hall table?"

"I'll go and see," said Rene.

She returned in a few moments.

"It isn't there, and the servants haven't seen it. It must be in your room, Mr. West."

"Oh, never mind it!" said Crown, jumping up. "We can't wait. I want to be in town by two o'clock. Let's go and find Sir Harry and make our adieux."

"I shall send it on to you," said West.

Rene thanked him with a glowing smile as she shook hands; and ten minutes later he heard the rattle of the drawbridge as Crown's scarlet sports model shot out upon its journey to London.

Pandora Hyde was the next to appear, followed by Cecil Sabelle and the Willoughbys.

They had all heard of Undine's strangely sudden departure, but politeness apparently forbade their discussing it.

West found Sir Harry in his pleasant little writing-room, whose leaded windows were embellished with shields of blue and amber glass. He was turning over his letters, but when West entered he looked up with thinly veiled anxiety in his face, and said:

"Undine didn't take a car last night. She must have *walked* away!"

"Or could someone have fetched her?"

"I suppose that's possible . . . but who?"

"She says she'll explain in a few days, Harry."

Sir Harry returned to his letters with businesslike absorption, as though to counteract any possible betrayal of anxiety by his previous remarks. He naturally would not want his friend to think that anything was amiss.

The Major walked in a quarter of an hour later, stuffing his pipe.

"Good morning. Have the papers come? No? I never can understand, when they get to Abertefn by nine o'clock, why it takes about four hours to bring them along here. I've asked them at the shop, and it's all the fault of the Great War, or Daylight Saving, or the Labour Party. Where is everybody this morning?"

There was an awkward silence.

"Undine has gone away for a few days," said Harry. "She went last night."

"Last night? But she was playing hide-and-seek!"

"She left this note."

A strange expression crossed the Major's face. Sir Harry was bending over his letters again. The man who was reading the note changed colour, fingered his tie, and shot a peculiar glance at his brother. He took out his handkerchief, replaced it, and catching West's eye, laid down the note and remarked casually: "I see."

He went hastily to a small cabinet, and pulled out drawer after drawer.

"Do you still keep matches here? I can't find any."

His nonchalance was overdone. West saw it if Sir Harry did not.

West sauntered over to the cabinet, holding out a silver match-case . . . "Have mine, Edward. Would you care for a stroll? Come along, do!"

His eyes carried a hint of urgency.

"I don't mind if I do," said the Major.

The two men emerged from the castle by a small postern

door, and found themselves upon a sunny, flagged terrace, out of sight of any of the occupied rooms. They walked up and down for a few moments, the Major drawing thoughtfully at his pipe, West with his hands in his pockets.

At last the latter said: "Harry's keeping the lid on. He's worried about his wife. Does she do this kind of thing? You gave me the impression — "

"I'm a bad actor." There was a grim note in Edward's voice.

West looked up sharply. "I'm sorry. I shouldn't have asked . . . But then, why should Harry have consulted me if he already suspected something?"

"Harry doesn't suspect anything. That's the trouble."

"Then there is trouble!"

"There's a lot, West; and it's bad . . . damned bad."

Edward glanced round to make sure they were alone. Above them frowned the massive east wall of the castle with its high arrow-slit windows; below, the grassy bank fell away to the black and silent moat.

"West, you've known us all our lives. You know I'd do anything to spare Harry trouble, but this is a case when I don't know whether I ought to spare him. You're a legal man; the right fellow to see round a problem like this. I've had it on my mind for a week. I never foresaw what would probably happen. Undine . . . was too deep for me."

He turned his back on the castle and stared across the moat to the few cultivated fields where rotting stalks alone gave indications of the summer's crop.

"Did Harry ever tell you how he met his wife?"

"Yes. At a village in the south of France. She was alone and an orphan."

"So she told him!"

The Major's teeth ground on his pipe-stem. Suddenly the words came with a rush.

"I had a friend once called Corbett. I discovered him at Marseilles when I came home a few weeks ago. He's a doctor . . . brother to Corbett the poisoner, who was sent to New Caledonia twelve years ago. You remember?"

"Corbett? A young English doctor practising in Toulon? He got – how many? – years' penal servitude for poisoning a Monsieur . . . Monsieur . . . I forget, but it was one of his patients, who had a pretty wife. Wasn't she the reason? You say you knew this Corbett?"

"I knew his brother. Yes, Corbett was put on trial – along with the pretty wife. She was acquitted; he got fifteen years after a recommendation to mercy. Who will ever know the truth of that affair? The wife was an Englishwoman, married to a French shipping merchant. Madame Abadie – now you remember all the case! Her maiden name was Wallace – Katherine Undine Wallace!"

"It couldn't be possible!"

"Wait! Madame Abadie disappeared after the trial; went into the country; called herself a poor, friendless girl, the daughter of an American – artist, wasn't it? – who had recently died, leaving her alone in the world. Pshaw! I must have a nasty, suspicious mind, West; I should always doubt a plausible tale like that. But then, poor Harry had never even seen an adventuress until he met this one. I told you that I met the other Corbett in Marseilles. He told me his brother's story, and reserved judgment on Undine. He was always a good-natured fellow. Said she was married now to a wealthy man of my name, and lived in England. I was bitter when I discovered her trickery. She had ruined Corbett; now it was my brother's turn. I faced Undine the day before yesterday. I'd been torn in my mind . . . I couldn't smash her without smashing Harry. She didn't say much; I couldn't understand what kept her so quiet. I know now! She was in communication with her lover. He has got a mitigation of his sentence, and is free. He came for her last night; sent her a message to be ready. The game of hide-and-seek was planned so that in the darkness she might slip away. All this flashed through my mind when I read the note she left. West! I've let you in on the responsibility now. What are we going to do?"

"Aren't you taking the worst possible view of it?"

"Of course! If you'd seen her as I saw her when I threatened her with exposure!"

"You threatened her with exposure? Then these two days she has known she was found out?"

"She deserved to be kept in suspense."

"I noticed that there was something between you," said West. "But why Corbett? Supposing fear of exposure has driven her to run away – alone?"

Edward gave an ugly laugh.

"Adventuresses do not run away alone!"

"You're very bitter, Edward."

"I am. I'm a hard man. I felt merciless towards her."

"Harry has no suspicion of false dealing," said West. "Can we keep this story to ourselves?"

"I warned you I'm no actor."

"Then for a few days, until Undine herself writes, or returns."

"Returns!" The Major's lip curled.

"Then, writes. She offers to explain. By the way, what do you make of that note? That reference to Miss Fullerton?"

"How should I know?" The Major made a gesture as though the whole subject nauseated him. "I suppose you'll agree that I've solved her disappearance?"

"I still dislike to take such an extreme view. I very much hope you are wrong. But we agree to be silent, Edward, until she writes?"

"She won't write."

They returned slowly to the castle. Almost against the postern door they met an agitated maid wearing the neat grey satin dress and cap peculiar to Lady Stacey's personal attendant.

She stopped them, and for a moment was too breathless to speak.

"Oh, Major Stacey!"

"What is it?"

"Sir Harry asked me . . . to find out what luggage . . . what clothes her ladyship had taken."

She grew calmer, and with one nervous hand upon the satin breast of her dress, added: "Please will you tell him she has taken no luggage, no clothes, but only her long mink coat and the blue velvet hat which hung beside it in the big clothes closet. No shoes, so far as I can discover. Her ladyship was wearing blonde crêpe-de-chine shoes with her beige dress of ring velvet. You will tell Sir Harry?"

"I'll tell him," said the Major curtly. He took West's arm as they moved away. "You see! She was fetched by a car."

"We heard nothing."

"You don't suppose he waited at the main gate!"

An hour later the guests were all packing, and at half-past twelve they sat down to an early lunch before leaving to catch the two o'clock train from Cwm Dyffod.

Lionel West, who had been pressed by Sir Harry to stay for a few days, said diffidently at lunch: "Forgive my mentioning it, but I can't find the emerald ring. It seems to have disappeared in last night's confusion; and I've promised to send it on to Crown, who won it by getting himself covered with ancient cobwebs in the organ loft."

"He's boneless enough to get inside one of the pipes!" said Cecil Sabelle.

"Does anyone remember seeing the ring just before we began to play?"

There was a moment's pause; glances flashed round the table.

Enid Willoughby, with a faint smile disarming her contrite expression, said: "Am I to blame? I picked up the ring from the hall table to examine it while Undine was explaining the rules. But I put it down again immediately, beside its case. Did anyone see it after that?"

No one answered.

Pandora Hyde was cutting a piece of cheese, and the knife slipped suddenly, so that the cheese was crumbled and fell in fragments on the table.

"Now then, Pan, own up!" cried the incorrigible Cecil. "I saw you with the ring on your pretty finger when we went to find Mrs. Willoughby in the powder closet!"

The girl flushed scarlet and turned furious eyes upon him; then gradually she recovered her calm, and the colour died from her ivory cheeks.

"Don't take any notice of him, Pan," said Jack Willoughby. "He's only raggin'."

She seemed to breathe more easily, and cast at Willoughby a decidedly grateful glance.

"But she was!" insisted Sabelle. "I'm not ragging. Pan, you can't deny it! You were wearing the ring!"

She laid down her knife, and said awkwardly: "I'm sorry, I put it on when Mrs. Willoughby laid it down to see if it would fit my finger. Just then Undine switched the lights out, and I forgot I was wearing the ring until after I was found. Then the next time I was passing through the hall I put it back on the table. That's all I know."

Her face was colourless, and she suddenly put her hands under the table. West had seen witnesses do that, to hide the clenched knuckles.

Everyone seemed satisfied, but West knew that he had been in the hall all the time, and he had not seen Pandora Hyde lay anything on the table. In fact, he remembered distinctly that she had remained standing on the lowest stair until the party was reformed to go in search of Basil Crown, and had then turned by the newel post and gone out with the others through the *portières* at the back of the hall. She had not gone near the table.

"You're quite sure?" he asked pleasantly.

"Oh, quite sure."

"It may have rolled to the floor and into a corner,"

suggested Enid. "Ask the maids to look."

Pandora rose.

"Will you excuse me? I haven't quite finished my packing."

"Hurry up!" advised Cecil Sabelle. "The prison van leaves in ten minutes. Line up for Holloway, Pentonville, and the Scrubs!"

It was an unfortunate allusion on the part of the Staceys' tame jester. West saw Pandora's lips stiffen as she rushed from the room, and from his long experience of the courts he was sure that she had lied about his ring. He knew nothing of the girl, whether or not she had kleptomaniac tendencies, but he could not accuse a fellow guest in a friend's house. It was awkward! Presently a man-servant appeared, carrying Pandora's bags, and behind him came the girl with a round, green kid hat-case slung on her arm.

"What's the matter, Pan?" sang out Jack Willoughby. "You look as if you'd seen a ghost."

"You have been an age!" complained Enid, who had come to lunch ready for the journey. "Does it take you all this time to pack your hats? Will you sit with Jack at the front? I prefer the back."

There was the usual confusion of luggage and farewells, and in a few minutes the Willoughbys, Sabelle and Pandora were carried rapidly away in Sir Harry's Rolls.

A quarter of an hour after they were gone West found the empty white case which had contained his ring in the pot of a palm which stood at the rear of the hall. He pocketed it and said nothing, ruefully convinced that the jewel itself reposed in that innocent green hat-box of Miss Pandora

Hyde.

Left alone with the two brothers he realised how deeply the three of them were concerned over the disappearance of Lady Stacey; he and Edward knowing the probable truth, Harry unsuspecting.

The guests had departed – even Enid Willoughby – little knowing that anything was wrong or that Undine Stacey had left her home under such sordid circumstances. What was the loss of an emerald ring compared to the tragedy which threatened Harry Stacey and which every day drew nearer to its disclosure?

The days went by. A time came when Sir Harry could not disguise the fever of impatience with which he waited for the daily post. He could hardly be induced to leave the castle lest a telegram should come in his absence.

A week lengthened into a fortnight, and then the third week was past. Edward Stacey and West could endure the strain no longer. The news was broken to Sir Harry of his wife's early deception and probable flight with her lover.

That was the end of Cleys Castle. Sir Harry could no longer bear the sight of the place. He took a small country house in Surrey and moved into it with his two children, their governess, and a suitable staff of servants. He did not even try to trace the wife who had so cruelly deceived him. He sometimes looked fearfully for her name in newspaper columns, but he never heard from her again.

Chapter VII
THE DISCOVERY

LIONEL WEST spent a busy winter. A returning desire for work indicated the renewal of physical energy, and he appeared as counsel for the defence in two cases of the first importance; besides engaging himself in writing the life of his old friend and legal adversary, Sir Cheston Thorp, most famous of barristers. In April he went to Cannes for a change of scene and revelled in scents and sunshine. Some people might have considered his holiday dull, and insisted that he was wasting all the advantages for enjoyment which Cannes offered.

The promenade saw him not at all; nor did he enter any popular restaurant to eat, dance, or stare. He rented a small villa with an exquisite garden; and there among the flowers he reclined with quantities of books, only emerging for his daily drive or to stroll inland to some secluded spot where he could stand and see, from a new point of vantage, the beauty of the bay and the pearly contour of the Cap d'Antibes.

His English paper – Continental edition with its attenuated version of the news – came to him every day, and as a rule he found little there to interest him. A sensational headline left him cold; and when one morning he was greeted by the flaunting message, "Gruesome Find at a Welsh Castle," he was about to turn hastily to the brief political column when his eye was captured and held by a name he knew; and soon with a growing sensation of horror he found himself eagerly assimilating a paragraph as dreadful as it was incredible:

"BODY OF MISSING PEERESS DISCOVERED IN A CHEST.

"Late yesterday afternoon, some workmen engaged in repairing the roof of Cleys Castle, on the borders of Radnorshire, were horrified to discover in an antique chest the body of a woman. The remains were identified as those of Undine, wife of Sir Harry Stacey, present owner of the castle, who disappeared from her home in October last and has not since been heard of. Pending the inquest, there is as yet no evidence to throw light upon this terrible occurrence. Sir Harry Stacey is the grandson and heir of the late Sir Digby Stacey, the multimillionaire shipowner; and it is said that he paid as much as a quarter of a million for the ownership of Cleys Castle, which is in excellent condition and a fine old relic of Norman times."

The trivial thought that crossed West's mind was this: "So they've made poor Undine a peeress!"

He laid the paper down. "I must get home and see Harry."

There were matters to arrange. It was a week before he reached London. At his rooms he found a summons to Cleys, signed by a Scotland Yard official. He wondered.

He went round to Edward Stacey's rooms; the Major had gone to Cleys. He rang up Whitelands, Sir Harry's house in Surrey; Sir Harry, the children, and the governess were gone to Cleys.

West was mystified by the trend of events. He sent a wire

to Cleys announcing the time of his arrival at Cwm Dyffod; and next morning he went down, to be met at the station by Edward Stacey, driving his own car.

The car swung out upon the long stretch of road between the looming mountain ranges.

West said: "Of course I know nothing apart from the bare statement of the discovery. I drew the obvious conclusion: that she perished the night we played that ridiculous game. That she hid in the chest and was unable to get out. It won't bear thinking of."

The Major's fingers tightened on the wheel; he trod the accelerator recklessly.

"You read about the inquest?"

"No. I was only in England yesterday morning. But, Edward, there's a mystery: that note to Harry! And we were wronging her: there was no lover. Poor Undine! Poor girl!"

"I can't pity her," said Edward, the muscles tightening round his jaw. "She deceived Harry. She met the end she deserved."

"Ah, you're ruthless!"

"My soldiering has made me ruthless. One isn't often privileged to view the intervention of such a timely Nemesis."

West was silent. Though inured to the sight of human distress by a career almost as hardening as that of the professional soldier, he could not view with equanimity the picture of the unfortunate woman stifling to death in the garret while her unhearing friends laughed and played below.

Major Stacey went on with a rather forced lightness: "I tell you, there's going to be the devil and all to pay. I'm sorry for you, West, as I am for all the rest of us. You're putting your head into the lion's den and your feet into the hornet's nest . . . Do I mean that? Let it pass. Personally I can face anything, even inquisitive policemen – except for Harry. It's hell for him. And now he knows that she didn't go away with Corbett, he's all remorse for having suspected her. He illogically and sentimentally overlooks the fact that her twelve years' life with him was one continual deception."

"Policemen? But the inquest is over."

The Major turned his head sharply and then swung it back to a concentrated scrutiny of the rushing road.

"To be sure! You never heard the verdict."

"What was the verdict?"

"Wilful murder against some person unknown!"

"You don't mean it!"

The Major's voice relaxed into an easy drawl.

"My dear West, the castle is full of detectives; inspectors, sergeants, footprint and finger-print experts, locksmiths, photographers, and every known variety of sleuth. Surely your own presence here was compulsory rather than voluntary?"

"I had an order to present myself."

"So had we all."

"All?"

"Every one who was in the castle at the time of the – murder."

"What! Enid, Willoughby, Crown — "

"All of them."

"And, Edward, why murder?"

"Because," said the Major tersely, "the lid of the chest was no automatic contrivance; it fastened with a hasp and bolt. The bolt was shot when the workmen found it! Understand? Secondly, the letter placed by *someone* in Harry's room to suggest a secret departure. There were two other curious circumstances. The mink coat and the hat in which Undine was supposed to have gone away were laid in the chest on top of her body; and on her finger was – your lost emerald ring."

"But Miss Hyde was the last person to handle that ring. How — "

"Ask the inspector. I'm no sleuth, but he'll be glad enough to start a fox, even a dainty little vixen like Pandora."

"You don't mean to say that anyone in the house is suspected?" said West thoughtfully.

"For an eminent barrister," said the Major with a sidelong twist of his lip, "your faith in your fellow-creatures is positively touching. You're a simple, guileless laddie, West. Far be it from me to open your eyes to the awful depths of depravity that underlie the apparent benevolence of every human heart! Who'd have suspected Undine of having a past? Our new friend, Inspector Sedley, is, alas, no gentleman. He has a nasty mind; he suspects everybody. To him we are all, from the least to the greatest, undiscovered criminals. Upon my word, Jack Willoughby drops a spent match and His Excellency pounces upon same and deducts from poor Jack's whorls that he is of a vindictive nature and disposed to sudden acts of violence. One up for the prosecution! I tell you, you can't imagine what an atmosphere awaits you at Cleys."

A quarter of an hour later the car ran over the drawbridge and crawled under the portal of the Norman gate. A policeman stuck his head out of the porter's window and the Major had to wait for the official wave before he could proceed. West realised then that the affair was serious and that he was entering a sphere of trouble and horror.

He was given his old room, and found to his joy that the service was as excellent as ever and the supply of hot water in the adjoining bathroom failed not under the dread reign of the law. He descended at the sound of the tea-gong to join the guests whom last he had met under such innocent and merry circumstances. He dreaded the first encounter, but forgot that after a week of horror and shock a reaction is bound to set in. There were neither fearful eyes nor hushed voices in the billiard-room. Sir Harry came forward to greet him with a hearty hand-clasp. Edward Stacey was turning the knobs of the wireless, while Basil Crown offered suggestions from the *World Radio*. Enid Willoughby sat at the low walnut table pouring tea, and Amy Farbell carried round the cups. Jack Willoughby, Cecil Sabelle, Rene Fullerton, and Pandora Hyde were engaged in an argumentative travesty of the game of bridge.

"I went to the hall first," said West. "You've changed the tea rendezvous."

There was a moment's pause. Enid made an expressive

grimace at Edward, who said easily: "Needs must, old man, when authority commands. This is the room officially allotted for our social amenities. You will discover later that we dine here, eh, Rene?"

Miss Fullerton giggled.

"It's like being in the Zoo," she suggested.

"A pretty analogy," agreed Sabelle. "We walk in lambs' clothing but inwardly we are all ravening wolves."

Enid's shoulders shuddered slightly under their delicate lace covering.

"Your tea, Lionel. Amy, give him something to eat. Edward, that loud speaker has been bleating about football the whole afternoon; turn it off, do! I can't stand it another minute."

"There's a good concert at Hilversum."

Enid spread her hands. "Basil, do get him away and turn the thing off! It's so rude when Mr. West has only just arrived."

There was an official knock at the door, and it was heavily opened to display the form of the constable who had inspected West at the outer gate.

"If Mr. West has finished his tea," he announced pontifically, "Inspector Sedley will be pleased to see him in the study."

Enid, who was evidently acting as hostess, replied acidly: "You may tell the Inspector that Mr. West has only just arrived."

She smiled cynically at West. "You're not to be allowed much grace. Do take your tea in peace; the man's a monster."

West drank his tea hastily, and refusing the plate offered to him, rose. He was already sensitive to the atmosphere of which Edward had spoken, the consciousness of a roomful of over-strained people, all hiding an apprehension too gloomy for words under a thin crust of forced frivolity.

When, a few minutes later, he was following the officer along a stone-flagged passage which rang hollow under his feet, he wondered if he walked above dungeons, and how many men long dead had gone to their doom within these gloomy walls.

A sunny, circular chamber in the north turret, where the ill-fated Undine had often gone to sew, had been hastily turned into an office of the law.

A broad table had been drawn across the windows, and behind it with his back to the light sat a tall man with stooping shoulders, a florid complexion, and a striking lack of hair upon a head which could not have owned to more than forty years.

West had known Inspector Sedley well, during the course of many criminal cases, as a tireless worker, keen as a sporting dog, but possessing also that quality which is known as firmness in a friend and obstinacy in an opponent. If he had a fault it was that he hated to share his spoils. Also his imagination was limited to the extent that although he could put two and two together with infallible precision, they always made four and never the inspired five.

He rose to meet West with instant recognition. When greetings had been exchanged, he said, "I must admit I'm glad to see you, Mr. West. There aren't many of my cases in which I'm able to have expert legal advice so close at hand. Perhaps you'll be able to see your way to talking things over occasionally?"

"I should like," said West, "to see this dreadful affair cleared up for my friend Sir Harry's sake. I have the main facts of the case from Major Stacey. It seems incredible to me still. I was a member of the party last October; I remember clearly the events of the evening upon which Lady Stacey disappeared. I was the first to be shown the note, which they tell me was an important factor in influencing the coroner's verdict. That note had peculiarities which may now be explained. What troubles me is this sinister suggestion of foul play in Lady Stacey's own household."

"Household?" The inspector's eyebrows shot up. "We've cleared the servants, every one."

He rose to his feet.

"Come up and see the room where it happened. My own mental processes always get active on the scene of the crime."

He held open the door for West to pass out.

"Take note of the way we go. There's only one route to this garret. Assuming that Lady Stacey went to the garret during the game of hide-and-seek, with the object of hiding in the chest, we shall now be covering the same ground that she did. This way!"

Sedley nodded to the constable in the corridor, who immediately took up his position at the door of the room they were leaving; and the two men proceeded along a short cross-passage and emerged upon a wide gallery which connected the north wing with the keep. Half-way along that gallery they turned again under an open arch, crossed a small stone chamber, opened a low door, and discovered an ascending flight of stone stairs.

West took careful notice of every turning, and in some places looked closely at the walls and the floor. They ascended to a higher story, left the stairs, and traversed a couple of rooms, to find another smaller spiral stairway set in the thickness of an angle of the outer wall. This stair led to a small landing from which sprang another flight – wooden this time and rickety – which was little better than a ladder. Through arrow-slits in the wall a little light penetrated, and a constable stood on guard at the foot of the stair.

"So this is the way she came," said West. "Circuitous! I doubt if I could find my way a second time."

They climbed the ladder-stair one at a time and gingerly, thrust aside a grating, scrambled through, and stood in an ancient garret under the very roof of the castle.

This was the scene of the crime which for six months had remained hidden from knowledge, and which was still to West mysterious and unproven. He was conscious of a quickening of his pulses, and the inspector too seemed more alert.

"Nothing has been moved," he said, gasping slightly from his climb. "Everything stands as it did on the day when the workmen found the body."

"Even this, I suppose," said West ironically, indicating the roughly boarded floor where the dust of centuries had been trodden and trampled as though by an army of feet.

"Unfortunately, yes. I questioned those fool builders – I fairly had 'em on the grill – to find out if they'd noticed any footprints in the dust when they first entered the garret, but, of all the unobservant cuckoos! Said they'd had their eyes on the roof, not on the floor! The foreman was the real culprit, being the first man in to see the damaged roof. To think, if it hadn't been for that prize star-gazer we'd have had the whole story of the crime written for us in the dust on the floor!"

West shrugged his shoulders.

"Finger-prints?"

"None! Would you believe it?"

"Oh, yes, I'd believe it. Even the densest murderer in these days knows to use gloves, or else a corner of his coat to obliterate his traces. You don't give this criminal credit for much intelligence."

"Criminals don't have what I call intelligence," growled the inspector; "I've known them give themselves away by carelessness that a babe would scorn."

West had no wish to argue, but he said quietly: "The crimes of intelligence are never solved. Let's hope this isn't one."

He cast a comprehensive glance round the garret. Mouldering, broken furniture was stacked round the walls where it had been left for centuries, but his attention was immediately held by the ancient chest which occupied a distant position under the down-sloping rafters.

"Is that — ?"

The inspector nodded. He strode over to the chest and flung up the lid. West followed with a reluctance that was almost disgust. The chest was quite empty, except for a torn and crumpled blanket which covered the bottom. The walls and lid were of solid oak, two inches thick.

The inspector pointed to the blanket.

"That rag is as old as the chest, I should say. The tears were freshly done, ripped by the woman's heels in her death agony. Her hands and arms were covered with bruises."

"And on her finger was the ring I lost the night before?"

"Hum . . . curious. The body was covered by a mink coat, well pressed down over the head and shoulders to prevent resuscitation, and the hat was thrust into a corner."

He gently let down the lid of the chest, raising and lowering it several times.

"You can see how easy it is to raise. It's impossible for the thing to fasten itself. It can only be secured by lifting the hasp from the outside and pushing in the bolt. The five workmen who made the discovery gave independent evidence that the bolt was completely secured – like this!"

The inspector swung up the hasp and shot the bolt. The lid of the chest was now immovable.

"What made them open the chest?"

"A thirst for knowledge, I presume," said the inspector dryly.

West smiled inwardly. It was a joke in the courts that Inspector Sedley, himself the most inquisitive man on earth, was merciless in his denunciation of this trait in others.

"I'm not giving anything away," said the inspector, straightening his back and dusting his hands, "by telling you the popular reconstruction of the crime. Needless to say, they all think I have a highly superior theory up my sleeve – and I let them think; but between you and me, Mr. West, I haven't yet seen my way to an alternative. As you were a member of the party on the fatal occasion, you'll remember that on the night of October 18th last the castle was darkened, all except the servants' wing, where the servants were all together, and Lady Stacey with nine other persons took part in a game of hide-and-seek. Major Stacey was left below in the hall, and Lady Stacey and the rest – including yourself – dispersed in all directions to hide. The prize for the person who remained longest hidden was to be an emerald ring, presented by yourself."

West nodded. "Good recapitulation. That's all I know, Inspector."

"The rest is theory – except that pretty soon I've got to have everyone of those people on the mat for the purpose of painless extraction. If – as is certain – there was funny work going on in the castle that night, one or another is bound to let drop a hint. But returning to the reconstruction; we'll conclude that Lady Stacey is anxious to win the prize. She thinks of this chest in the garret and decides to hide there – quite a good spot to lie *perdu* if you consider it from that angle. The murderer follows her . . . now I see you opening your mouth, Mr. West, to ask me why! I don't know why! If I knew why, I should have my man and the case would be tied up and pigeon-holed . . .

"He follows her to the garret, sees her enter the chest, creeps up and secures the chest, and makes his retreat – if he's one of the guests, and who else could he be? – to select his own hiding-place far enough from the scene of his crime. Well, Mr. West, I've been in that chest, I've hammered at the lid, and shouted myself hoarse; and while my man at the foot of the stair could hear me fairly well, another man across the passage-way there, with a door between, heard nothing. That speaks for itself. After a short period of suspended animation life would become extinct. Meanwhile the murderer has to cover his tracks. He gets that note – and my theory is, it was part of a letter at some time sent to him by Lady Stacey — "

"Or picked up in her own boudoir. It's a clumsy trick, but it served its purpose of gaining time."

"If you like . . . He plants it in Sir Harry's room; gets the coat and hat from Lady Stacey's apartments, first things he could lay hands on to support the theory of departure; and likewise, by some means, your emerald ring – by the way, I've got an idea about that; and during the hours of the night – here's nerve for you! – returns to decorate the body of his victim with the proofs that a crime has been committed. Silly, that! Those finishing touches put the lid on it."

"What about my ring?"

"Oh, that! My idea is, that was pure malice. Lady Stacey had won the ring; she should have it, and much good might it do her! Points to somebody with a grudge; woman, I should say."

"Woman? Possibly. The very nature of the crime; furtive, sly, mean. Does a man slink after the woman he intends to kill, and creep up to latch her into a living tomb? He'd shoot her, strangle her . . . not this. And yet to return at dead of night . . . it's a woman with a man's nerve, Sedley."

"There's something in what you say," replied the inspector, non-committal. He might adopt someone else's idea, but he would never acknowledge it.

West began to walk slowly round the garret, examining the sorry collection of ancient furniture.

"I suppose you've examined all this for fingerprints, Sedley?"

"Yes . . . but it isn't suggestive. It's all well out of the direct line from the door to the chest."

"Oh, but — "

West had paused before a narrow, upright cupboard of rough finish and splintered panels, which might once have contained the robes of a Norman châtelaine.

"I should like to know," he said, as though to himself, "why the latch of this family pew should be almost free from dust, while the rest of the exterior is so thickly coated that I can't see the colour of the wood. Did those workmen paw the entire contents of the garret?"

"They swore they touched nothing but the chest, and that was within half an hour of entering the garret. Crompton may have tested the latch for prints."

West took out his silk handkerchief, and using it to cover his fingers, gingerly lifted the latch and poked his head into the interior of the narrow cupboard, which suggested nothing so much as a coffin set on end.

Immediately he made an exclamation.

"What do you think of this, Sedley?"

He pointed to the floor of the cupboard where the ancient dust was stirred as though a pair of impatient feet had shuffled there.

"Looks like feet," admitted Sedley grudgingly, "but there's not a print. Tells you nothing."

"Are the marks new or old?"

"Pretty recent."

"And look . . . the wooden sides here are brushed, as though by a pair of elbows. Have you a torch?"

West seized the torch and flashed it over the inside of the cupboard. The whole of the interior was coated with dust and mildew, except at the top where the wood was brushed clear with a similar mark to those which appeared on the sides.

West's eyes gleamed, as often they did in the hearing of a difficult case when a witness's evidence gave him the chance to score a point. He was quick of intuition, and was sometimes criticised for jumping to a conclusion before he had even prepared the steps to take him there; but one thing not even his opponents could deny, his intuitions nearly always proved to be right ones, and eventually he was able to clinch them by logical methods.

"See where he shuffled his feet? See where his elbows rubbed the sides while he waited? See where he bumped his head on the ceiling? . . . Sedley! This is where our friend waited in the garret for Lady Stacey!"

"He?" growled the inspector. "I thought you said it was a she?"

He would not admit that he was impressed, but it was plain that he was so, for he examined the cupboard eagerly; and taking the torch, scrutinised every inch of the floor, ceiling, and walls, without, however, adding anything to his knowledge.

"I'll have the finger-print expert up – Crompton. Why couldn't this fellow – sorry, lady – have left a little souvenir? A cigarette end, for instance."

"I didn't cotton on to that following her upstairs business," said West, rubbing the dislodged dust from his eyes. "It seems so purposeless. How could the murderer know she was making for this inaccessible garret, for the purpose of hiding herself in so convenient a death-trap? It doesn't make sense. Now supposing the murderer was here already when Lady Stacey arrived, hiding in this cupboard, watching her through a crack, seeing her enter the chest, seizing the opportunity for – revenge, retribution, what you will. Or another theory. Lady Stacey and the murderer, whom we'll call X, come upstairs *together*, wanting a very private interview. They have their talk here. When it is over and the result, to Lady Stacey at least, is satisfactory, she hides in the chest and X in the cabinet. Seeing his opportunity, X slips out and fastens the bolt. Or X may have hidden in the cabinet *after* the crime to avoid contact with some other person."

"Whom we will call Y," said Sedley ungraciously. "All right. I'm convinced. He stepped out of here, slipped the bolt of the chest, and made his escape."

"I'll show you."

West stepped lightly into the cupboard and drew the door close. There he remained for a moment while the inspector waited to see him emerge; but when he did not do so, Sedley impatiently opened the door of the cupboard, and demanded: "Aren't you coming out?"

"Yes," said West.

His face had lost a little colour and his mouth was tight. His eyes seemed to have retreated into his head, blank and dark behind their lowered lids.

The inspector looked at him sharply. "What's the matter? Did you find that place conducive to thought?"

West, with the ease of an actor, was himself again. He shrugged his shoulders. "There's nothing to see."

The inspector, still suspicious, stepped into the cupboard and drew the door close; and West, relaxing for a moment his assumed ease of manner, bit his little finger savagely, aghast at a revelation which only too appositely closed the chapter of events in Undine's sad drama. From the moment that she and Edward burst into each other's lives, the tide of hate and retribution had swept inevitably to its climax in that dark garret. Her deception; his ruthlessness; her defiance; his devotion to Harry's ends . . . And Sedley was still in that revealing cabinet!

If only he could get away from Cleys . . . that was impossible. He would have to play his difficult part to its destined, dreaded end. West kicked out suddenly at a rickety Empire chair with tarnished gilding and tattered brocade, and it collapsed with a crash.

Out darted the inspector. "What's that?"

"I've knocked a chair over."

"So I see. I didn't suppose it was the Prussian army." He smiled to show that the joke was purely humorous and not sarcastic.

"There's nothing more in there" – he jerked towards the cabinet – "Mr. West, do you remember how that fool game began? I mean, someone must have made good speed to get here ahead of, or along with, her ladyship? Did she start up the stairs alone?"

"Yes. She was alone."

"Sir Harry said you were in the hall all the time. You'd know."

"Oh, yes. She was alone."

West paused, and then said suddenly: "Has anyone been admitted to this garret since the discovery of the crime? What people have been here besides yourself?"

"Only police officials, and Sir Harry Stacey. You don't think I'd allow that gang in from downstairs! I have a man on duty day and night below."

"Has anyone tried to gain admittance?"

"No. Your 'lady' was clever enough not to drop the pink rose from her gown, or she might have had to return for it and walk into our arms. That's what you were meaning, wasn't it?"

His "lady"! That which he had put down to the furtive malice of a jealous woman, the sly fastening of the lid, the secretive slipping on of the emerald ring, might equally well have been performed in the cold-blooded rage of an iron-nerved man; the bolt driven in with all the strength of a powerful wrist, the ring forced upon a finger that had long worn the jewels of deception.

They left the garret and went slowly down through the winding mazes of the keep.

"Come in here a moment," said Sedley; "I want you to take a look at Lady Stacey's apartments, particularly the clothes closet."

West followed reluctantly.

Undine's rooms had been left unchanged in every detail from the time she had last occupied them. Next to her boudoir, which contained her writing-desk and the famous tapestries, was the door of her bedroom, and directly inside that door was a deep clothes closet with sliding panels.

The inspector pushed the nearest panel which – a testimony to good workmanship – slid open with the greatest ease, and no noise. Within were hangers holding light dresses; and at the back of the closet was a row of coat pegs. There, a conspicuous object, hung the mink coat. On the next peg was a hat of sapphire blue velvet, underlined with cream lace.

West took it off its peg and examined it with dissatisfied scrutiny . . . "Unsuitable confection for an October night!" He scanned the back row of pegs with a care which the inspector judged to be purely academic. *He* knew what was on those pegs. Nothing had escaped his eye. In order: a green wool coat; the mink coat; the blue hat; another hat, black; a purple suede golf coat; a purple suede hat; and a fawn dust coat.

"It's obvious," said Sedley, getting impatient. "Took the first things that came to hand. Naturally would be in a hurry." West emerged from the clothes closet.

"I've finished," he said with unusual curtness. Sedley lowered his voice.

"That's how I felt, Mr. West; completely in the dark! Isn't it a teaser? But I've only scanned the surface, so to speak. To-morrow I'll get down to the human element. Then we'll have some surprises!"

The two men descended the worn stone stair and emerged into the outer bailey, where West was glad to make his escape to his own room.

Shortly before dinner Sir Harry visited him.

"I saw Sedley by himself," he explained, "so I concluded he had finished with you."

He paused, as though wondering whether he dare ask what had passed between his friend and the detective; and then, resting one arm along the mantelpiece, he said: "West, it would be a great weight off my mind if you would watch this affair for me. I'll retain you professionally, if you prefer it."

It was the last thing in the world that West desired, but how could he refuse Harry?

"It's hardly feasible," he said. "I can take a semi-official interest in it on your behalf, if you like."

"I feel tremendously cheered since you came," said Sir Harry. "To have the advantage of your experience, your – sanity. This place is virtually a prison; none of us are allowed to leave. The police keep us in the dark; we don't even know what is being done. It isn't conducive to our mental ease! What do you know of Sedley? Is he the right man?"

"He has a number of cases to his credit. I suppose he has his own methods. I know he would very much resent interference from me! If I am permitted to watch him at work – which he has already graciously promised me – I shall have to do so in silence. I mean, if he had any suspicion that his professional skill was being challenged, he'd deliberately pursue his own way, even if in his heart he knew it was the wrong one. You get the type of man? But don't misjudge him. He's straight, and you'll get – justice."

West dragged out his pipe. He wished the interview was over.

Sir Harry struck the mantel restlessly with his clenched fist.

"If only it were all over! The mystery is as impenetrable as it is awful. Undine had no enemy; everyone loved her for her beauty and sweetness. And I can never forgive myself that I thought evil of her while she already lay dead in the house! Why did I ever listen to Edward?"

West was silent, remembering Edward's theories the morning they walked on the terrace under the castle wall. Edward's theories! . . . Sir Harry, being the one man in a thousand, had already forgiven his dead wife everything – and forgotten the sin!

Chapter VIII
INQUISITIVE SEDLEY

NEXT morning after breakfast a policeman came to fetch Lionel West to the inspector's room. Everyone knew what that meant. The Scotland Yard inquiry was about to begin.

Some of them had appeared in the witness box at the inquest, but there the questioning had been perfunctory and the full seriousness of the charge unrevealed. It was a different matter now, to be under direct suspicion, to have to face the gruelling, searching probe of a detective who was renowned for his tenacity and a certain horrid skill in exposing the secrets of a human mind. The tension at breakfast was great. Edward Stacey strove to lighten the atmosphere.

"What would you say are the chances of a quiet game of golf this afternoon? There's a tidy little club three miles away."

Cecil Sabelle flicked a bread pellet at him, and shrilled: "Anybody would think you were taking a country holiday instead of doing time!"

"Sorry, Sabelle! I keep forgetting. You see, I haven't had your experience!"

"I've got an appalling headache," drawled Enid Willoughby. "I'm sure I shall tell the man anything he wants, just to get it over."

"There's nothing to be afraid of!" declared Rene Fullerton, with a toss of her tawny head. "We can't tell him anything, because we don't know anything, do we, Basil?"

"Sickening business!" growled the immaculate Crown, with a disgusted compressing of his eyebrows.

Rene cast him a doubtful glance. He had been urging their marriage for the last four months, while she, young, untamed and adoring her gay freedom, insisted on a two years' engagement, which did not at all suit Crown's plans. Her fortune would have settled them both in luxury, but it was no pleasure to him to be dragged about London by this madcap girl with his diamond ring on her third finger. Rene the heiress was desirable as a wife, but impossible as a fiancée. Basil Crown was beginning to sulk.

Pandora Hyde sat silently over her breakfast, with a perceptible pallor even in her usually ivory cheeks. Her eyes looked larger than ever, and there were blue shadows under them as though she had not slept.

"Oh, do cheer up, Pan!" said Enid impatiently. "We all loathe it, but there's no need to give ourselves away. Stand up to the man! Show him you don't care a row of pins for him!"

The girl looked up with a flash of spirit.

"It isn't your business how I look, Mrs. Willoughby."

Enid shrugged her shoulders with an amused glance at Edward.

"Outbreak of second World War!" chanted Sabelle. "Amazons of all nations take up arms!"

"You idiot!" flared Pandora.

"Pan will go in with that suspicious look," said Jack Willoughby maliciously, "and the inspector will say, 'Guilty or not guilty?' And Pan will reply, 'Father, I cannot tell a lie. I did it with my little hatchet'."

There was a yell of laughter from those who saw humour rather than bad taste in this remark, and Jack grinned with delight at his own cleverness.

"So this is how they talk when Harry isn't here!" thought West.

"Inspector Sedley's compliments, and he'll be glad to see Mr. West in the office as soon as may be!"

The constable mouthed his message and withdrew.

West had a curious feeling that all eyes were upon him; some openly, some secretly, veiling fear, curiosity, distrust, resentment, innocence, guilt.

He slowly drained his coffee cup, set it down, and left the room. Directly he had closed the door a babble of voices broke out among the seven people round the breakfast table. Sir Harry had breakfasted alone at a much earlier hour.

"So they're going to turn that fellow loose on us, what?" exclaimed Crown, jauntily lighting a cigarette. "King's Counsel; regular ferret."

"I 'ates lawyers," observed Sabelle gloomily.

"I think he's got a nerve!" cried Rene Fullerton. "Sticking himself among us as a guest and hearing all we say, and then pumping us as though we were criminals!"

"He will pump you too," drawled Enid. "I've heard our good Lionel at work on a sticky witness!"

"I shall ask him what the blazes he thinks he means by it!" blustered her husband.

"Don't make a fool of yourself, Jack. After all, he represents the law. He's got to find out who – I mean — "

"You mean, who murdered Undine," said Crown bluntly.

121

"Why can't we all say what we mean? I'm sick of beating about the bush! We're all in this mess together. We might as well put our cards on the table. The inspector thinks that one of us did it – one of us seven, if we're to leave out Sir Harry and the Legal Ferret; Major Stacey, Mr. and Mrs. Willoughby, Sabelle, Rene, Pandora and myself."

"Thanks awfully!" said Pandora touchily.

"Oh, my dear Pandora, don't make a song and dance! I don't believe any of you did it. It's too absurd. I know I didn't."

"Well, I jolly well know I didn't!" shouted Rene Fullerton.

"I didn't!" put in Jack Willoughby.

Enid raised her eyebrows, and said icily "Surely there's no need for us all to proclaim our innocence! So crude!"

Major Stacey looked at his wrist watch.

"West has been gone twenty minutes. I wonder what's happening? I vote we disperse. We weren't told to stay here."

When Lionel West reached the inspector's room he was greeted with businesslike curtness, and introduced to a second official sitting by Sedley at the table – Detective-Sergeant Ward, of the Metropolitan Police. There was also a shorthand clerk with horn rims and a notebook.

"Will you sit there?" said Sedley, indicating a chair placed a little apart from the official body, as though to suggest delicately that West's was only a watching brief. Sedley need not have been afraid. West had no desire to assist in interrogating his fellow guests.

"We'll have Sir Harry in, please."

Presently Sir Harry came in accompanied by a plain clothes man, who might have been a reporter or a finger-print expert.

"Sit down, Sir Harry." Sedley greeted him with a touch of deference. "I'm not going to trouble you much, but just one or two questions . . . Since I first asked you, have you thought of anyone who might have had a grudge against your wife?"

"Indeed, no!" said Sir Harry, in a firm, emphatic voice. "She had no enemies. Everyone who knew her admired her. She was exceedingly popular – though I dislike the word."

"With all her guests, for instance?"

"Certainly. They were her chosen friends."

Sedley made a few notes, and while he scribbled, Sergeant Ward asked: "What was Lady Stacey's manner on the day of her death? Did she appear worried at all?"

"On the contrary; she was always particularly happy when she was entertaining friends. She had been a little upset earlier in the day, so she told me, over a very slight matter which could have no bearing — "

"What was that?"

"Oh, nothing really. Mr. Crown and Miss Fullerton had announced their engagement, and she did not approve of it. She told me before dinner that she had spoken rather strongly to Crown – but I can't say she was worried. She was gay enough when we began to play that damnable game!"

Sedley stopped writing, thanked him, and sent him away. He turned to Ward, with whom he seemed on excellent terms.

"Prejudiced evidence, of course. Let's see what the brother has to say."

Major Stacey's eyes as he entered the room met those of West in a glance of amused intimacy. He advanced to his chair with the easy swing of a soldierly bearing, and faced the inspector with mocking coolness, as though he were the inquisitor and Sedley a hostile Indian tribesman.

"Major Stacey!"

"Inspector Sedley!" rapped out Edward in the tones of the parade ground.

The inspector frowned. "Please remember that you are before a British legal tribunal!"

"That doesn't worry me," said Edward blandly. "Carry on!"

"Did you admire Lady Stacey?" Sedley flung at him without further preliminaries.

Edward was clearly taken aback, but he was keenly intelligent and answered without hesitation: "Now, Inspector, I ask you, knowing what I did about Lady Stacey, and what everyone now knows, could I conceivably have admired her?"

"I'm asking you!" snapped Sedley, with barely concealed anger. "Did you admire her?"

"No. I despised her."

"You knew about her past, previous to the night of her death?"

"I knew when I landed in Marseilles, six weeks before."

"Ah, yes. That all came out at the inquest, I see from Sergeant Ward's papers . . . Now, Major Stacey, what part did you play in this game of hide-and-seek?"

"Me? I was the Big Noise. I had to find all the others."

"Tell me what you did, from the time the guests dispersed to hide."

"Lady Stacey switched the lights out," said Edward easily, his eyes fixed on a spot two inches above Sedley's inquiring glare, "and people started making for the stairs. I was sitting in the hall in a sort of half-light that came from the windows. Undine seemed to linger about a bit. I heard her – in fact, I saw her go upstairs a few minutes after the others — "

"After the others? She was the last to leave the hall?"

"Oh, yes, quite. After the others."

"Note that . . . Go on!"

"Well – the arrangement was that I was to wait fifteen minutes and then strike the gong before starting the search. See? . . . So I – well – I just waited fifteen minutes and sounded the gong. Then I went straight upstairs to the Priest's Hole in the East Wing. There I found Willoughby."

"How long did it take you to reach the Priest's Hole?"

"Oh, three minutes."

"Making eighteen minutes in all," said Sergeant Ward, noting it down. "What made you go straight to the Priest's Hole?"

"It seemed such a likely place. I thought of it while I was waiting."

"You may go," said Sedley . . . "Blackmore, send John Willoughby."

Edward Stacey turned carelessly to leave the room, and passing West flashed upon him another friendly glance. He was met by a keen look of such puzzled sternness that he turned his own eyes quickly away and the muscles of his jaw stiffened perceptibly. Had he forgotten that West had been sitting in that hall all the time? Or was he deliberately lying in the easy certainty that his friend would never give him away?

Already West was realising with dismay the tangle of loyalty and justice into which this inquiry was leading him. From his seat on the settle by the hearth he had seen Undine, the last to leave the hall; and a moment after, Edward had quietly left his seat and disappeared up the stairs. It was twenty-five minutes by West's watch before he had returned to bang the gong!

Jack Willoughby walked in, one hand at the lapel of his coat, and diplomatist sticking out all over him.

"Which is Inspector Sedley? . . . You are Inspector Sedley? Well, I'm Willoughby of the Diplomatic Service. What is it you want to know?"

"Sit down," said Sedley bluntly.

Jack draped himself over the chair, and shot at West a look of haughty defiance, which was wasted.

"Now, Mr. John Willoughby!" began Sedley dryly. "The Diplomatic Service is apparently not above a game of hide-and-seek. You hid, we understand, in a cavity in the east wing called the Priest's Hole. Did you go straight there from the hall when the lights were turned out?"

"Yes, I did. Filthy hole, it was. Most insanitary!"

"Then you'd pass . . . let me see, twelve rather unpleasant minutes there before the gong sounded?"

"Twelve!" protested Jack. "It felt more like half an hour!"

"I dare say it seemed a long time," said Sedley smoothly, "but it couldn't have been more than twelve, allowing you three minutes to get to the Priest's Hole?"

"I suppose you're right," agreed Jack, "but I was glad when Edward came and let me out."

Ward suddenly leant forward and pushed a piece of paper under his colleague's nose.

Sedley glanced down.

"Mr. Willoughby, tell me, did you admire Lady Stacey?"

Jack smiled confidingly.

"Well, between you and me, Inspector, she was a bit overpowerin'. Not my type at all. She managed things, if you know what I mean, and wasn't afraid to speak her mind – sort of cross between Xantippe and Queen Elizabeth."

"Then you didn't admire her?"

"Not so you'd notice."

The inspector stifled a smile, and resuming a businesslike manner asked: "After Major Stacey found you in the Priest's Hole, what exactly happened?"

"We got out and went along the passage, and I put out my hand to feel round a corner in the dark, and got hold of Pan Hyde's foot. She was standin' high up in a window niche."

"How long would you say it was before you found Miss Hyde?"

"I should say, five minutes."

"Thank you, Mr. Willoughby . . . Blackmore, we'll take Miss Hyde."

The girl walked in with a face as white as paper. Her hair was flung back damply from her brow and her eyes were wide with apprehension. Her hands fingered the folds of her blue skirt. She was the first woman witness to be called, and it was plain that the summons had given her a shock.

West cast her a reassuring glance as she passed him, but she gazed at him blankly.

This time it was Sergeant Ward who nodded to her to be seated.

Ward was used to nervous witnesses. He leant over and, with a disarming smile, asked: "Now, Miss Hyde, are you a good judge of time?"

She jerked up her head, and a faint colour swept into her cheeks, as though she were relieved at the innocence of the question when expecting something far worse.

"Why, yes, I think so."

"Then tell us, how long did it take you from leaving the hall at the beginning of the game of hide-and-seek, to find your own hiding-place?"

"I should think – about five minutes. I climbed into a window embrasure."

"And how long did you have to wait there before you were found?"

"Oh, a long time!"

"Ladies aren't very definite, I fear. Would it be twenty minutes?"

"Much longer than that," said Pandora calmly. "Why, it must have been half an hour *before even the gong sounded!*"

Sedley, who had been scribbling, shot up his head and interrupted sharply: "It was only fifteen minutes before the gong sounded! You're speaking at random."

"Oh, no, I'm not."

Pandora had recovered herself, and was speaking with the directness which often characterised her remarks.

"Just before Lady Stacey turned out the lights I looked at the hall clock. It was twenty-five minutes to nine. I went up and hid in the window and waited for ages. It was frightfully cold, and I kept thinking the gong would sound. I heard the big gateway clock toll the quarter-to, and then nine o'clock. It was several minutes after that that the gong sounded."

"About thirty minutes altogether? You're sure?"

"Quite sure."

Ward paused to turn back to the notes of Jack Willoughby's evidence. He gave a grunt of satisfaction.

"Miss Hyde, did you admire Lady Stacey?"

"No! I hated her!"

The directness of the girl's reply took everyone's breath away; it was the last thing in the world they expected.

Her eyes gleamed and the hot colour rushed to her cheek-bones.

"I'm not going to tone it down! If I pretend I loved her I shall only give myself away later, so I'm telling you now!"

She spoke quite recklessly, as though some pent-up force within her had suddenly found its outlet, impossible to check.

Sedley was anxious to put her at her ease and maintain this flow of candour.

"That's right, Miss Hyde," he said approvingly. "If you're straight with us you won't regret it. Now tell me, you must have had some good reason for this aversion, hadn't you?"

"Indeed I had!" The girl's lips wore a touch of scorn.

"You knew something, perhaps, to the detriment of Lady Stacey's character?"

"That Marseilles affair? Oh, no!" Pandora looked genuinely surprised. "Nothing like that."

"Then you hated Lady Stacey for a personal reason. What was that?"

"Oh, I shan't tell you that! There's no reason why I should."

"My dear Miss Hyde!" Sedley's voice was dry. He could afford to be pleasant when he was getting what he wanted, but he could not bear a check. "Remember this is a police inquiry. It is for me to decide what information is necessary, and you will kindly answer every question."

"Not that!" said Pandora with cast-iron defiance. "The row's over and done with. I shan't tell you or anyone what it was about."

"Row?" muttered Ward, with a questing eye.

"Wasn't it a peculiar thing," said the inspector smoothly, "that when you were on such bad terms with Lady Stacey – when, as you imply, you had actually had a serious quarrel with her – you should be staying in her house as her guest?"

"I wasn't on bad terms with her when I came."

"No? Then the quarrel took place after you arrived at Cleys?"

"Yes," said Pandora sullenly.

"Just when – I'm sure you remember?"

"One afternoon . . . I don't remember."

"On the very afternoon of her death?"

"Oh, no, it wasn't!"

"You seem sure about that!"

"I don't really remember," said Pandora, a little less boldly than before.

"Now, Miss Hyde . . . this quarrel was about a man, wasn't it?"

"I shall not tell you." If looks could have killed, her black eyes would have been two sword-points in his heart!

"All right, Miss Hyde. I've finished with you."

She rose, trying to control her passionate breathing and to look sufficiently unconcerned as she left the room. At least it was all over, and her luck had held. Nothing to have worried so much about!

When she was gone, Ward pulled the notes over to him and examined them, tapping his teeth with a pencil.

"Nothing much emerged so far," he said thoughtfully, "except that Sir Harry was either misinformed or exaggerating about the lady's popularity! Those three witnesses taken at random hadn't much of an opinion of her, what?"

"What about that chronology business?" grunted Sedley. "That's what we've got to check up. Either the Major lied about his fifteen minutes, or else Willoughby and Miss Hyde put their heads together before they came in. I incline to the former theory. In any case, there's something to hide, and we may get on the mark. What about having the Major back?"

Ward tapped his teeth.

"Leave it till after lunch. I'd like them to get together and realise they've given each other away. It may scare them, and help the next lot to come across clean. I've get this Sabelle next on the list – in order as they were found on the night. Shall we have him in?"

Cecil Sabelle's lanky body was even more sketchily clothed than usual, in a flannel cricket shirt open at the front because it had no buttons, and open at the back because of a large rent; and a pair of tweed trousers which looked as though they had been drenched in the moat and hastily dried over a smoky fire. His countenance, however, was clean and frank; and since his forelock persisted in tumbling into his eyes, he thrust it back before the gaze of the astonished inspector, and secured it with a safety-pin.

"All ri', guv'nor," he droned huskily. "I took the sparklers ter feed me hungry kids."

"Sit down, Mr. Sabelle."

Cecil obliged, after grinning wickedly at West.

"Chuck it, Cecil!" said West suddenly. "Be sensible now."

Sedley looked across sharply as though resenting the interference, but seeing that his unruly witness had already assumed a more serious demeanour, he even vouchsafed West a grateful nod.

"On the night of the 18th of October, Mr. Sabelle, you went upstairs to hide yourself, along with other members of the party, leaving the hall at 8.35. Can you tell me how long it was before you were discovered?"

Cecil looked slightly pained.

"I say, inspector! I know something about the law. You haven't warned me!"

"That's all right, Mr. Sabelle . . . I was asking you — "

"I'm not bound to answer your questions?"

"You are not, as you say — "

"And everything that I say will be taken down and used as evidence against me?"

"Quite so."

"But if I refuse to answer, you'll make it jolly uncomfortable for me until I do?"

"Dear me!" said Sedley softly. "You do know something about the law!"

"Very well, then . . . I didn't know it was 8.35, but I'll take your word for it. It would be well over an hour before they found me; nearer an hour and a half."

"Ah! . . . say ten o'clock. Where were you found?"

"Sir, I was bestriding one of the rafters in the Long Gallery."

"Now, Mr. Sabelle, what were you doing between the hours of 8.35 and 10 o'clock?"

"Verily, sir, I was hiding of myself and awaiting the seekers, who, in sooth, were tardy. Jolly tardy! I got splinters from that darned rafter stuck all over me!"

"You were on that rafter for an hour and a half?"

"Well, it took me a few minutes to decide where to hide. You see" – his tone became confidential – "my big idea was to get far enough away from Willoughby. Just before dinner he said to me: 'Cecil, old top' " – this in a spirited imitation of Jack's affected tones – " 'What about you and me doin' a bunk to the cellar when this darn silly kids' game starts, and havin' a lap at Harry's fizz before the hounds draw cover?' Well, I wouldn't have minded the suggestion, but two hours of old Jack 'ud be worse to me than Monday morning with an overdraft and a sick headache. What'll they do without him at Bukarest? . . . Poof! I like Mrs. Willoughby and I can't blame her. But to resume — "

"You can't blame Mrs. Willoughby for what?" interrupted Ward gently.

"Did I say that?" Sabelle looked annoyed. "As you were!" He dug his hands in his pockets.

"A moment," said Sedley, and scribbled upon his pad: "Relations between Mr. and Mrs. W. Another man?"

"Go on, Mr. Sabelle . . . You avoided Mr. Willoughby, went upstairs, took a few minutes to choose your hiding-place, and finally climbed on to a rafter in the Long Gallery where you remained for an hour or more. Is that correct?"

"Word perfect, Inspector."

"Did anyone see you during that time, anyone who can support your statement? Or did you see anybody?"

"I didn't see any of our crowd, and the servants were all in their own quarters – you know their wing, on the west side of the inner bailey. Undine had told them they had to keep there until our game was over."

"Who found you?"

"Edward Stacey, and Willoughby, and Pan Hyde."

"When did you last see Lady Stacey?"

"When she was turning the lights out in the hall."

Sedley turned to Ward. "Anything more to ask this witness?"

"Did he admire Lady Stacey?" muttered Ward.

"Did I?" Cecil, like his predecessors, looked surprised at the question. "Oh, rather! She was no end of a sport!"

Sedley looked relieved, as though he had feared the

revelation of yet another mysterious aversion.

"We'll stop for lunch," he announced. "Clear the room, Blackmore."

West had heard all he wanted to hear, but as he was going out, Sedley hastened after him.

"Mr. West! There's that emerald ring business. We must tackle that. You said Miss Hyde was the last person to handle it?"

"Yes." West turned back into the room, and closed the door. "She admitted that she was wearing it after they found Sabelle in the Long Gallery. He saw it flashing on her finger. She says that she then came downstairs and placed it on the hall table. She didn't. I was watching her all the time. I don't want to get the girl into trouble, but there must be a reason for her evasion. I wish witnesses would tell the truth! It would be better for them!"

"She'll have to come across with it," struck in Ward. "I let her off lightly this morning, because I saw she was a twister, and it paid to restore her confidence. When she's recalled, she'll have to go through it about that ring. Why won't she tell what she did with it? I'm watching that girl!"

"I think myself she stole it," said West, and told the episode of the green hat-case.

Ward was not impressed. "Well, it got on to a corpse's finger!" he said ominously.

The inspector studied his colleague for a minute, and said: "That girl has got me too – hot! She and Lady Stacey quarrelled over a man, and the girl was still furious, showing she was the injured party. Know anything about it, West?"

"The man would be Crown."

"Crown? Good! . . . What do you say, Ward? How do I know what they quarrelled about? My good chap, when two women quarrel and refuse to tell what it's about, it's always a man! That girl had it in for Lady Stacey! Hatred like hers is abnormal."

"She couldn't have done it. She hadn't time."

"Time? She had over half an hour, by her own estimate."

"That's in her favour. If she'd done it, she'd have made the time out to be shorter, not longer."

"We'll settle that definitely after lunch, with the Major."

West went out, in no mood to join the party at lunch. The gong had not sounded, and on a sudden inspiration he ran down to the billiard-room, where lunch was laid, and pocketed a roll and an apple. He then made his way to the keep, and picking his steps carefully up a spiral staircase of crumbled stone trodden by the feet of centuries, he came out upon the peaceful isolation of the roof. He leaned upon the battlemented wall and ate his apple very thoughtfully. The sun was sparkling in a sky of sheerest blue, and the spring light illuminated all the distance of plain and thicket and mountain. It was a lovely sight for a day in spring, that country-side which swept away from the foundations of the old fortress; a sight which in happier days Lionel West would have loved, recalling tales of romance and remembering the lovelorn ladies and the men-at-arms who had stood where he was standing now, and leant upon these very stones looking out for a lover or awaiting a hostile army. An adventurous life, that of the old Sabelles, placed here in this stubborn fortress to guard the marches for their royal master. Sabelle! Lord of the Marches! How proudly must that title once have been worn! Young Cecil playing the fool, idling through life, and amusing himself on his share of the proceeds from the sale of his birthright – how could you account for his lack of sensitiveness, his absence of even the merest shred of sentiment for the home which forty generations of his ancestors had guarded, often with their lives? One could only say that there were people like that, devoid of romance and feeling, or even reverence for tradition.

West munched his roll. A fleet of snowy cloud galleons closed in above the purple mountains of Wales and advanced in mass formation towards the sun.

Edward! Why had Edward told that silly lie, or rather suppressed the truth? Was he going to lie his way through the whole hideous affair? It was not like him. And should West seek out his friend, or avoid him?

He went quickly down the winding, dangerous stair, too quickly for safety, and landed at the bottom dizzy and reeling. He put out a hand to steady himself against the wall.

"Now, Lionel! Who's been having a secret orgy?"

Edward Stacey stood laughing under the portcullis at the gate.

West was himself again. He said coolly: "Hallo, Edward! I wanted a word with you. Come to my room."

"Why not a stroll round here?"

"No. It's important."

There was a second's pause, full of meaning. For an instant West thought that Edward was going to refuse.

Then he shrugged his shoulders and said lightly: "Lead on." They walked silently across the sun-splashed flags, and turning into the cool, tunnelled passage on the opposite side of the court, they heard the children's voices, and came upon Rita and Nicholas playing at ball while their governess leaned against the archway watching them.

She seemed startled by the sudden appearance of the two men, and West noticed that while her gaze flew to the face of Edward and fastened there, he made no sign of recognition, rather – though it seemed far-fetched – it was as though he deliberately avoided the girl's eyes.

They passed on, and suddenly looking back from the far end of the tunnel, West saw that the children had run on and Miss Farbell, pressed back against the wall, was still staring after the two men. When she saw West turn she looked quickly away, and began to call to the children.

West remembered that he had not noticed her since the day they played hide-and-seek. She had brought Rita and Nicholas down – rather a pretty, silent girl – and as suddenly disappeared.

Edward sauntered into West's room, glanced from the window, lit a cigarette, and said: "Well? Have they unearthed anything?" He laughed, and added: "The idea of Jack, Pandora, and Cecil Sabelle as witnesses is too farcical! Their evidence must have been marvellously funny! Really, though, West, if that's a typical detective-inspector with his regular way of doing business, one can't be expected to take even the elucidation of the family crime seriously. To take a group of absolutely harmless people like Enid, and Crown, and Pandora, and the rest, and pump them, and worry them, and scare the women until one of us admits to losing a handkerchief on the night of the crime – faugh! It's an insult to our intelligence! I'm fed up, West. How long is this nonsense going on?"

"Is it nonsense?"

The Major grinned, and drew on his cigarette until it sparkled merrily.

West steeled his heart.

"What were you doing upstairs, Edward, to make you late sounding that gong?"

"Bad break, wasn't it?" Edward still grinned a little as he spoke. "Just my luck that you should have been watching me, you old spoil-sport! But they don't know anything, do they?"

"Of course they know!" There was a rasp in West's voice in spite of his care. "Jack and Pandora both knew it was half an hour before that gong sounded, and they said so . . . They're recalling you this afternoon."

"Oh, la, la ! I'll have to think up something!"

"You'll be a fool if you don't tell them the truth!"

"My dear West, I've no real objection to telling the truth. It's all perfectly harmless. But it would be far more of a lark to make up a story, something really sensational to intrigue Sedley. However, I'll tell you what really happened, to avoid mistakes, and you can pass it on to Sedley if he'll accept it secondhand."

"I shall have to take it down, read it over to you, and have you sign it."

"All right. It makes no difference to me. You're making a fuss about a small matter. Sometime before dinner that

139

night I promised Miss Farbell – the kids' governess, you know – that I'd go up to her room and fetch her down to join in the game of hide-and-seek. You know what a memory I've got! I forgot all about it until the lights were out, and I was sitting there waiting for the folks to hide. So I thought I'd have ample time to slip up to the East Turret, tell the girl to hide, and get back and ring the gong. Which, West, to cut a long and thrilling story short, was exactly what I did."

He stopped with a smile, threw away the stub of his cigarette, and lit another.

"Miss Farbell was not in the game," said West, without lifting his head from his notebook.

"Oh, didn't I say? She didn't want to play, after all."

"It wouldn't take you getting on for half an hour to get to the East Turret and back . . . Sorry, Edward, but I've got to have this properly."

"Of course! I stopped there talking to Amy, looked at my watch, found I'd overdone it by a quarter of an hour, dashed down, and sounded the gong. I'd have preferred not to have brought Amy into it – it's quite unnecessary – but I see if I don't you'll all think the worst."

"This doesn't involve Miss Farbell."

"Oh, I'm glad of that!"

The Major spoke nonchalantly; it was impossible to tell what was in his mind. He bent over and scrawled a heavy signature across the paper, under a falling shower of cigarette ash.

"No mystery, old man!" he laughed. "It must be a disappointment when the witnesses don't even try to conceal their suspicious behaviour!"

West folded the paper and put it in his wallet. He half hoped that his friend would go away, but he had reckoned without Edward's love of congenial company.

The Major settled down comfortably in a long basket-chair.

"I'm in Harry's bad books," he said suddenly.

"Yes?"

"You see, I blackened Undine rather badly, didn't I? Of course, I really believed she had gone off with Corbett. It was the obvious conclusion. And, after all, she was an adventuress; he seems to have overlooked that fact. He's got such an overwhelming, such a wholesale-scale of a forgiving nature. Lionel, I feel rather rotten about it. It wasn't an easy job to break that news to Harry all those months ago. You were here at the time; you remember how it happened. I first told you the story as we walked out there on the terrace. It was an ironical trick of Fate. There was I, in the days before Undine's death, watching her, bewildered, up against a tougher problem than I ever faced in India . . . my one desperate idea being, at any cost, to keep the tale from reaching Harry's ears. And in the end it was I . . . who had to strike the blow!"

West looked up sharply, with a wary glint in his eyes. "It was I who had to strike the blow!" What a sinister double meaning! Did Edward realise what he was saying? Or was he on the point of confession? Supposing he should confess now to his friend that he had murdered Undine? What ought West to do? If Edward wanted to confess, let him have the decency to go to Sedley, and not put a pal in the horrible position of choosing between friendship and duty!

"I'm such a blunderer!" said Edward. "I only wanted to spare Harry."

So he was not going to confess. West sighed with relief.

"You don't mean there is ill-feeling between you and Harry?"

"No, never. But we are no longer friends. He associates me with that horrid moment when he learnt of Undine's deception. He knows of the horrible ten minutes I gave her on the day before her death when I faced her with exposure, and let her go – at a price! I suppose he realises that her last night on earth was a sleepless one, and I was the cause. He knows I did it for his sake – and yet he can't forgive me. Do you understand?"

"He will understand himself soon. Just now he is too shocked."

"Do you think so?"

"I'm sure of it."

But as he spoke the words, West's eyes dropped. He had forgotten for a moment in speaking to Edward, his friend, that he was speaking to one the whole of whose future life would be a deception, supposing this police inquiry proved fruitless and the death of Undine Stacey were added to the long tale of unsolved crimes. Renewal of friendship and understanding between the brothers? It was hideous . . . unthinkable. How could Edward suggest it? And yet for twelve years Edward had lived with a wild and uncivilised people, governed by strange laws and savage codes of justice. Perhaps he had actually brought himself to think that in ridding the world of Undine Stacey he had committed an act of righteous judgment and saved his brother from future distress. Men had strange ideas, and no end would ever be discovered to the variety and fantastic nature of their motives. The last word in the history of bizarre crime would never be written so long as human nature remained the greatest enigma of the universe.

Another idea flashed into West's mind. Why should he tolerate any longer this talk at cross-purposes? Should he not here and now tell Edward that the hidden game was revealed, that he had read his secret in the Norman cabinet?

And what would happen? Edward would smile . . . big, handsome, debonair . . . would smile lazily, frankly, and say without surprise or malice: "Well, Lionel, old man, and what are you going to do?" And then the old battle of conflicting loyalties!

Edward's voice broke in on his thoughts.

"Lionel, you were here when all this happened. You understand my motives . . . everything. If Harry should talk to you about me . . . will you put in a word for your old pal?"

How naïve he was . . . how boyish!

Like a flash West's memory flew back to a scene beside a river years and years ago. Two boys in flannels were sitting on the bank, himself and Edward, twelve years old.

"Harry's mad," said Edward, "and it's all my fault."

"You mean about the village match? But he was run out."

"Yes, but I got him run out. We were both in together, and I had only four to get to make my fifty. I couldn't wait; I was sneaking runs. I knew he'd be run out, but I shouted

'Yes,' and he had to come. I ought to have waited and given him a chance. He'd only been in one over."

"He'll get over it," said Lionel West callously.

"Yes . . . but I hate it when Harry and I are out. Look here" – the boy Edward rumpled his hair with a grubby fist – "can't you go and find Harry, and put in a word for your pal? . . ."

In West's room at Cleys Castle after more than twenty-five years the scene was repeated, but with what dreadful significance. A word for Edward . . . knowing as he did of Edward's greater, concealed crime? How could he!

He mumbled: "It would be difficult for me to interfere."

And for the first time in his life he knew that he had failed a friend.

Edward changed the subject suddenly.

"Here's a queer thing," he said. "The police have got hold of a cheque that Enid cashed in London a few days after Undine's death last October. The cheque was payable from Undine to Enid, and the sum was big – five hundred pounds. With their usual thirst for knowledge they immediately wanted to know what this was all about, and they put the question to Jack. He, like the fool he is, shouted out, 'Good for Enid!' or words to that effect, and then denied all knowledge of the transaction, and shut up like a clam. Now wasn't that enough to turn any respectable policeman into a bloodhound? What it all means, I don't know, but what I fear is that there's trouble brewing for Enid. I wish I could be more definite in what I'm telling you; what I'm doing is merely hinting that you might keep a fatherly eye on Enid and see that she isn't bullied."

"Then what do you suspect?"

Edward's eyebrows shot up. "Oh, you wily crittur! Who said I suspected anything?"

"You implied that there was something between Lady Stacey and Enid that might not look nice in the light of day!"

I won't go so far as that . . . but five hundred pounds! It's rather more than lend-me-a-fiver-till-Monday-darling, which I believe is the common formula between women friends. And there's something else to the story which I didn't bother to tell Mr. Sedley. Undine borrowed that cheque from *me* on the afternoon of October 17th. She said she wanted it for herself, and hadn't one of her own. I tore it out of my book. Sedley showed me the actual cheque, in a burst of confidence, and it was dated October 17th. Oh, I'm making a lot out of nothing. It's the suspicious atmosphere of this abominable place! All I want to repeat is, don't let them bully Enid. She's ill, poor kid!"

"I thought she looked so."

"Nerves, I suppose. I don't know of anything else to account for it."

From where he sat Edward could see out of the window, for he suddenly said: "Ha-ha, Lionel! Here come your friends!"

Sedley and Ward were coming out of the gate-house, Sedley cupping his hands round a lighted match and having terrible trouble with a playful breeze, which light as a fairy leapt from the innocent blue sky to plague him.

"Why 'my friends'?"

Edward shrugged his shoulders, and smiled slyly.

"Only – that the people downstairs are wondering whether you are their friend, or ours." West studied his finger-tips.

"Why should you be antagonistic to the police officers? Isn't it to everyone's benefit to see this business cleared up?"

Edward's jaw tightened. West faced him squarely.

"Don't you want to see this affair cleared up?"

Edward swung round with a face like flint.

"No! I do not!"

There was a moment's pause in which anything might have happened, any irretrievable word been said. West turned, and went out, and left Edward in his room.

A few minutes later Sedley was reading Major Stacey's signed statement with approval.

"It's simple and straightforward," he admitted grudgingly. "Why couldn't he have told us in the first case? Some of these people are deliberately confusing the issues."

"He didn't want to involve Miss Farbell."

"But this doesn't involve Miss Farbell – at least, only remotely."

"I suppose it was natural reluctance on a man's part to introduce a girl's name."

Sedley looked blank. "I don't see it."

"Just an elementary idea of honour," said West dryly.

"Oh, so I gathered! But I still don't see it. Apparently in polite society one may murder and lie about it, but one may not mention a lady's name. That's my experience. Still, you've done a useful bit of work. We'll file it for reference."

West went out into the garden and found a shady lawn where Rene Fullerton and young Sabelle were unconcernedly playing clock golf with the cheerful vigour of perfect youth and innocence.

He sat down on an iron seat to watch them. The tow-headed young man was tidier than he had been in the morning. West was irresistibly reminded of a grubby child who has been taken in hand by his nurse and turned out comparatively respectable, only to plunge once more into the happy task of bemiring himself and rending his clothes.

At least, Cecil could play clock golf. With a steady hand, a perfect eye, and no particular care, he was consistently getting them down in one.

Rene wore a blue tweed skirt and a golf jacket of the same colour, with neat white buckskin shoes strapped with brown. Her cheeks were scarlet, and her tawny locks rioted in the breeze. She played in a gay, reckless, abandoned manner which never seemed to bring her ball within a yard of the hole, and all the time her tongue wagged like the clapper of a bell.

"O, Cecil, why can't I do it like you?" she shouted. "Look, the beastly thing always goes a hundred miles!"

"Well, don't hit it so hard, you idiot!"

"I'm not hitting it hard!"

"You are! You're clouting it as if you were playing hockey at a kids' boarding school! And that's no way to hold a putter!"

"Oh, you are clever, aren't you?"

"Sure, baby. You've said a mouthful."

They were like a couple of ten-year-olds, thought West.

Their company pleased him, like a refreshing bit of honest fun clapped into the middle of a grim tragedy.

At last Rene flung down her putter and ran to perch on the iron seat.

"It's a silly game, anyhow. I wish I could go for a long tramp. I should like to explore those mountains."

"There's nothing to see," said Sabelle, "except sheep."

"Oh, but I've heard the Welsh scenery is magnificent!"

"Farther north. You're thinking of the Snowdon country. Tourists don't come here."

"All the better. I don't want to go where tourists go!"

"They always seem to find the best spots, nevertheless."

Sabelle picked up the two balls. "I'm going in; I'll take the putters."

When he was gone, Rene turned impulsively to West.

"Mr. West, I wish you'd speak to Basil. He's behaving so badly."

For the moment West was nonplussed. Basil? Oh, yes, Crown! This girl was engaged to Crown, the young man who looked down his nose and drew duchesses.

"I hardly understand," he parried smilingly.

"He says he won't be questioned by anybody. And he loses his temper so easily! And . . . oh, I'm so miserable! Everything's so – so hateful!"

She clenched her fists and kicked savagely at the turf with her little shoe.

"But, my dear Rene, surely this is a matter between yourself and your fiancé? I can't interfere!"

"But you're going to do the questioning, aren't you?"

"Oh ! . . . You mean the police inquiry?"

"Of course. What did you think I meant?"

"I thought you were referring to a – a private quarrel. The police inquiry! But I have nothing to do with that. Nothing at all!"

"But Mrs. Willoughby said . . . that is, someone said . . . that you'd put us through it. That you — "

"Mrs. Willoughby is entirely misinformed." She looked at him suspiciously, only half convinced.

The castle clock struck two.

"At the same time," said West, "I should advise you to warn Mr. Crown to tell the truth, and all of it. This isn't a joke."

"When shall we be allowed to go home?"

"I couldn't tell you."

"Do you mean you can't, or you mustn't, or you don't want to?"

"I mean, Rene, that I haven't the least idea."

The girl bit her lip, and her eyes clouded.

"I want to go to London. Cecil would run me up."

West rose.

"I must go. I shall be wanted inside."

She sat where she was, with tangled hair and mutinous eyes. Already the gay interlude was over, and there was a part in the tragedy even for this "ten-year-old" child.

Chapter IX
THE BREAKING STORM

"Mr. Crown?"

"That's my name," drawled Basil, in a fearful but controlled rage.

Inspector Sedley himself was in a vicious mood that afternoon, for Mrs. Willoughby, who was due to appear as first witness after lunch, had retired to her room to lie down, and flatly refused to come down until she was ready to do so. This defiance was going to make things worse for everybody.

Sedley set his jaw and lashed out.

"On the day of Lady Stacey's death, you and she had a violent quarrel. On what terms did you part that afternoon?"

Crown's face grew white with rage.

"Are you accusing me of murdering her? If so, charge me and prove it; and if you don't prove it, you'll be actionable for defamation of character! I'm not compelled to answer your questions, and you know it!"

Sedley half rose from his chair.

"Are you saying you murdered her? Don't sit there chewing your lip, you young fool! If you come across me you'll be sorry for it! Quarrel with a woman on the afternoon of the day she was murdered, and a temper like yours! I've a good mind to charge you and risk it!"

Crown, his bluff called, sprang up, overturning his chair with a crash. The afternoon inquiry in its first three minutes had become cyclonic.

"Who's been telling you this, anyway?" he cried. "Who's been spying on me and making a lot out of a little? Edward Stacey? He's a fine critic! Undine would have done better to keep her virtuous matron manner for her own family. What about Edward's little affair with the governess? . . . And you, Inspector What's-it! . . . I see your game! Getting us in here one by one and bribing us to split on the others!"

West jumped up, and his compelling voice rang out: "Sit down, Crown, and hold your tongue, or you'll be put under arrest!"

Crown turned on him with twitching hands. Nothing could stem the torrent of his coarse rage when once the veneer of the gentleman was gone.

"Right you are, lawyer! Lock me up! Ask me why I did this, and why I did that; but you can also ask Enid Willoughby if she's sorry that her rival's out of the way, and what sort of a brew she's going to drop into Jack's coffee; and you can ask Pandora Hyde what she meant when she told Undine Stacey to her face that she was going to kill her – I was under the window and I heard her; and since Edward Stacey was so interested in my affairs, and my room being in the East Turret underneath Miss Farbell's, you can ask him where he had been when he came down the stairs of the turret at midnight on the night of the murder! Is that your money's worth, Mr. Inspector, or have I left anything out? . . . If you think I killed Undine Stacey after that, you're the biggest mug on the Force!"

"Put him out, Blackmore!" snapped Sedley. "And tell one of your men not to let him out of sight . . . Gunson, did you get all that down?"

West interposed.

"Sedley, you're never taking note of that young ruffian's ravings! A lot of malicious gossip! You'd not admit such stuff as evidence?"

The inspector said stiffly: "You'll excuse me, Mr. West, but we may even have to use some of these unpleasant remarks later on if they seem suggestive. Besides, I haven't finished with that young fellow by a long way. He's the most likely subject I've seen so far."

"Crown the murderer?" West waved the idea away with one of his famous gestures. "Why, the youngest student of criminal psychology would dismiss him at a glance. You can't connect a cunning, cool, and secret crime with a hot-headed fool who loses his temper and breaks into vulgarity and bluster at the first hint of interrogation! I wouldn't give him the credit of an ingenious affair like this!"

He stopped, for Sedley, conferring with Ward, was not even listening.

West was conscious of a feeling of dismay; not that he personally cared about the implied slight, but knowing too well that all his future suggestions would be met in the same way. It didn't promise hopefully for the future when Sedley really got to grips. What innocent persons might yet suffer for this wretched crime!

"Mrs. Willoughby next," said Sedley. "She'll have to come now, if I go and fetch her myself. Ward, this is the lady you're interested in, so I'll leave you to work the preliminaries . . . Oh, she's here! Blackmore, show Mrs. Willoughby in."

Enid came in slowly, her fair hair smoothly brushed, her face freshly powdered, wearing an elaborate black gown with a stiff Medici collar of scarlet and gold embroidery.

She ignored the police officers, and approaching West with a languid air said: "Well, Lionel? Where do I sit?"

He silently indicated the chair facing the paper-strewn table.

She raised her eyebrows petulantly, and twisted her fingers in a long string of crystal beads which she was wearing.

"I'm afraid," she volunteered dryly, "that I'm not a good witness. I never seem to see or hear things that aren't intended for me, and I hate anything sensational."

West read in this ultimatum: "Don't you think you'll get anything out of me!"

But Sedley was ready even for this attitude. He said just as dryly: "Would it be too sensational, Mrs. Willoughby, to ask if it is correct that you are first cousin to the Stacey brothers?"

She replied coldly: "Second cousins. We were brought up together."

"At your home, wasn't it?"

"Yes."

"And Sir Harry Stacey lived there until his marriage twelve years ago?"

"Yes."

"Didn't the family consider that marriage rather sudden?"

She looked annoyed. "Why should we? Aren't all marriages rather sudden to one's family?"

"But the circumstances in that case were unusual. Were

you yourself married when Sir Harry brought his wife home?"

"His fiancée. They were married from our house. No, I was not married then."

"Is it true that you and the future Lady Stacey became great friends from the first?"

"Yes, we were very friendly."

"And your friendship continued to the last without a break?"

"Certainly."

"You never suspected her of concealing the truth about her past?"

"Oh, never! Really, Inspector, the average person does not pride himself on having a suspicious mind!"

Sedley sat back in his chair as though satisfied that the way was prepared, and nodded to Ward to continue.

To Ward's preliminary questions Enid replied in tones of the utmost boredom, and as tersely as possible, that on the night of the game of hide-and-seek she had hidden in the powder closet of the so-called Royal Suite, and had remained there all the time until she was discovered. Not caring whether she were found or not, she had switched on the lights to examine the old furniture. The servants' hall was in an opposite angle, and someone there would probably be able to corroborate her evidence that the lights were on. She had seen no one, nor heard anything, until she was discovered by several people.

"Were you," inquired Ward, "one of the persons who afterwards joined in the search for Lady Stacey?"

"No. I went to bed. I was tired."

"Being a close relative, Mrs. Willoughby, wasn't it unusual that you should have displayed so little anxiety about Lady Stacey's disappearance as to go off to bed without knowing what had happened to her?"

Enid's eyelids dropped, and she played with her crystal beads.

"I didn't know there was any cause for anxiety. I thought she was hiding."

"Mrs. Willoughby!" Sedley suddenly struck in. "You say that you had been on friendly terms with Lady Stacey ever since her marriage . . . In what way could it be suggested that you were – a rival of Lady Stacey?"

Enid's eyelids flew up. She bit her lip, as though in surprised annoyance, and said: "In no way. I don't know what you mean."

"Do you suppose that Mr. Willoughby would have any idea of what I mean?"

Enid's pale face flushed scarlet, and she flung up her head with haughty defiance. She cast a half-glance at West, who was looking down at some notes upon his knee. He, too, was angry that Sedley should already be trading upon a random suggestion thrown out by that scatterbrain, Cecil Sabelle.

But Enid was clever, far too clever to lose her temper or give herself away.

She answered in a level, cold voice: "My husband makes a great many indiscreet remarks; not always reliable ones."

"I see . . . Mrs. Willoughby, you are the proper person to ask. Is it true that you and Lady Stacey were – or had been – rivals for the affections of Sir Harry?"

"Certainly not. That is absurd!"

"Why absurd?"

"Because I regarded both Harry and Edward Stacey as brothers."

"Then it would be untrue to say that you were ever jealous of Lady Stacey?"

"Most decidedly it would be untrue."

Sedley leaned back, and Ward, taking an envelope from the desk, opened it and unfolded a pink cheque which he held out to Enid.

"Do you recognise this cheque for five hundred pounds? It was made payable to you by Undine Stacey, dated the day previous to her death, and cashed by you four days later at the branch bank in Leadenhall Street. You remember this?"

"Yes."

"Under what circumstances did Lady Stacey give you this cheque?"

"It was a private affair between herself and me."

"A friendly affair?"

"Perfectly friendly."

"What was the nature of it?"

"I shall not tell you," she said in the same cool tones; "and since I am neither in the dock nor the witness-box, you can't make me!"

"In dealings of this kind," went on Ward calmly, "in *normal* dealings, Mrs. Willoughby, where a large sum is involved, there is usually a receipt given by the recipient. Now, Lady Stacey was evidently methodical about her receipts; there was a file of them on her desk, but no receipt for this cheque! Did you not give her one?"

"I should have done later. I had no opportunity."

"I see . . . It must have been a very private affair . . ."

Again Ward lifted a small, covered object from the desk and held it up. It was a powder compact of gold and blue enamel.

"Is this yours, Mrs. Willoughby?"

She allowed her eyes to rest on it, rather disdainfully.

"I have one like it."

"Where is yours?"

"In a bag in my room."

"Has yours any distinguishing mark?"

"Not that I know of."

Ward looked at her keenly. "This one has E. W. scratched on the bottom. Is it yours?"

She hesitated a moment.

"As far as I know mine is in a bag in my room."

"What kind of a bag, and where is it?"

Again Enid hesitated.

"A silver mesh-bag, in the top right-hand drawer of my walnut chest."

"Blackmore," ordered Ward, "go to Mrs. Willoughby's room and fetch the bag."

There was five minutes rather uncomfortable silence. West was ill at ease, knowing nothing of the evidence collected by the police, seeing that the strain was telling upon Enid. He knew that her heart was weak. Her face was colourless, except for dark stains under her eyes. Her head was less erect, and her fingers clutched the crystal beads as though they must have something on which to fasten.

The constable returned with a silver mesh-bag which he placed on the desk before the detectives.

"Now, Mrs. Willoughby," commanded Ward. "Empty out the contents of this bag."

She did so slowly; a lace handkerchief; a cigarette-case; a shilling and four coppers; a screwed-up counterfoil of a theatre ticket; and a small blue enamel powder compact.

Ward pounced upon it. "This is not in the least like the other!"

She compressed her lips.

"They are both yours, of course?"

Enid said deliberately: "I remember now. I lent that other to Undine."

"When?"

"Oh, ages ago!"

"You mean when you were down here in October?"

"Possibly it was then. We were out motoring. I'd forgotten all about it, but she never gave it back to me."

"No? So Lady Stacey forgot to give it back to you? . . . Were you in the habit of visiting her rooms?"

"Yes."

"You knew her bedroom?"

"Yes."

"Were you ever inside the closet where she hung her clothes?"

"Not that I ever remember."

Two scarlet spots suddenly appeared in Enid's cheeks; she gave a sudden sigh and collapsed in her chair.

West came quickly to her assistance, but she was unconscious, and water poured gently between her lips failed to rouse her. West and Blackmore between them carried her to her room and laid her upon the bed.

After about ten minutes she opened her eyes in a wide, fearful stare and started up with a cry of fright.

"It's all right, Enid," said West. "You're in your own room."

"Has the policeman . . . gone?"

"Yes."

She shuddered and seized West's arm violently.

"Lionel, I was terrified. Did I show it?"

"Not in the least."

"Oh, I was a fool over that compact! I knew it was mine and that I'd lost it here in October. I did lend it to Undine; but I was afraid they'd found it on the scene of the murder, or some awful place. I lost my head . . . trying to put them off. Lionel! How much do they know? It's so terrible! Where did they find the compact? In Undine's clothes closet?"

"Perhaps, Enid. It must have fallen out of one of her pockets."

"They'd believe that, wouldn't they!" She gave a hysterical sob; but suddenly, with a tremendous effort, pulled herself together and sat up.

"I'm all right now. Thanks very much, Lionel. I'll bathe my head and lie down till dinner-time."

"You're sure you're fit to be left?"

"Quite sure, thank you."

When West arrived back at the inspector's room he found the witness's chair empty. Rene Fullerton, he learned, had occupied it for a few minutes during his absence without supplying any information except – indignantly – that she was certainly not involved in any quarrel between Pandora Hyde and Lady Stacey about Basil Crown, nor even knew of any such disturbance.

"And she looked," explained Ward, "as though she were going straight downstairs to see into the matter. She's a forthright young woman is Miss Fullerton, and if she and Miss Hyde and Crown get together now there'll be as pretty a little circus as you'd wish to see!"

"Then they'll have to wait for one of the gladiators," announced Sedley, "because I'm having Miss Hyde back here just now!"

"About that emerald ring?"

"Mind-reader!"

"Do you think she stole it?"

"No, I think she lost it and daren't tell; and I've a very good idea who found it."

Pandora recalled, had a look of stony defiance in her dark eyes. To West's experienced gaze it was the look of one who has rehearsed a plausible story and means to stand by it. She was instructed to sit down, and as she did so a bar of sunlight slanting from the long window fell across her face and seemed to add to her discomfort, for she lifted both hands impatiently as though she would like to brush away the too-revealing light.

"You'd like the curtain drawn, Miss Hyde?" suggested Ward suavely.

"Oh, please!"

She watched him stretch out a hand to the long velour curtain, and as she did so her eye fell on the extended palm of Inspector Sedley. Upon it, in all the impudent glow of its green fire, lay the emerald ring.

She gave a glance aside.

"When did you last see this ring, Miss Hyde?"

"On the night we played hide-and-seek," she replied promptly.

"During the course of the game you were seen wearing this ring on your finger. When did it leave your possession?"

"I brought it downstairs," she said sullenly, "and laid it on the hall table."

"And did you at the same time throw the velvet box which belonged to it into a big plant-pot at the back of the hall?"

"No, I didn't!"

Sedley leaned back, tilting his fountain pen between his fingers.

"You didn't do the hall-table bit either. You were watched."

She sat in stolid silence.

"Come, Miss Hyde. What did you do with the ring?"

After a long pause she said: "I've told you."

"Oh, yes? Then shall I tell you what you did with it? Didn't you slip away from the others and creep to the garret, and place it on the finger — "

"I didn't!" the girl flashed. "Oh, you don't think I had anything to do with that, surely! Listen! I . . . I lost it out of my bag."

"That's better. And might I ask," went on Sedley ironically, "how Mr. West's ring came to be in your bag?"

A sudden scarlet dyed her cheeks. She hesitated an instant too long for innocence, and said: "It was too big. It kept falling off my finger. You see, I tried it on . . . down in the hall . . . and forgot . . . Cecil Sabelle saw it when we were looking for Mrs. Willoughby, and he said, 'You'll be losing that.' I took it off and dropped it in my bag. I – I forgot all about it then until I got to my room at night. When I looked in my bag the ring was gone. The bag had an open top, and it could easily have fallen out. I was frightened then . . . and when Mr. West asked us all at lunch about the ring, I said I'd put it . . . on the hall table. I still thought I might be able to find it, and—"

"And drop it on the hall floor, where it would look natural?"

She gulped. "I pretended my luggage wasn't ready, and I went up and had a long search in the wing, but I couldn't find it."

"And when you couldn't find it you left the house without saying anything at all?"

"Yes."

"Odd behaviour . . . Did anyone see you put the ring in your bag?"

"I don't think so."

"H'mph! I suppose you took good care they didn't! Where was your room?"

"In the guests' wing of the new building."

"And who had the rooms on either side of yours?"

"There are only three rooms in that wing; mine and the Willoughbys' and Mr. West's."

The girl's head had sunk lower and lower, and by now

she was whispering her answers. It was obvious that she had made a pitiful and futile attempt to steal the ring.

"Have you ever been in the garret, Miss Hyde?"

She lifted her head, and said with a plaintiveness that rang true: "No, I haven't. I didn't know there was such a place. I don't think any of us knew."

"All right, Miss Hyde; you can go."

She jumped up with such pathetic haste that she almost overturned her chair, and almost ran out of the room, carefully avoiding West's eye.

"And that's all we can do now," said Ward, relaxing in his chair and clearing a space before him on the table to accommodate his pipe and tobacco pouch. "We've seen them all – and no further. That girl's shady."

Sedley made no reply, but after fidgeting with his note books he cast at West a glance which was obviously a suggestion to retire. But West had no intention of retiring; he was compelled to be in the background, but they would not force him off the stage.

"Well? Is the girl guilty?" he said quietly, his eyes following the flight of a house-martin swooping under the eaves.

"No. But the woman is."

"The woman?"

"Excuse me, but is Mrs. Willoughby anything to you?"

"To me? Why, yes – an old friend."

"Then I'm sorry, Mr. West, but old friends are apt to prove disappointing. I read her like a book. Honestly, now, didn't you? Are you surprised to hear that Mrs. Willoughby herself would have been Lady Stacey if that pretty adventuress from France hadn't cropped up twelve years ago? She was particular to lay stress on her sisterly relation to Sir Harry, didn't you notice? Well, a woman doesn't forgive that sort of thing. It rankles. And she was insanely jealous of Lady Stacey. Probably you didn't know that either about your old friend! And here's the tit-bit. She'd got hold of that story of Lady Stacey's past and calmly used it the day before the murder to extract five hundred pounds from her ladyship. What do you think of that? Blackmail!"

"You surprise me!" said West.

"Motive for murder?" put in Ward.

"Blackmail just in time; story about to leak out; no more money forthcoming. Jealousy motive predominates. Mrs. Willoughby accompanies Lady Stacey upstairs on the night of the game. Some argument takes place in the garret and they fail to come to terms. The gong sounds, and realising that the searchers will be at work the two women hide, Mrs. Willoughby in the cabinet — "

"Oh, no!" interrupted West blandly.

"Mrs. Willoughby in the cabinet!" blared Sedley; "and Lady Stacey in the chest. Then all Mrs. Willoughby's pent-up resentment flares up, and she takes her chance. Having fastened the chest she steals downstairs and has plenty of time to hide herself in the powder closet, where she is eventually found. When the party returns to the hall she finds she is emotionally exhausted and cannot face the prospect of a search for the missing lady. Instead she goes to her own room. Now comes a test of her nerve. Having committed an unpremeditated crime, she finds herself faced with the preparation of many details. But she is a clever woman. That final sheet of one of Lady Stacey's letters to herself is a lucky idea; it postpones inquiry for a few days. You remember it was signed 'With love from Undine.' That's just the way Lady Stacey would sign herself to Mrs. Willoughby. She takes that letter along to Sir Harry's pillow; then she goes to Lady Stacey's rooms – and who knows them better than she did? She takes the coat and hat from the clothes closet and – she drops this!"

He triumphantly flicked with his finger the blue and gold powder compact.

"She gave herself away to-day when we faced her with it, in spite of that quick story about lending it to Lady Stacey."

"I thought she took it remarkably calmly," suggested West.

"At the time, yes; but she fainted when the emotional strain relaxed." Sedley thrust out his underlip shrewdly. "I've seen a murderer in France faced with his victim's corpse – it's the custom there – and never turn a hair or lose a drop of colour; but back in his cell half an hour later, when he thought no one was looking, he fell into a fit. You've heard of their system in France? They have a recording instrument to the pulse and heart of the suspect. Then they throw a picture of the murdered man on a screen, and the pulse and heart register normal; two minutes later they put a photograph of Queen Victoria on, and the mercury boils up and nearly bursts the glass. Relief from strain, you see. Well, Mrs. Willoughby gets the hat and coat, and has the nerve to toil up to that garret in the middle of the night and bung them into the chest on top of the corpse. The ring, of course, she found when Miss Hyde lost it. That was intended for the victim's finger. She had won it; she should have it, and much good might it do her."

"Why?" asked West innocently.

"Why? Why?" Sedley stared. "Don't ask me why! I can't follow all the workings of the mind of a jealous woman and a murderess at that!"

"You ought to be able to," said West with disarming meekness. "You see, the psychology of a crime and the psychology of its perpetrator coincide in every detail, so you have to be able to understand them both to link them together. There's such a lot of malice in this crime! Malicious devilment. That ring, for instance. Now, is Mrs. Willoughby capable of malicious devilment? Oh, no! I know her too well for that . . . Another point, quite apart from that. Mrs. Willoughby couldn't have done it the way you suggest. It was too risky. Suppose the search-party had discovered the chest and released Lady Stacey before any harm was done; she would know who had fastened her in."

"I'm not arguing it," interrupted Sedley, snapping his notebook and fastening the band.

West bit his lip at the snub; another intimation that he might keep his theories and suggestions to himself.

"There are other things to be explained," said Ward thoughtfully. "Confound these medieval barracks! There's nowhere for a fellow to knock a pipe out. How does a window like this open itself, anyway? All those little blue and yellow shields, they're getting on my nerves. Do you remember what that young savage, Crown, said? What was Major Stacey doing in the East Turret at midnight on the night of the murder? There was nothing about that in his signed statement, Mr. West. Where is it? . . . Oh, here . . 'Went up to the East Turret to ask Miss Farbell – governess – to join in the game.' Time about 8.45. Stayed talking for a quarter of an hour or so; returned to hall to sound gong at about 9.5. No midnight perambulations there! Inspector, don't you feel you'd like to have another heart-to-heart talk with Major Stacey?"

Sedley shrugged his shoulders.

"Humph! Sounds to me amorous but immaterial."

West frowned and left the room, strolling out into the cool stone-flagged passage. It was of no interest to him that his friend had been overheard while playing the fool. He would hardly have suspected Edward of liaisons with governesses, and he was not anxious to be present at the extraction of details.

"Mr. West! Whoo-ey!"

A flying, tawny-headed vision in green whirled to a standstill before him, and Rene Fullerton poised there scarlet-cheeked and flashing-eyed.

"I suppose I must get permission from you to go up to town," she said. "Well, I want it now, this minute! And I'm not coming back!"

"I'm afraid it isn't in my power to give, Miss Fullerton," he replied with a smile. "You must see the inspector."

"Which? That mouldy old giraffe who won his teeth in a raffle? I guess I can do without his permission! I'm going. Cecil will run me up. I've finished with all the crowd down here. I've broken off my engagement, and I've told Miss Hyde she can have her precious Basil, and long may she live to enjoy him! Just pass that on to the inspector, Mr.

West; and tell him that Cecil will be back after he's dropped me at my address!"

West smiled again with some amusement.

"Really, Miss Fullerton, I'm afraid it isn't possible for any of us to leave until the police inquiry is over. In any case, I haven't the authority. You'll have to interview the giraffe."

She tossed her tawny locks and grinned fiercely.

"Oh, very well! If I must, I must!"

And she marched away with a fine swagger of defiance.

West stood where she had left him. He found it difficult to understand this girl. Was she very frank . . . or was she subtle? The atmosphere of gloom and death which hung over the castle seemed to have no effect on her too exuberant gaiety. Was she hard . . . was she callous – as one read about the girls of her generation? Certainly she could not have been very fond of Lady Stacey, to treat this whole gruesome affair as a mere interference with her personal arrangements.

He did not suppose that Sedley would allow her to go; and then he must watch how she took the refusal. Oh, this hideous atmosphere of suspicion ! Did he really believe that everyone in this house wore a mask? This afternoon he had seen some of the masks stripped away, and it had not been a nice experience. Basil Crown shrieking in vulgar rage; Pandora Hyde trembling with fright, her eyes still furtive, trying to hide the evidences of a mind which could not always be relied upon to act honourably in any situation; Willoughby, boastful and suggestive; young Sabelle, of a piece with Rene, light-hearted young fools who made a jest of everything – even death; Edward, the friend, fallen from his high place; Enid – poor girl – with some unconfessed, unguessed-at misery in her heart, and now to bear the burden of an intolerable accusation. He wondered how she was, and if he might go to see her again without appearing to presume. No one else seemed to understand her. To whom else could she turn? Willoughby . . . a fine help he would be to any woman in despair!

He wandered into a little book-lined room and sat down, glad to be alone. Too much had emerged to-day for his peace of mind. He slowly recalled every moment, everything that had been said and done. If one day could produce so much dismay, he hated to think of another . . . and another. Yet in his profession he had heard so much of this kind of thing, and it had moved him very little. He was surprised at himself . . . but, after all, when it came into one's own life . . .

He looked through stained windows upon a garden border, just daffodils in a tangle of brilliant gold at the foot of a crumbled wall, the wind lightly stirring them, the western light emphasising their lovely, ethereal air. Think of anyone trying to find consolation in the works of Nature! That cruel perfection would drive a man mad.

There was a shuffling at the door, and the two children, Rita and Nicholas, came in. They approached West carefully; he was to them an unknown quantity.

"Hallo!" he said.

Rita, with the superb assurance of a little girl of ten, frowned at him. Nicholas, not so critical, said: "Can you tell us a yarn? Nobody seems to bother with us much nowadays."

He was rather touched, reading his own mature feelings of gloom into these pathetic infants. He cast about in his mind, frantically trying to remember some of the things that King Arthur's knights did.

"What kind of a story?" he asked, playing for time.

"Something you did at school," demanded Rita promptly, and with a touch of scorn, as though challenging him to rise to the occasion.

"Something bad," amended Nicholas, "not good."

He went racing away back to his schooldays. All he could remember of that glorious, high-hearted time of which poets sing was a series of feeble jokes which at fourteen he had considered flashes of inspired humour, and a general depravity of conduct which made him wonder that decent citizens were ever evolved from such unpromising material. He recalled a rather lurid practical joke which he and others of his kidney had practised on a young master whose nervous mannerisms had simply asked for it, and which had ended in the poor fellow's dismissal for inefficiency to control the boys. Disgusting thing to do, to lose that chap his job. He related to Rita and Nicholas a purified version of the incident, which they received with approval.

"Now another," said Rita. "Did you never do anything worse than that?"

He felt it his duty to lift the minds of Harry's children to higher things.

"Have you never thought," he said, "of the great and noble deeds which have been done within these very walls? I feel sure that such a fine old castle has many stories connected with it. You must ask your friend, Mr. Sabelle."

They looked blank.

"Oh, he tells us better stories than that!" boasted Nicholas. "About a gentleman jockey called Guido."

West thought it a pity, and said so, but they remained politely bored with his suggestions. Another of his illusions was exploded. He had thought that the minds of nice children would gravitate naturally to the heroic characters of the history book. But had his own? He remembered Deadwood Dick, tattered and thumbed, secreted between his mattress cover and the ticking.

He abandoned his attempt to elevate, and told them cowboy stories until the first gong sounded. He felt better for this interlude, but unfortunately it was not Life. The harsh cries of the rooks above the castle walls seemed to remind him of that.

Chapter X
A SILVER PEPPER-POT

THE sound of the dinner-gong clanged and echoed through the hollow corridors of the castle. West descended, and found to his surprise that he was to share a *tête-à-tête* meal with Jack Willoughby. The entrée followed the soup and fish, but no one else appeared.

"Harry is dinin' in his study," explained Jack, "and Enid's havin' half a lemon in her bedroom to soothe a fit of the megrims; but as for the others, search me!"

The butler placed port on the table and was about to withdraw.

"Where is everyone?" asked West.

"Mr. Crown is having dinner in his room, sir; and Miss Hyde is in her room. Major Stacey is in the small library with the police officials; Miss Fullerton is packing her clothes; and Mr. Sabelle is looking over his car preparatory to running her up to town, sir."

"Oh, then she's going to town?"

"I understood her to say so, sir. In fact, her exact words to me were, 'Give us a bun to eat in the bus, Patterson. The 'tecs have given me my ticket-of-leave'."

"So Rene's got permission to depart!" exclaimed Jack. "I wonder if there's any chance of Enid and me gettin' away?"

"Better ask," said West casually, making his escape.

He wandered out into the formal garden where clipped yews were trailing their angular shadows over the golden grass. The neat precision of that enclosure contrasted strangely with the wildness of the land in which the castle was set. The mountains frowned against the sunset as though their black and barren rocks resented the coloured softness of a daffodil sky. They bristled cruelly, scoffing at the fading splendours of the daylight, knowing that the hours of night were still theirs, and theirs the triumph of tempest and thundercloud and the powers of darkness.

It was better here in the cool garden than inside that house of dark history and present fear. He did not want to see anyone or be led into talk. There could be only one topic now, and that full of horror and suspicion among friends. Already yesterday's cloak of forced gaiety was torn away, and the castle was full of secretive creatures who hid their thoughts and avoided one another's eyes.

"West! . . . Lionel!"

Sir Harry had come quietly, unheard across the darkening grass. His voice was low and lifeless, with a hint of unbearable distress.

"Yes, Harry."

"Lionel, this is awful! They say that Enid – Enid! – was blackmailing Undine over that – that affair of hers in France. That she got five hundred pounds out of Undine the very day before her death! It can't . . . it can't be true! Enid!"

"Have you asked Enid for the truth about that cheque?"

"Of course! I went straight to her. She won't admit anything – or deny it. Just think . . . she won't deny it! I told her I wouldn't believe it; that I didn't want to believe it. She had the money – she admits that – but she won't tell me what it was given her for. Surely she could trust me, if it were nothing discreditable! I'm like a brother to her!"

He dug his toe savagely into the perfect turf, making a hole which would cost any proud gardener his reason.

"And I'm bothered about Edward too," he went on; "or rather the insinuations that Sedley is making about Edward. They've just had him on the carpet again. It seems he was fool enough to pay a second visit to the governess about midnight on the night of the – of the . . ." His throat contracted and he fled from the dreadful word. "It may have been perfectly harmless, but it was indiscreet. The police are making capital out of the story, though we can't imagine how they got hold of it. Edward says he didn't stay ten minutes with the girl. That doesn't matter; but Ward – Ward! A smug-faced policeman! – had the nerve to tell me in my own house that my own brother was under suspicion of having been concerned in the death of my wife!"

Sir Harry's voice rose dangerously and cracked with an ugly sound.

"Rubbish!" said West sharply; but somehow his tone was not convincing. He realised it, and suddenly a cold wind seemed to swoop from the battlemented walls and icily envelop his shoulders.

"Come inside, Harry. It's cold."

"It's the night wind. It comes off the mountains."

That same night wind had already caused Enid Willoughby to shudder under her flimsy kimono and close her window tightly against the oncoming dark. Life had again become too difficult for Enid. Her ordeal of the afternoon had proved the final snapping of her quivering nerves. She had seen the lust of the captor in the cold eyes of her inquisitor; he had not been able to conceal the fact that he had chosen her for his victim. And that hideous interview with Harry had been the very end!

She felt the net closing about her, the final act in her life's tragedy. She was crushed; she could not even make a struggle for her own vindication. She was physically ill. Her spirit was broken. And again the money problem, the sordid question of ways and means, was assuming vast proportions. She could not face it again; she had not the strength to plan and struggle and cope with the kind of situations which would periodically embarrass her path so long as her life with Jack Willoughby continued. She sat with her elbows on her dressing-table in the attitude of despair; her wrists pressed against her temples, her fingers thrust into her fair, dishevelled hair. She stared at the thin-cheeked, dull-eyed creature in the mirror and her lips twisted in a cynical smile.

"You're done, Enid! Old . . . ugly . . . raddled . . . haggish! It isn't worth it, my dear!"

There was a sharp knock on her door. She winced and caught her breath . . . "Come in!"

It was Sedley. Her lips went dry and hard. "Oh, good evening, Mrs. Willoughby . . . Thank you . . . I will sit down."

Like a cat with a mouse! She folded the kimono across her throat and clutched it defensively.

"People don't usually intrude on me here, Inspector!"

He ignored her last pathetic flash of defiance.

"Sorry, Mrs. Willoughby, but if you'd been franker with us in the first place we might have avoided this. I warned you that everything would have to come out. I've been talking to your husband. To give him his due, he didn't come across easily, but when I suggested that you and he were on the blackmailing game together it seemed to loosen his tongue."

Enid gave a strangled cry.

"Don't you think you'd better admit that you blackmailed Lady Stacey?"

"No! I did not!"

He leaned forward, shaking a menacing finger.

"Come, Mrs. Willoughby, you are not helping yourself. Your husband has told everything — "

She cried: "But there was nothing to tell!"

"Nothing? . . . You were in low water; in debt. Your husband had embezzled public money. You had to get five hundred pounds, and you took a chance at holding Lady Stacey up."

"I did not! She gave me the money of her own free will."

He smiled sardonically. "She was careful not to tell her husband about the affair. That doesn't sound very innocent."

"It was I who asked her not to."

"Why not?"

"I shall not tell you!"

"Your husband suggested, Mrs. Willoughby" – his eyes probed her – "that being in love with Sir Harry and anxious to appear well in his eyes — "

"Does Jack think I blackmailed Undine?"

"What else should he think?"

"Oh, what a farce!" She flung her hand to her mouth and

collapsed in a chair.

Sedley rose. "So we have the story at last. I can go to Sir Harry now."

"You wouldn't do that?" Her voice was shrill.

"I keep nothing back," he said dryly. "There have been enough evasions in this case already."

"Oh, but this can't serve any purpose! I beg you! I beg you!"

"You beg me – what? To save your face? Under ordinary circumstances, perhaps; but to-day I'm investigating murder."

He went away, vaguely conscious that with distorted face Mrs. Willoughby had fallen on her knees. He was used to such scenes.

When the door had closed she dragged herself to her feet, and with tragic calmness flung back her tangled hair.

She rummaged in her drawer for paper and pencil and wrote in an unsteady hand which was still recognisable as hers:

Dearest Harry, —

When you read this the inspector will have told you how I shamed myself for love of you. I have kept up this pretence for twelve years. I have made you think I was happy and prosperous. I have kept Jack out of public disgrace, and I went to Undine for the money to do it. I told her my trouble and she gave me five hundred pounds. I didn't care what she thought of me because I hated her. I hated her, but I didn't kill her. The police will tell you I did, but I shan't care now. I have kept one thing back from *the beginning. When I saw that note Undine left behind I knew it wasn't genuine. She left me in her room on October 17th, while she went downstairs to get a cheque from Edward. I was looking at some things on her desk and I saw that letter lying there, as though she had forgotten to put it in its envelope. There were two sheets, and it was meant for Sharlie Wright. It was about a charity matinée, and Undine suggested that Rene Fullerton should be asked to act in it. I don't know why I didn't speak at the time, but I never suspected anything so bad as Undine's murder. Perhaps this may help to clear up the affair—*

She stopped, for her frantic scribble was becoming illegible, and read over what she had written. The sudden back-firing of a car brought her to her feet, and tremblingly to the window. A dark-blue coupé – Cecil Sabelle's two-seater – with Cecil and Rene Fullerton aboard, was crawling under the main gate.

"Beyond those gates is freedom!" thought Enid Willoughby.

Meanwhile, Sedley, meandering thoughtfully towards his office, was surprised to meet his subordinate evidently in search of him and in a state of suppressed excitement.

"Here!" Ward jerked a thumb. "In this junk-hole for a minute. I've got an idea."

He led the way into an alcove where some broken screens of mediaeval carving leaned drunkenly against the wall in company with the stained fragments of many suits of armour, looking like so much scrap iron abandoned to rust away.

"I've got a strong and unaccountable desire," said Ward, "to meet a lady whose name keeps cropping up in this case with quite humorous regularity; and she is the Major's lady friend, Miss Amy Farbell, or, the Intriguing Governess."

"But I counted her out with the servants," said Sedley impatiently. "She didn't take part in the game."

"Not exactly, but" – Ward could not restrain his triumph – "she was another one of those interesting persons who had a regular stand-up row with Lady Stacey on the day before her death!"

"She did? The governess? Who presented you with that?"

"It was Miss Hyde. That girl's frightened, and wants to get on the right side of us. She came sidling up to me a while ago and told her tale. It seems that on the afternoon of the 17th – day before the murder – Miss Hyde proceeded to Lady Stacey's room to apologise for the little dust-up she'd already had with her ladyship."

"Apologise!" Sedley snorted. "That little tigress apologise? Sounds to me sort of sweet!"

"M'm . . . well, we can pass that. Because when little Hyde got to the boudoir she never went in; because her ladyship was in the middle of dismissing the governess, and the governess was throwing 'em back hell for leather, telling her ladyship off."

"And what was it all about? Did Miss Hyde tell you that?"

"Yes. It seems that Lady Stacey had just found out about the governess's affair with the Major, and she was very properly giving the girl the sack, while the girl was protesting her innocence and vowing she'd see Lady Stacey in – well, Jericho, before she'd shift a yard. Miss Hyde says she never would have guessed that meek little thing had it in her. Now, can't you think of anything you'd like to ask her personally? I can!"

"And I might," said Sedley thoughtfully. "Have Blackmore send her down."

The two detectives hurried to their office; while at the same time Lionel West, not thinking that the inquisition was to receive new impetus at this time of the night, was sauntering towards his own room with the growing conviction that there was nothing left for him to do but to go to bed.

The moon was newly risen and shafts of greenish light from the high windows gave him all the illumination he required. Suddenly he realised he was looking through an open doorway at a superb view of the mountains. The highest peaks against a pall of black sky were burnished by the moonlight to an awful and revealing splendour. He strode across an empty room and stood before the window, gazing out from the castle wall across the grey and silver wilderness of the plain to where the mountains with their gleaming crests bristled in darkness.

Turning again, he realised that he was in the room recently occupied by Rene Fullerton. The girl had packed and left in a hurry, leaving doors and drawers indiscriminately open. One could not expect spoilt heiresses to be tidy, thought West. Crumpled wisps of tissue paper strewed the bed, and the moonlight falling on the floor showed a white ball which proved to be a pair of soft doeskin gloves rolled up carelessly and abandoned by their scatter-brained owner. Miss Fullerton *had* gone away in a hurry! Was that typical of her? Or . . . no! He would not give way to this horrible house's atmosphere of suspicion.

On his way to the billiard-room he was button-holed by the conscientious constable, Blackmore.

"Could I have a word with you, Mr. West?"

"Of course. What is it?"

Blackmore lowered his voice.

"It's about some thefts. Mr. Patterson's very worried – the butler, you know, sir – and he doesn't like to trouble Sir Harry. I said I'd mention it to you."

"But what thefts? I haven't heard anything."

"No, sir? Well, it seems a lot of little silver things have been taken out of the drawing-room – 'articles of virtue,' they call them. They're supposed to be in Mr. Patterson's care, and" – Blackmore rolled a conspiratorial eye – "he suspects Miss Fullerton who's just gone away!"

"It seems a strange story. I — "

"Oh, there is Mr. Patterson! Excuse me, sir, for interrupting you. I'll call him."

The butler joined them, his habitual air of calm rotundity gone. He looked worried; no longer a butler, serene and stable as the British Empire, but merely a hot and bothered, middle-aged man.

"Now, what's the trouble? " said West kindly. "Take your time, Patterson, and tell me the whole story."

"Well, sir, I didn't like to worry Sir Harry, but it's beyond a joke, and that's a fact. It's like this, sir. There's a lot of valuable things in the drawing-room, including two cabinets full of little antique silver things – spoons, and cups, and bits of jewellery – some with quite a history to them, I believe. Well, with such a lot of things lying about we've always been in the habit of keeping the drawing-room door locked, and I have the key. The room's never used to sit in. Her late ladyship didn't like it because it faces north and never gets any sun. However, every day at some time or other I open that door and have a look in to see that nothing has been disturbed; so this evening, after I'd seen Miss Fullerton and Mr. Sabelle off, I went into the drawing-room, and at first everything looked just as it always does. I should never have noticed anything amiss, except that there's a little silver pepper-pot that I've always had a great fancy for. It was supposed to have belonged to Queen Elizabeth, so her late ladyship told me, and it had E.R. scratched on it, which they say the queen did herself. I generally have a look at that pot before I leave the room, but this evening, sir, to my surprise it wasn't there! And if I hadn't been looking for that in particular I should never have seen anything wrong with the appearance of the cabinet, because all the other things had been rearranged to fill up the empty space! It seemed to me queer, so I went off to my pantry and fetched the drawing-room inventory – oh, yes, I keep that for my own satisfaction. Would you believe it, sir, no less than twenty-two small articles had been taken from the two cabinets! I doubted my own eyes at first. And, sir, behind the velvet curtain of the door I found the Queen Elizabeth pepper-pot; as though somebody had had her arms too full and dropped it in making her escape!"

"*Her* escape? Now, what do you mean by that,

Patterson?"

"Just this, sir. Between you and me, there's only one person I know that ever took an interest in the drawing-room, and that was Miss Fullerton. Always worrying me to take her in, she was, because she'd heard about the 'articles of virtue' – as her late ladyship called them – and she wanted to see them. So two nights ago I took her in, and I could hardly get her out again. She asked me endless questions that I couldn't answer: where did all the things come from, and what was their history, and how much were they worth? And foolishly like, I told her what I've told you, that the room was never used, and I was the only person who ever entered it; and she saw me put the door-key in the inner pocket of my dinner-coat that I keep hanging in my pantry at night! And tonight she's off and away at a minute's notice, and I even carried her bag out for her to Mr. Sabelle's car. What do you think about it, Mr. West?"

"Were these cabinets kept locked?"

"No, sir; they had sliding glass panels."

West frowned. "You say twenty-two articles were missing. If they were packed together, wouldn't they take up a considerable amount of room?"

"Well, yes, sir. They'd fill a suit-case."

Blackmore broke in. "I think what's wanted, sir, is for me to mention it to Sergeant Ward and get him to organise a secret search of the castle. We can go through everybody's things without them knowing it. If the silver isn't in the castle, then it's been taken out and Miss Fullerton is the only one who's tried to do a bolt."

"Have you that silver pepper-pot?" said West to the butler.

"Yes, sir. In my pantry."

"Then please go and fetch it, and take it to my room. Put it in the top left-hand drawer of my dressing-chest."

"Very good, sir." Patterson bowed and departed.

"Queer business, isn't it?" said the constable, wrinkling his brow. "I never was in such a house! Why, sir, there's a full-blooded torcher chamber down in the basement; Mr. Patterson was showing me. He wanted to Demon Strate on me and all, but I was afraid as the thing was Haughty Mattic – one of them what won't stop, you know." He blew his cheeks full of air, and released it with a significant pop. "Aren't you going up to the office, sir? I thought you were listening in to it all?"

"But the detectives aren't there now, surely?"

"Oh, yes, sir; they're hard at it. I gathered they were on a new trail."

"But who are they questioning now?"

"It's that governess, sir; Miss Farbell."

Five minutes later West slipped quietly into his seat.

"No," Amy Farbell was saying, shaking her fair head; "I was not dismissed. Lady Stacey withdrew that. She never intended me to leave. It was all settled."

"Do you mean you parted on friendly terms?"

"Yes," said Amy, with just that tiny lack of enthusiasm which betrayed the half-truth to the watchful detective.

Amy, in a short brown frock with a fichu of white georgette, sat under the full glare of the electric light, wondering how she had found her way into such an unpleasant position. She was facing the detectives, and was conscious that another man had come into the room and taken a seat behind her. She dared not turn her head to see who it was, but her heart missed a beat and the scarlet rushed to her cheeks at her own fond conjectures. Could it be Major Stacey come to see that they did not bully her? Did he really care for her so much? Incredible! She had been rather miserable since they all came back to Cleys ten days ago, for it seemed as though he had deliberately avoided heaven-sent opportunities of a few minutes alone with her. Perhaps that was just his caution; but last October he had not cared about caution!

At the thought that he was now sitting behind her, her heart beat so excitedly that she hardly heard what the detectives were asking her. Unable to bear the suspense any longer, desiring just a look – a smile, she flicked a tremulous glance over her shoulder.

It was Lionel West! Her heart dropped into the toes of her shoes. She didn't care what happened to her.

"Miss Farbell! Will you attend to me, please! . . . I asked you, did you after all take part in the game of hide-and-seek on the night of October 18th last?"

"No, I didn't."

"Why not?"

She hesitated, and finally said: "Lady Stacey didn't want me to."

"And were you always so particular as to Lady Stacey's wants?"

"A governess has to be," she replied serenely.

Ward smiled knowingly.

"Did you spend the whole of that evening in your own room?"

"Yes."

"Now, Miss Farbell — " Ward cleared a space on the table for his clasped hands to rest. "About those two visits that Major Stacey paid you on the night in question. I want you as nearly as possible to tell me the exact time" – he broke off sharply. "Well, Miss Farbell? You look very blank! You remember those visits surely? In any case, we know all about them, so you needn't be shy."

She moistened her lips with the tip of her tongue; and it seemed to Ward that her face was blank with surprise rather than reticence.

"The first time Major Stacey went up to your room — "

"He didn't come to my room."

"Don't try to deny it. We know all about it!"

She made a determined gesture with both fists.

"He did not come to my room that night, or any time!"

"My good girl, we know the approximate times! At a quarter to nine, and again at midnight — "

Suddenly a look of sheer horror flashed into the girl's eyes and the colour wavered in her cheeks.

Sedley with a keen expression put his hand on Ward's arm.

"Stop! We're getting to something now. The girl's speaking the truth. Blackmore, fetch Major Stacey here at once, whatever he's doing!"

Amy jumped to her feet, clasping her hands.

"Oh, but he may have come when I was asleep. I went to bed very early. I didn't hear him."

"My good young woman!" said Sedley dryly, "he is supposed to have held conversation with you on both occasions. One of you is lying! Sit down! . . . Lying! And I'm here to find out" – he thumped the table and roared "what you're trying to hide!"

Amy collapsed on her chair and her fingers picked at the velvet upholstery.

"Major Stacey!"

Oh, he was there! He was behind her!

"Your Majesty desires?" said the Major lightly.

"We have your written statement here," said Sedley, "that on the night of the 18th of October you paid two visits to Miss Farbell in the East Turret, of twenty minutes and ten minutes duration respectively, and held polite converse with her on each occasion."

"Well? " said the Major brightly, "what about it?"

"Miss Farbell denies that you ever paid her these visits!"

There was a minute's dreadful pause. Then Amy, turning to Edward with outflung hands, cried: "Oh, what have I done? Forgive me! I didn't know . . . I don't understand . . ." She buried her face in her hands. And the Major's face, wiped of its debonair smile, was a study in consternation. Under his breath he whispered to West: "Well, she has gone and put the cat among the pigeons!"

West studied his finger-nails. Sedley pounced like a panther.

"Now, Miss Farbell! What have you to say?"

Amy almost shrieked, "I must have been away from the room for a few minutes when he came!"

"Then why does he not say so? Why make up an

imaginary conversation?"

Ward struck in, with tones as smooth as cream: "Naturally, because Major Stacey found Miss Farbell absent from her room on both occasions, and in the light of after events he did not choose to say so. May I say, Major, that your chivalry has given us a good deal of unnecessary trouble, and done Miss Farbell more harm than good?"

West saw Edward clench his fists, and his eyes smouldered fiercely.

"Am I right, Major? . . . I thought so! And of course not only was Miss Farbell absent from her room at nine o'clock and at twelve o'clock, but she was absent all – or most of – the time between. Weren't you, Miss Farbell?"

The girl set her lips tightly. One could hear her little teeth grit.

"Weren't you, Miss Farbell?"

The girl sat in frozen silence.

"You won't speak? That speaks for itself. I wonder what Major Stacey thought you were doing during that rather sinister three hours? You know, we're looking for someone who can't explain their movements — "

"You rotten little rat!" suddenly exploded Major Stacey. "You'd suggest that against her, would you?" His outflung hand suddenly flicked Ward on the cheek. "That's for you, sir! Now come outside and fight, you insinuating devil! You'll leave that girl alone!"

Ward scratched his insulted cheek with the utmost calmness.

"We're not in a melodrama this time," he said. "Take him out, Blackmore; and keep him out!"

There was every indication that the Major would go berserk. West hastily interposed and induced him to leave the room quietly.

"I will if you'll keep an eye on that kid, West. See she gets fair play!"

"Of course I shall."

Edward dropped his head and whispered, "I'm horribly afraid she's guilty!"

West avoided his old friend's eyes and said tonelessly, "Is that why you lied for her?"

"Of course. Any soldier would . . . a woman's honour . . ."

Meanwhile Amy, her last defence gone, felt the palms of her hands go damp against the rough velvet of the chair. The sergeant's face hung before her like a vast china plate full of expanding and contracting eyes. Her heart was leaping hideously somewhere at the base of her throat. Frantically her mind raced back to that dreadful 18th of October. She had not even the excuse that the events of that day and night were by now vague in her mind. She remembered every detail of it only too clearly, from the time that Lady Stacey had forbidden her to play hide-and-seek and Edward had so consolingly kissed her in the stone passage, to the cruel moments when, after her early dinner with the children, she had lain sobbing with childish hysteria because it was past eight o'clock and he had forgotten to come for her as he had promised. She knew he had forgotten, for she had crept to the head of the stairs and seen them all laughing in the hall and getting ready for their game; and Edward was lounging in a big chair, fastening a bracelet on the pretty wrist of Miss Fullerton, who perched on the table beside him in her beautiful Paris dress. And what had happened after had all been part of Amy's foolish despair. She had been ashamed by the next morning of her temporary madness.

"Now, Miss Farbell," Ward was demanding briskly, "we shall want you to give an account – as every member of the house party has done to-day – of your movements on the night of the murder" – he brought out the word deliberately – "of Lady Stacey, between the hours of 8.30 and the time you got back to your room. When was that?"

She dug her nails into her palms. How much did they know? No use to deny that she was out of her room!

She answered, "It would be – just after twelve."

"Just after twelve! And where were you – don't be afraid! I'm sure you haven't anything to conceal! – between 8.30 and just after twelve?"

"I was . . . just about the castle."

"Oh, you were just about the castle! Well, so was everybody else. Supposing you're a little more explicit. In which rooms of the castle?"

"In . . . in the library . . . and in the sewing-room."

"And in the dark?" struck in Sedley with malicious intent.

"I . . . don't understand."

"No? Because the whole of the castle was in darkness, you remember. Or rather, you don't remember, or you wouldn't have given yourself away like that. Now! Supposing you give us the truth! Where exactly did you go when you first left your room?"

"Nowhere in particular . . . I can't remember."

"Do you mean you won't remember?"

She shook her head dumbly.

"You refuse to tell . . . quite within your rights, you know! We'll change the subject . . . Have you ever been in the garret?"

She hesitated a moment. "Yes."

"When?"

"That day . . . in the morning."

"What were you doing there?"

"I was with Lady Stacey, getting out a costume she was going to lend to Miss Fullerton."

"Did Lady Stacey keep this costume in a chest in the garret?"

"No. In a hamper."

"Did you notice the chest?"

"Yes. There was a lot of old furniture."

Sedley leapt in: "Miss Farbell! What did Lady Stacey say when you suggested that the chest would make a good hiding-place for the game at night?"

She stared at him as though he were a magician. The lucky shot, like the skilled plunge of a rapier, seemed to have hypnotised her.

"Oh, I didn't suggest it! She did. I told her not to."

"Why did you tell her not to?"

"I said it was too much like that horrible story of the 'Mistletoe Bough'; and she laughed and said that this chest couldn't fasten itself."

"So then she showed you how the bolt worked in the hasp!"

Amy's lips moved, but no sound of disclaim was heard.

"Of course, as well as knowing the garret, you would be

familiar with Lady Stacey's own apartments?"

She swallowed hard and said, "Ye-es."

"And you were absent from your room on the fatal night from 8.30 until after midnight, and you refuse to tell us where you were?"

Sedley turned over a page of his notebook and wrote at the head of the virgin leaf, "Mrs. Willoughby. Blackmail only. No other evidence against."

As though she had suddenly realised the peril of her position, Amy cried desperately, "I wasn't doing any harm!"

"Then what were you doing?"

She shook her head, and suddenly catching West's eye, flung at him a glance of wild appeal.

"You had better let this girl go," he said quietly. "She is overwrought. She doesn't know what she is doing."

Sedley did not hesitate.

"You can go, Miss Farbell," he said stonily. She rose nervously and stood with her hand on the back of the chair.

"You can go," repeated Sedley, "but if you'll take my advice you'll go to your room and stay there. Ward – go with her."

He turned to West. "Now you can see why Major Stacey didn't want to involve the girl. He knew well enough what was happening while she was away from her room that night! I don't mean he knew at the time – I'm not going so far now as to say that he was her accomplice, but he knew after the crime was discovered that she was the most suspicious person in the whole party. He's done his best to shield her. He knew he was the only person who could give her away. He didn't count on her giving herself away! She never would have done if he could have warned her of the bluff he was suddenly having to put up on her behalf. But I arranged for a bit of staff work. From the minute you came and told me that the Major wanted to keep Miss Farbell's name out of this business, I put a man on to see that they didn't get together. It sounded harmless that he should want to keep her out of it; probably it was harmless; but one never knows. So early this afternoon Robinson put himself on duty at the foot of the stairs of the East Turret. At ten minutes past two Major Stacey appeared, and was considerably taken aback at the sight of the constable. He made some remark about looking for Mr. Crown and went away. Just before tea he tried again. Robinson was still there. This time the Major started up the stairs. Robinson called after him that Crown was not there. The Major looked angry and hesitated, but evidently decided that he dare not say it was Miss Farbell he wished to see, made some excuse, and again went away. Robinson then turned his report in to me. I knew then of course that there was something between the Major and Miss Farbell, and that it had something to do with both their movements on the night of the murder. This information came to hand after I had dealt with Mrs. Willoughby. It made me not so sure about Mrs. Willoughby. One has to be open-minded. Earlier in the afternoon I had expressed a theoretical case against Mrs. Willoughby. That meant nothing; I believe in expressing my theories. I turned my attention to keeping the Major and Miss Farbell apart until I could have them here separately and work them off against each other. That sort of thing doesn't always come off, I may tell you, but on this occasion you saw for yourself it worked like a charm! I did think the girl might have had a plausible story to account for her absence from her room during the vital period. I can only think she imagined herself quite safe and was utterly taken by surprise."

West had not spoken throughout Sedley's harangue. At last he said: "Are you going to charge this girl?"

"Oh, no, no! We haven't the evidence yet."

"You sent her to her room with Ward. You can't keep her there without charging her."

"I'm not keeping her there. She can come out as soon as she chooses, but I don't think she'll want to. Of course she will be under observation, and so will Major Stacey. I shall give her every chance to make a statement which will clear her. If she's innocent, what more can she want?" And Sedley screwed up his fountain pen with the air of a judge of ancient times who thought that ordeal by fire, water, or battle was mercy's greatest privilege to any suspected man.

It was almost midnight now, and Jack Willoughby, miserably bored by his lonely evening in the billiard-room, crawled up to bed. Outside the bedroom door he paused, and with a single thump on the panels shouted: "Cheer-oh, old girl! It's only me!"

There was no reply. Pining for human society, even his wife's, he opened the door and discovered darkness within. As his eyes grew accustomed to the gloom he saw Enid sitting with her back to him, her shoulders bent over her dressing-table, her head down among the enamel-topped trinkets.

He snapped on the light. Was she asleep? Her cheek rested upon a pencil-scrawled sheet of note-paper. Jack read, "Dearest Harry — " The fingers of her left hand stiffly grasped the neck of a small blue bottle – empty!

He withdrew softly, closing the door, his prominent eyes flickering nervously. The corridor was dark and still. Miss Hyde's door was closed and there was not a sound within. He ran on tiptoe through the wing, wondering whom he ought to rouse, and where everyone's rooms were, and what on earth Enid had meant by it, and if he would be involved. He had already decided that she had let him down badly, and he was seriously annoyed with her. In any case, nothing would induce him to go back to that room. He hoped he wouldn't have to see her again; he didn't like the association of ideas. First Undine; then Enid . . .

He ran through the black cloisters with their ghostly central lawn and up the first flight of stairs he came to. A door up there was ajar, and within he beheld Patterson the butler in blue-striped pyjamas and an overcoat, making ready for his final locking-up round. Poor Patterson was having a trying time in these days, when people refused to go to bed and policemen roamed about the premises to all hours of the night. His urbane manner was a little strained as he confronted the pale and panting Willoughby.

"Is that you, Mr. Willoughby? Haven't those detectives done yet, sir? I can't go to bed until I see that everything's safe!"

"I don't know." Jack tried to be both commanding and casual. "By the way, you might find Major Stacey for me, or Sir Harry, or both . . . and will you tell them — "

His nerve cracked. He began to shudder from head to foot. He whispered in a strangled voice: "My wife is in her room – dead!"

He had a confused impression of Patterson's face looming towards him like a film close-up. He fled again, and roamed about the gardens for a long time, wondering what was going on inside. At last he found his way to the billiard-room, switched on the lights, and got a drink. He heard confused noises which died away. No one came near him. He thought it very callous of them; after all he was a bereaved husband.

Chapter XI
WEST MAKES A CHART

THE next day dawned in a dazzling wealth of spring colour, as though the universe must show its aloofness from humanity by countering the tragedies of mankind with a display of solar radiance. The far mountains wore the bloom of grapes as they melted into a pure amethyst sky. The spreading waste of country around the castle had become vividly green as though in a single night. From the triumphant sun there poured down a flood of golden splendour which hour after hour, without stint or effort, sparkled from the castle's grey and hoary walls. The air was rich and sweet with the smell of spring earth and bursting buds; the gardens ran wild with blue and yellow flowers; a light wind carried down the lively tang of the moorland, and the crimson banner on the keep streamed out bravely as though Cleys were a place of festival instead of a tomb.

As the sun was westering, Cecil Sabelle's blue car came bounding towards the drawbridge, ran through, and neatly stopped beside the gatehouse for inspection.

The young man popped out his head.

"All serene? Good. Nothing to declare, sergeant."

He climbed down. "I've had a splendid run, but I'd like to have stopped in town. London's looking lovely; I'll make all their mouths water to-night when I tell them about the lights of Piccadilly. Where is everybody, sergeant?"

"Well, I don't know, Mr. Sabelle . . . but there's Miss Hyde!"

Pandora came across the courtyard and greeted Cecil without enthusiasm.

"Hallo! How's everybody?" he greeted her. To his surprise she pressed a handkerchief to her lips, mumbled vaguely, seized a letter from the rack at the gate-house, and ran away without looking back.

"I expect," said Blackmore, whom Sabelle had dignified with the rank of sergeant, "that she's upset about Mrs. Willoughby. It's been a shock to them all, as you might say."

"Mrs. Willoughby! What's happened? Do you mean they've arrested her?"

"No, sir; oh, no! She's dead. She's committed suicide. Last night."

"I say! That's a facer! . . ." He pulled off his driving gloves and his candid eyes narrowed. "Why did she do that?"

Blackmore lowered his voice and gave a sidelong glance to make sure that his superior officers were not in sight.

"I don't know, sir; and I understand it won't come out. She left a letter, but Inspector Sedley is the only one who's seen it besides Sir Harry Stacey, and he's promised Sir Harry it shan't go any further."

"You mean . . . something to do with the crime?" Sabelle whispered.

"I couldn't tell you, sir, really."

Sabelle went to his own room without seeing anyone. The castle was strangely quiet, and in it somewhere Enid Willoughby lay dead. He felt a slight qualm; he had liked Enid . . . but then he liked most people and most people liked him. Everyone liked a harmless fool, which, he decided, was one of the compensations for being a harmless fool.

He went downstairs in search of tea, and met Lionel West pacing the Long Gallery.

"How long have you been back, Cecil?" West asked.

"Only a few minutes. Had a good run, too."

"Have you heard our bad news?"

"Yes . . . from the fellow at the gate." Sabelle shuffled his feet awkwardly and unhappily. "Why did she do it? I liked her."

"She did it for a reason that needn't ever be known. It's better so."

"Then it was nothing to do with — ?"

"With Lady Stacey? No."

The young man tugged his forelock apprehensively, and said in what was for him a very subdued tone: "Mr. West, did she kill Undine? You must know."

"No. She did not."

Sabelle gave a sigh of relief which resembled the roar of a young tiger. "Then that's all right! I'm glad! . . . My stars, I could drink tea if there were any!"

"Did you get Miss Fullerton safely to London?"

"Oh, yes, we had a splendid journey. No trouble at all, at least no more than the trouble one expects with Rene and me driving in turns half across England . . . Has anything else happened while I've been away?"

"Nothing of any great importance."

West was not anxious at this point to enter upon a discussion of Amy Farbell's position or the new suspicions of the detectives. The death of Enid had been a great blow to everyone, especially to Harry when the sad story of her last years had been revealed by the letter on which her tears were hardly dry. To his relief, the police officials had been considerate, and after making a copy of the few lines of the letter which might affect the case in hand, they allowed Sir Harry to keep the original and its secret.

Jack Willoughby was very subdued and had lost all his jauntiness. The law reigned now at Cleys Castle, and those persons who were still compelled to remain there as unwilling guests avoided each other as much as possible and were conspicuously guarded in their actions and remarks, in contrast to their former almost blatant frankness. Pandora Hyde was the only woman left among six men.

The inquest on poor Enid was held, and the facts being in the possession of the police, a verdict of suicide was quickly returned, and she was buried the next day in the little churchyard at Abertefn, where Undine already lay. And so those two women, so strangely brought into one another's lives by Fate, so inevitably antagonistic, at the end lay side by side, still in their youth and beauty, in a lost village churchyard in Wales.

Meanwhile Ward was energetically conducting a secret search of the castle for the missing silver articles from the drawing-room, which Patterson the butler still insisted had roused illegal desires in the breast of the departed Miss Fullerton.

West was interested in observing the methods of the police, the astute way in which they took advantage of anyone's absence from a room to ransack it from end to end and leave it suspiciously neat. That no one should suspect what was going on he could hardly believe; but at least everyone either respected the machinery of the law or else thought it safer not to protest, for not one word was heard about the peculiar proceedings of Ward and his minions.

The search went on by night also. It reminded West of Poe's classic description of the police hunt for the "Purloined Letter," and it was almost as thorough. Ward would have said scornfully that he had nothing to learn from the Parisian police of the mid-Victorian era. But, alas, thought West, there was no Dupin here to make the Great Find! Places obvious and obscure received equal attention. Open shelves in public sitting-rooms were scrutinised as well as cellars, vaults, and dungeons, unexplored for many long years.

At last Ward admitted that he was satisfied with his men's work and that they had done everything that could be done, although in vain. All that gruelling work for nothing!

"It's gone out of the castle all right! " he declared firmly; "and I'm authorised by Sir Harry to investigate the loss. Not that it isn't a great nuisance, all the same, coming when we're so busy. I feel like an insurance inspector!" He paused. "What do you know about this Miss Fullerton, Mr. West?"

"Very little, really," admitted West. "Her father was a good fellow. And she has plenty of money of her own and seems a frank, open girl."

Again there flashed through his mind Rene's sudden interest in the drawing-room silver and her abrupt departure. Coincidence, of course! Candid young heiresses like Rene did not develop attacks of kleptomania when left within reach of their host's possessions. Under ordinary conditions he would have dismissed the matter from his mind; but in this atmosphere of strange happenings, death and suspicion, he could not help wondering whether such trivial events as the disappearance of an heiress and twenty-two silver pepper-pots had a deeper and more sinister meaning.

He could not discuss the matter with Sir Harry, who was prostrated by the additional burden of Enid's tragic end.

Cecil Sabelle, tow-headed and melancholy, whistling a plaintive air, suddenly presented himself.

He examined Patterson's pepper-pot with – for him – serious interest.

"Why, of course! This is the Queen Lizzie mug from the drawing-room, though I haven't seen it for years! On the floor behind the door curtain, you say? Well, I don't know who dropped it, but Rene – oh, that's absurd! Really, Mr. West, you don't think a girl like Rene Fullerton goes around snooping valuable silver out of people's houses! I drove her up to town, and I assure you she didn't strike me as an escaping thief. I'm ready to swear there was nothing in her box but her frocks."

"That's exactly how I feel about it," said West with a legal frown. "But someone certainly dropped that pepper-pot in the drawing-room, and it rolled under the curtain unnoticed. Unnoticed because the thief's arms were already full with the other twenty-two articles."

"But who in this house would do such a damned silly

thing – and why?"

"It's as big a mystery to me, Cecil."

The young man dug his none-too-clean hands into his pockets, and corrugated a forehead which was not accustomed to serious concentration.

"I'll tell you what I'll do, Mr. West. I'll phone to Rene now, and see what sort of a reply I get. I have her number – Knightsbridge 2266. I'm not much hand as a sleuth, but I ought to recognise guilty accents when I hear them. There might even be a scream and a dull thud as she smashed the receiver. Shall I?"

"What are you going to ask her? It's a delicate matter to approach."

"I shall tell her the silver has disappeared, and ask her if she knows anything about it, and if she says no, I shall go on asking her awkward questions until she contradicts herself. That's your way, isn't it?"

West grimaced at his impudence.

"Very well. There's nothing like doing a thing thoroughly, is there, Cecil?"

Sabelle ambled off with the graceful gait of a giraffe, and West paced slowly along his favourite walk, the secluded terrace under the western wall whence the grassy hill-side ran so sharply down that no other defence was needed.

He was not alone for long. He saw an upward curl of blue tobacco smoke, and presently Inspector Sedley, off duty, appeared to disturb his pleasant privacy.

The inspector was in a friendly mood, or rather, being a little proud of himself, was inclined to be confidential.

"You'll be interested to hear that the girl has talked. A

little wholesome fright brought her to her senses. Meanwhile the Major has made two more attempts to get at her. There's something between those two, remember; they want to make their story agree. Now, Miss Farbell has had three days to think, and this is the gem of imagination she places before us. She says that she was unhappy at Cleys – no intelligible reason given – and decided to run away; all this quite suddenly at 8.30 p.m. on the night of the murder. She packed two suit-cases and left the castle, walking in the direction of Abertefn. It is three miles to Abertefn, and about a mile on the other side of the village she knew there was a farm where there lived a young man who plied a Ford car for hire. She intended to get him to drive her to Cwm Dyffod station. In the middle of the night, I ask you! She walked the four miles carrying her luggage, and it took her two hours. When she got there *she couldn't find the farm*, so she turned round and came back! She passed twice through the village of Abertefn, but saw no one who can prove her story. I asked her, had no motorist passed her? She jumped at it, and said yes, one, and he had slowed down and stared at her. He would probably remember the incident, but, of course, she had not noticed his registration marks! In fact, that journey of hers was altogether too solitary to be convincing. She says she got back to the castle about twelve-twenty, midnight. I gave her a slight shock by asking her how she got in unseen. She said by the little postern in the north wall. Now, Patterson, the butler, says that he bolts and locks that postern door every night of his life at eight o'clock, and has never missed doing so. He even remembers particularly the night of the murder, because two of the maids had gone on their bicycles to sing at a village concert a few miles away. He left the postern open for them, and they returned just after ten o'clock and came to his room to tell him they had fastened the door behind them. He was not satisfied and went himself to make sure that all was secure. What was more, the door was still locked and barred next morning; he would have noticed if it had been otherwise. I went back to Miss Farbell and asked her how she reconciled her story with this. She insisted that she had found the postern door unlocked at twenty past twelve, and had come in and left it unlocked behind her."

"Unless she was not telling the truth about the time. She may have returned before the maids."

"She couldn't have walked eight miles between eight-thirty and ten o'clock. And what was she doing between ten and midnight? We have her both ways."

"It seems a harmless story," said West. "Why was she so averse to confessing it before?"

"She *says*," confided Sedley with meaning emphasis, "that she didn't want Major Stacey to know that she had tried to run away. My explanation is that she wanted three days to concoct her scenario."

West snapped his fingers wildly.

"I can't accept the girl's guilt. I can't, Sedley; it's all wrong. There's one fact lurking in the back of my mind, and Amy Farbell doesn't fit it. Can I see her?"

"Oh, yes, you can see her!" Sedley drew airily at his pipe. "But if you'll forgive me for saying so, Mr. West, I know you barristers are never satisfied with a case unless it's trimmed up with a lot of fancy details and artistic festoons. To a plain policeman guilt is guilt, and the less trimmings the better. Why, I've known a barrister defend a fellow because his hair wasn't the right colour for a murderer, or some such nonsense! I'm just telling you, in case you're thinking something of the kind about Miss Farbell — "

"Hair? Miss Farbell?" West came back to earth with a jerk, and began to walk slowly away. "What has her hair got to do with it?"

"Mad as a bat!" snorted Sedley, flopping down in the sweet, lush grass.

"Coo-ee!" A voice was ringing through the stone-flagged passages . . . "Mr. West!"

"Here I am!"

Cecil Sabelle burst into view with Rita hanging on to one hand and Nicholas dragging at the other.

He turned on them fiercely. "Oh, go away, you beastly kids! Your Uncle Cecil's busy. I'll give half a crown to the one who cuts off cook's apron strings when she isn't looking!"

"Hurrah," yelled the children, and darted off immediately in the direction of the kitchen regions.

"Doubtful suggestion," ventured West.

"Oh, Cookie won't come to any harm! She always boxes their ears at sight. Those children are getting too much for the servants now their governess is in quod. I say, do you think she did it? The police are rather mugs, aren't they? But what I want to say is" – went on this incoherent young man – "I've got Rene on the phone and she wants a word with you. I'm afraid I haven't been tactful. She's as mad as a wet cat."

West took up the receiver. "Is that you, Miss Fullerton?"

"Yes, it jolly well is!" came with battering force against his tympanum. "Cecil's just been telling me that you accuse me of stealing some silver from Cleys! I suppose you've missed a teaspoon. What do you take me for? A runaway housemaid? . . . I never was so — "

"I'm sorry, Rene. You've got it wrong — "

"I should hope I have got it wrong! I never stole anything in my life; and as for the silver from the drawing-room cabinets at Cleys, what makes you think I should even want such things? If you're serious, I can only tell you I haven't got them. And I'll add that I think it's abominable of you to suspect me just because I happen to have left the house."

West said, "Wait a minute, please, Rene," and putting his hand over the phone, said to Sabelle, "What can you have said to her? I'm afraid you've overdone it this time!"

Sabelle's face was wrinkled with dismay.

"I'm horribly sorry," he said with frank contrition. "I only meant it as a joke. I thought she'd really taken the things for fun, and I told her the game was up and you were coming with a warrant to fetch them back. I — "

"You really are a tactless young fool, Cecil!"

"I know . . . I didn't think she'd take it seriously . . ."

"Not take an accusation of theft seriously! Well, be careful in future . . ." He turned back to the phone. "Are you there, Rene? Listen! Forget everything Sabelle said. He was trying to be funny, and I'm furious with him. But the theft is a genuine one, and we're really troubled about it. I only want a little information. Will you be kind and give it if you can?"

"Of course," said Rene; and added, "If it's reasonable!"

"Patterson, the butler, says you were the last person to see the little silver articles in the drawing-room cabinets. Is that so? When did you see them?"

"It was two nights before I went away. I'm interested in old silver, but I don't collect it. I wasn't even particularly impressed with that at Cleys – though don't tell Sir Harry so. I never saw the things again, much less touched them!"

The girl at the exchange asked, "Do you want any more?" and mistaking West's answer, cut them off.

He hesitated, and then hung up the receiver. Was Rene genuine? It was so hard, so very hard to tell. One could be greatly deceived by a frank young voice and unclouded personality.

"One has to believe her!" broke in Sabelle, subdued into seriousness. He hesitated a moment, and then said in a voice which was unhappy and low: "I say, Mr. West, I'm not exactly superstitious, in fact I've always laughed at such things, but do you think there might be some sort of a – Demon wandering about this awful old place?"

"Spirits?" West gave a bark of laughter. "I think you'd better go and play with the children!"

West found Amy Farbell in the East Turret, in her small, littered room, which it seemed she had no heart to keep tidy. He noticed a little bed, a chair, and a round table upon which stood a dish of fruit, a travelling clock, and a few books.

Amy, still wearing her brown frock, was leaning against

the window when he entered. Her face was pale and expressionless and she had recently been crying. Her utter friendlessness caught at his heart. He sat down on the chair and patted the bed beside him.

"Come and sit here, Amy. I want to talk to you."

She obeyed listlessly, sinking unhappily down with her hands clasped before her.

"They won't believe me!" she murmured.

"Are you sure you are telling the truth, Amy?"

"I am sure!" Her voice shook with emotion. "If you'd tramped all those miles carrying two heavy suit-cases, you wouldn't forget it! And then I couldn't find the farm. Besides, I started out in a rage . . . and it gradually cooled, and I saw what a fool I was, setting off to London with nowhere to go when I got there . . . so I deliberately turned back. I couldn't explain all that to the inspector. Haven't you ever done anything silly yourself when you were angry, and then stopped when you realised how absurdly you were behaving?"

"I believe I have, Amy."

The touch of human nature about it all had gone far to convince him that the girl was telling the literal truth.

"It's a pity," he suggested, "that you didn't see anyone in Abertefn or on the road who could prove this for you."

"It is a pity," she said bitterly; "but things do happen like that. If I'd known – if I'd guessed – I'd have knocked up every house in Abertefn. And the motorist who passed me on the road was drunk. I was terrified he was going to annoy me, and so glad when he drove on that I never thought to read his number. One doesn't. But then one doesn't expect to be suspected of murder!"

She suddenly broke down and cried noisily, as much from anger as despair.

"I don't seem to have anybody! Nobody cares if they hang me!"

"Don't get hysterical," ordered West sharply, "I thought — "

He stopped, for he did not know what was the relationship between Edward and the girl, or whether they had a mutual secret. And if Edward could deliberately stand by and see the girl in this position, then West's hands were tied.

"About that postern door," he said. "Are you quite sure of the time when you returned and found it open?"

"I'm certain. The big clock struck twelve when I was a quarter of a mile from the castle. I was too glad to find the door open to bother about why it was open at that time. It seemed as though Fate were on my side."

"What made you go to that door? You knew it would be fastened early?"

"Yes, but I wanted to get in without being seen, and the servants use that door. I knew that Patterson would be up late to serve drinks after the game, and I meant to ring and ask him not to tell."

"Have they made you comfortable up here?" asked West awkwardly.

She lifted her hands in a hopeless gesture.

"They've given me everything I needed, but I haven't eaten or slept for three days. Could you?"

"Oh, but look here, Amy! You're innocent. Why behave

as if you weren't? It's bound to come right soon."

She gazed at him incredulously.

"You believe I'm innocent? Oh, Mr. West – Mr. West!"

"I do. And what's more, if the worst comes to the worst, I'll defend you in court and get you off. Now do you feel better? Eat one of these nice oranges before I go."

"I couldn't."

"Yes you could. Look, I'll peel it for you, like Nursie did."

He turned his back on her because his kind words were having rather a melting effect, and when he faced her again with the peeled orange she was dabbing her eyes and there was a faint pink in her icy-pale cheeks.

"Mr. West, I can never thank you enough! You are wonderful!"

"That's all right, child. Keep that orange juice off your little bib."

He patted her vaguely, with promises of another visit the next day, and departed in search of Sedley, whom he found stretched out where he had left him, blinking in the rays of the setting sun as they flamed beyond the mountains and were flung back from the castle's silvery walls.

West lowered himself to the grass beside the detective.

"Sedley, I've already told you I believe that girl is innocent. You'll allow me my little opinion, won't you? Well then, just by way of mental exercise, can you evolve a theory to account for that open postern door?"

Sedley being in a malleable mood thought for a moment, and then replied, "Her accomplice could have opened it for her and fastened it after her."

"By thunder, he could! Who's her accomplice?"

"We'll have to find that out."

"And what was she doing outside at all if she hadn't been to Abertefn?"

"That's another of those things, Mr. West, that you'll be able to answer better than I can."

West said with great deliberation, "Now, Sedley, will you please listen to my theory, and I'll tell you now, it's the right one. Just as you know when you've got the right answer to a crossword clue, I know I've got the right answer to the puzzle of the postern door. Here you are. The murderer got hot after his horrible job, and he unfastened the postern door and slipped out for a breath of cool air. While he was outside Amy returned and entered by the open door. The murderer went in too, and fastened the door behind him."

There was a thoughtful silence.

"It's ingenious, I'll admit," said Sedley, with considerable indulgence; "and under other conditions I might consider it, but look at the case against the girl!"

West sat bolt upright and crossed his legs stiffly.

"What exactly is this great case against the girl?"

"You can read it for yourself. It'll take a bit of explaining away, even for a barrister."

He drew from his inner pocket a pad of typed sheets and laid them on West's knee.

CASE AGAINST AMY FARBELL

MOTIVE

On the day before the murder Lady Stacey (*a*) had discovered the existence of a clandestine love affair between Amy Farbell and Major Stacey.

(*b*) In a violent quarrel had dismissed Amy Farbell from her post as governess.

N.B. – Farbell makes the unsupported statement that the dismissal was withdrawn, was not in fact seriously meant.

Lady Stacey showed evidence of an estrangement by refusing to allow Farbell to join in the game of hide-and-seek.

MEANS

Farbell was in the garret with Lady Stacey on the morning of the murder and suggested the chest to her mistress as a possible hiding-place.

N.B. – This more likely than Farbell's statement that suggestion came from Lady Stacey.

Lady S. demonstrated the use of the hasp and bolt.

Farbell familiar with Lady Stacey's rooms, clothes, letters, etc.

OPPORTUNITY

Farbell was absent from her room during the whole of the vital period of the murder, that is from 8.30 p.m. until past midnight, and can give no explanation of her movements other than an alibi which it has taken three days to produce and which cannot in any way be proved or disproved.

N.B. – Discrepancy of postern door.

SUGGESTED SEQUENCE OF EVENTS

Farbell knowing that Lady Stacey intended to hide in the chest, made her plans for the murder during the day. She had the half-letter in her possession, having abstracted it from Lady Stacey's room, where it was exposed on the writing desk. (See Mrs. W.'s last note.) Before the game was due to begin she went to the garret and concealed herself in the cupboard, where we found footmarks.

Lady S. arrived and hid in the chest, which Farbell then secured.

Later she was able quite safely to abstract the hat and coat from Lady S.'s room and convey them to the garret, and place the letter on Sir Harry's pillow, the house being in darkness and the guests otherwise engaged. Had it not been for Major Stacey's visits to her and lies told on her behalf, would never have been discovered.

"You've missed something out," said West without lifting his eyes from the sheet.

"What is it?"

"The emerald ring. Miss Farbell never even knew of its existence."

"How do you mean?"

"She was not in the room when I displayed it, and no one mentioned it to her since it was known she was not taking part in the game."

"Miss Farbell probably knew a great deal more than you give her credit for!" snapped Sedley. "I haven't any time for minor possibilities."

"You seem to make time," West flung at him, "for the deliberate evasion of essential facts."

Sedley smoked on placidly, knowing that he held the whip hand.

West, chafing at his limitations, knew it too.

"Amy Farbell could not possibly have been the person who hid in the Norman cabinet," he said sharply.

"Indeed? Why not?"

West ground his teeth. "You'll have to find that out for yourself!" He suddenly checked his anger, and said coolly,

"You had just such a case against Mrs. Willoughby. Each bubble you blow is larger and finer than the last!"

At dinner that night West saw Pandora Hyde wearing for the first time in his acquaintance with her a look which was more than cheerful, positively triumphant. The look of sullen fear which usually characterised her features had disappeared, and she had suddenly changed from an unapproachable young savage into a tolerably attractive girl.

Being the only woman among six men she chose her own seat at table, and to-night she had placed herself, with a slightly proprietary air, next to a bashful and unusually silent Basil Crown, who ate with his eyes on his plate and gave no sign that he shared the secret of his companion's vivacity.

When Pandora's left hand came into view with its fish fork the mischief was out. The observant West noted at once that third finger flaunting Crown's cornelian signet ring. So Pandora had succeeded in enticing back her errant lover.

"Poor little fool," thought West, who had no great opinion of Crown. "She's happy now. In five years' time, perhaps another Enid. But who dare croak treason to an infatuated girl?"

He was not in any mood for the announcement of engagements, and immediately dinner was over he escaped to the quiet of the little study to embark upon a serious piece of work.

West realised as well as anyone the value of getting a difficult situation down upon paper; and knowing the cold and material aspect of figures with their lack of emotion and appeal to pure reason, he commenced to draw up a chart which would indicate the possible value as a suspect of all the persons concerned, not even omitting himself and Sir Harry.

He made a list of ten names, and three columns headed respectively, Motive, Opportunity, Suspicious Behaviour, and to each heading allotted a maxim of ten marks.

The fourth column he headed Total, with the idea that the final list of totals might contain some startling revelation.

He spent almost an hour over his chart, carefully considering all circumstances before allotting the marks.

The final result was as follows:

Name	Motive	Opportunity	Suspicious behaviour	Total
Harry Stacey ..	0	10	0	10
Edward Stacey..	10	10	10	30
Lionel West..	0	10	0	10
Jack Willoughby..	0	10	0	10
Cecil Sabelle..	0	10	0	10
Basil Crown..	5	10	3	18
Enid Willoughby..	10	10	5	25
Pandora Hyde..	5	10	5	20
Rene Fullerton..	0	0	3	3
Amy Farbell..	10	10	10	30

It was evident at once that the blackest case lay between Edward Stacey and Amy Farbell. Add to that that West had the strongest of reasons for awarding Edward full marks in each section, and that he was personally convinced that

Amy Farbell was innocent, and it is easy to understand why he now bit his pipe-stem in two and nearly tore the list to fragments without studying it further.

However, he read it through again with a faint gleam of hope that another trail might emerge, and his spirits only sank lower. Enid came next with a total of twenty-five; and not only was she dead but no one could seriously consider her as having had a hand in the murder. Next, Pandora with twenty marks and Crown with eighteen. This to Sedley would look almost like collusion. The rest of the men, Harry, Jack, Cecil, and himself had ten marks each, for opportunity. Actually they had all had the same opportunity; but there was nothing else against them.

Rene Fullerton was conspicuous for having the lowest total, only three marks against her name. Even those three West was inclined to strike out, for in allotting them he had been thinking of her abrupt departure following the thefts, of which she had definitely disclaimed knowledge in her telephone conversation. Rene also was the only member of the party who had no marks for opportunity; her alibi seemed sound enough, for she had been in the servants' hall from the commencement of the game until her discovery.

The list in the purpose for which it was intended had failed; though being compiled from West's own limited knowledge there was still a hope that further facts would emerge. He hesitated to tear it up, and was placing it in an inside pocket when he heard running footsteps and the sounds of an excited meeting not far from the room where he sat.

"That you, Sir Harry?" It was Sabelle's voice. "Have you heard? . . . No? . . . The police have caught somebody on the garret stairs! . . . Yes . . . Patterson told me . . . No, I don't know who it is . . . I say! . . . Shall I go and see?"

West somehow got across the floor and out into the gallery.

"What has happened?"

Sir Harry looked round.

"Cecil says they've caught someone trying to get up the garret stair. There was a policeman on duty there."

"Who was it, Cecil? A man?"

"I don't know." Sabelle cocked an eyebrow. "It wasn't any of us three, thank goodness!"

There was a slight cough in the background, and Patterson stood there, the back of one hand nervously flickering across his lips.

"Oh, Sir Harry! The inspector says . . ."

"Well, Patterson?"

"Will you come, sir? And Mr. West? . . . It's Mr. Ed – they've caught the Major, sir!"

West was dumb. What he had feared and dreaded so long had come to pass. It was the end. His only doubt was whether Edward had been making a last bid for his own safety, or whether Amy Farbell's danger had finally decided him to give himself up.

Sir Harry kept perfectly calm. He said, "You can go, Patterson . . . Cecil, you go too. I'll come soon."

He turned to West. "What does it mean? Do you know anything about this? Are you keeping anything back?"

West said non-committally, "We don't know yet what

has happened."

"Ah, but we do. This means something . . . that I hate to think about. Good God, Lionel, I didn't think another blow could fall on me! Undine . . . Enid . . . and now, Edward."

And still West was silent. He had no word of hope for his friend, for he feared that this last blow would prove the worst of all.

Chapter XII
FOR WHAT MOTIVE?

THE captive, refusing to behave with the struggling abandon and guilty dismay of a prisoner, leaned his broad shoulders against the worm-eaten panelling, very handsome and very bored. Under the spotlight effect of two electric torches – for there was no light laid on in this part of the castle – Robinson, the young constable, waved his hands in excited demonstration at the foot of the garret stair.

Blackmore, slightly envious, kept ostentatious guard over the prisoner.

Sedley, in his glory, dominated the situation. Ward, determined not to occupy the background for long, waited eagerly for a chance to trip his superior.

"It was just as I was going off duty at ten o'clock," spluttered Robinson. "I went to meet Blackmore, who was coming up the stairs to relieve me. He gave me a packet of cigarettes he'd bought for me at Aber – that place, you know – and at that minute I heard the garret stair creak loudly. We both ran, and saw a Dark Shape half-way up the stair. We fell upon him immediately. The prisoner made little resistance, realising that the Game was Up. By the light of my torch we both recognised Major Stacey. He must have Approached Surreptitiously from the other direction and hidden in the Adjacent Doorway until I went off duty. The prisoner has made no statement of any kind."

Robinson ceased reluctantly, disappointed that his big

speech was over.

"H'mph!" grunted Sedley, turning with great satisfaction to the lounging prisoner. "Major Stacey, you have heard the statement of the constable. What have you got to say?"

"It's quite correct," said Edward calmly.

"Quite correct, is it? Then I think you've got a good deal to say! Why did you want to get into the garret?"

"Curiosity," said Edward.

"Just that? You could have asked my permission, you know. I'd have gone with you."

"That wouldn't have suited me at all."

"No?" Sedley's narrow gaze was full of triumph. "You're not telling me, Major Stacey, that your errand wasn't a perfectly innocent one?"

"You know quite well," said Edward, with a slight smile and a shrug, "that I was out to destroy a piece of incriminating evidence."

The two young constables goggled.

"Ah!" said Sedley, "we're getting warm. You didn't want to see Miss Farbell in the dock!"

"I certainly didn't."

"And you know of something that would incriminate Miss Farbell — "

"Oh, no!" Edward's voice had a haughty ring. "I am not in the least concerned with Miss Farbell."

"That remains to be proved."

"You can take my word for it and let her go. I confess to everything!"

"Everything? You confess to the murder of Lady Stacey?"

"Yes."

Sedley remained admirably unexcited. "Will you make a written statement?"

"Yes, if you'll take me where I can do it."

Sedley swung round to Ward. "Well? Are you satisfied?"

"I am," said Ward. "I've had him in my mind from the first."

Sedley signalled to the two constables.

"Take him away. Fetch Gunson with the typewriter and let him dictate his confession. You know what directions to give him. Then bring it to me."

Edward swung right-about with his splendid military bearing, and marched away between the two policemen like a conquering Titan escorted by two pygmy slaves.

"There we are!" said Sedley when he was gone. "I suppose we ought to have known it. He's a hardened soldier; no nerves."

The two detectives went down, and in the Long Gallery met Sir Harry and Lionel West. They had already heard the news.

"Sorry this has happened, Sir Harry," said Sedley. "It's a nasty blow for you, but the truth's out at last, and you'll be better satisfied to have this atmosphere of suspicion cleared away."

"Then it's true that you've arrested Edward!" cried Sir Harry. "I'll never believe anything against him!"

"You'll have to accept your brother's own word," Sedley pointed out. "We shall have his written confession in a few minutes."

"I shan't accept it. He's doing it to save the girl. Don't you think so, Lionel?"

West was silent.

"You mustn't delude yourself, Sir Harry," broke in Ward, not unkindly. "A man won't put his head in the noose for a woman, except in novels."

"But you don't know Edward! He's got the most exalted notions of chivalry. Can I see him?"

"Not yet, Sir Harry. You can see him tomorrow."

When West arrived alone at the office half an hour later, he found Ward placidly smoking and Sedley sitting on the table with the slow smile of toil well ended spreading towards his ears.

"We've got it, Mr. West; as pretty a little document as ever you did see. I never remember handling a neater confession. The Major is doing the thing thoroughly, and I guess we were wise in watching the girl. He wouldn't have spoken if he hadn't thought we were in earnest about her."

He handed West a typewritten sheet. West took it grimly and began to scan it over.

"It's very short!"

"Ah, but it's all there! We can do without the heretofores and the whereas-be-it-knowns."

West read to the end of the short document and then looked up, his face full of conflicting expressions, of which amazement and incredulity were uppermost.

"Major Stacey says here, 'I determined to kill Undine before my brother could discover how she had deceived him.' That, of course, is the obvious motive. But this, 'Undine lingered behind after the others had gone upstairs to hide. After a few minutes she went up and I followed her. I followed her to the garret, and when we got there she turned round and saw me. She screamed, and I seized her. She then fainted, and I put her in the chest and fastened it. On the way downstairs I knocked at Amy Farbell's door, but she was not in. I do not know where she was. I never saw her until the next day!' . . . Sedley! I'd be willing to swear this is impossible. To follow Lady Stacey up to the garret, keeping her in sight on a strange and complicated journey through the castle, in the dark, without her knowledge! Along those winding galleries, through doors, up stairs – and then she is so surprised to see him in the garret that she screams and faints in his arms!"

"Well, he did it, didn't he?" drawled Sedley. "And not a word about the cabinet where we know the murderer stood! Major Stacey seems to have a very poor recollection of his own crime!"

Sedley heaved himself off the table with a touch of impatience.

"Our theory was wrong, that's all! Great Scott, Mr. West, you can't boggle over a man's confession because it doesn't tally with your own tentative reconstruction! Stacey's explanation is good enough for me. He hasn't omitted anything; describes how he got the hat and coat, the letter, and the emerald ring — "

"I noticed," said West, biting his lip, "that he'd made a neat and comprehensive job of it. But he doesn't say why he wanted to get into the garret to-night! It's odd that he should be so reticent on a minor point."

"It's odd enough," broke in Ward with a puzzled frown. "He said himself he was after a piece of incriminating evidence, but he won't say what, and I've had my men strip every splinter of that garret and they haven't found a thing. You'd think if he had left something on the night it would have been well in sight."

"Unless," chimed Sedley, "those workmen took it when they found the body."

"No, that won't wash. He knows it's still there, or he wouldn't have made a desperate dash for it to-night."

"He was a fool," growled Sedley, " to attempt it when he must have known that garret stair creaked fit to wake the dead."

"What did you say?" West suddenly sprang to life. "The garret stair creaked? Of course it did! Edward wouldn't forget a thing like that. And why did Undine scream at the shock of seeing him in the garret when she must have heard him, minutes before, toiling step by step up that creaking stair? . . . Where is he? Can I see him?"

"Not to-night, I'm afra — " began Ward; but Sedley, probably for the pleasure of overruling his subordinate, pulled his lower lip and drawled: "You can see him in here for a few minutes if you like."

"Please!" said West, and sat down to wait.

When Major Stacey appeared he had adopted a changed manner, as though realising that his previous lofty bearing was out of keeping with his role of confessed criminal. His shoulders drooped, his hair was disordered, and he kept his eyes lowered. When he saw West he brightened for a second, and a half- smile crossed his mouth, but he quickly took himself in hand and assumed an expression of sullen obstinacy.

West went up to him and put a hand on his shoulder.

"It's all right, Edward. I'll do my best for you, old man."

Edward stiffened, and edged away from the friendly hand.

"You needn't trouble. I'm guilty."

"Will you answer a few questions?"

"No. I've said every word I'm going to say – there." He pointed to the typewritten sheet on the table, which he recognised as his confession.

"But there are some points I don't understand," began West.

"It isn't for you to understand, Lionel. It satisfies Sedley."

"Edward!" A hint of tremendous eagerness crept into West's voice. "Why have you confessed?"

"To save Amy, of course."

"You mean quixotically! You've taken the blame on yourself!"

"Certainly not. I couldn't let her suffer any longer for what I'd done."

"What did you want in the garret to-night, old man?"

"It doesn't matter in the least what I wanted!" said Edward irritably. "If they must know, let them find out. And it's no good hurling questions at me, Lionel. I know you mean well, but I refuse to say another word!" He snapped his lips together.

Sedley nodded. "Take him away." . . . He turned to West: "I shouldn't complicate matters if I were you."

In the blue and gold radiance of the next morning West walked out early into the parterre, sniffing restlessly at the breeze from the mountains, noticing how the flower-beds were all a-tangle with weeds, for Sir Harry had ceased to take any interest in the garden and the gardeners were getting slack and lazy. He stooped and pulled a great, straggling trail of chickweed, and the effort seemed to do him good. He cleared a whole bed before he paused, panting, and recognised with glad surprise the slender figure of Amy Farbell standing at the edge of the lawn, as though too timid to join him.

When she saw him smile she ran to join him with a glad cry, her eyes bright and sparkling.

"Oh, Mr. West! They've let me go; I'm cleared!"

"I'm very glad."

She clasped her hands. "After you came to see me I never felt afraid. I knew you would look after me. But you won't let them keep Major Stacey, will you? Make them let him go! I'd rather they took me back again. I asked that horrible inspector if I could go and see Ed – Major Stacey, and he said only if he went with me, and that wouldn't do at all."

West pulled thoughtfully at a venturesome dandelion.

"Why not? What did you want to say to Edward?"

"Only that I was so very, very grateful that he'd taken the blame instead of me, and that I'd soon get him free by finding the real murderer!"

West suffered a slight shock of surprise.

"The real murderer? Do you suppose then that Edward is not the real murderer?"

The colour rushed to her cheeks.

"Suppose? I know! Don't tell me that you thought he could be guilty of such a sneaking, Borgia-like crime!"

For a moment West was thrilled by a wild hope. Did the girl really know anything?

"Amy – speak low – and tell me, how do you know he is innocent?"

She looked up with glowing, guileless eyes.

"I know because he's the most brave and wonderful man in the world, and he couldn't do anything that wasn't fine and magnificent! I know . . . here . . . and here . . . in my heart and my head!"

West rolled his eyes to heaven and weakly flapped his hands in despair.

"Oh, *ciel!* She knows in her heart and her head!" He recovered from the shock of this anti-climax, and said in his normal voice: "I'm afraid Sedley won't accept either your heart or your head, except on a charger. I thought you were actually going to hand me a piece of evidence! Have you any idea why Edward has made this mad confession?"

"To save me!" she whispered in excited pride. "It was a noble thing to do, but I wouldn't have allowed him if I'd known. Now he has done it, there's no good in my confessing or your confessing. Sedley wants blood this time, and he's got to have the right blood! Mr. West, we must find the murderer! You can, I know. And oh, be quick, before they take Edward away!"

"I'm only too anxious, Amy." He sighed. "Go away – there's a good girl. I want to think. I've got a big think hammering against my brain, and if I don't let it in it may go and attack Sedley and rob me of my legitimate victory. You wouldn't like that!"

"If only I could help you." She broke off suddenly, and West saw her shrink as, at the same moment, he caught sight of Sedley himself standing in the low stone doorway which led to the parterre.

Amy was already slipping away across the turf towards the ruined wall. She climbed over some fallen blocks of masonry and soon reached the grassy parapet, along the height of which she ran noiselessly out of sight.

West nodded to the detective, but being more inclined for constructive thought than for destructive argument he followed Amy; and since she was not to be seen he stood upon the parapet, leaning over the battlemented façade, and watched a troop of threatening thunder-clouds advancing from the ambush of the mountains, as centuries ago some armoured defender had watched with apprehension the furtive advance of the savage Welsh hordes. Soon the sky was overcast, and steely lines of rain slanted upon his lofty and exposed position, so he followed the wall's rectangular circuit until a flight of worn steps led him down to the doorless entrance of the ruined banqueting hall.

Through great rents in the roof the rain splashed down upon the flags, upon which were carved inscriptions almost too ancient and mouldy for West to decipher. A horrid and chilly desolation pervaded the place. The long window arches were tangled with ivy and stuffed with rope-like branches and decayed leaves. The drip of water was answered by the stealthy beat of some creature's wings in the black vault of the roof. High over the chimney there still drooped a tattered, colourless rag, stained and sodden, writhing under its oaken staff, a banner of ancient days condemned to live on in this tomb of history.

West felt the depression of the place enwrap him like a

mantle. There was something foul and tainted in the atmosphere which emanated from these broken, fungus-ridden walls, a breath of some cruel secret of the Dark Ages. He shuddered, and turning to depart found Inspector Sedley at his elbow.

"Not much idea of comfort, they hadn't, in those days," declared the detective genially. He was evidently in a good mood.

"I was glad to see Miss Farbell at liberty," was all the reply West made.

"There wasn't any point in watching her further."

"There wasn't any point," said West, "in watching her at all."

"And yet one couldn't tell," pursued Sedley. "If it did nothing else, it brought the Major out of his hole. And in the first case, Mr. West," he added pointedly, "it was you that suggested a woman had done it."

"That," said West guardedly, "was only because of the stealthy nature of the crime. Women hate anything so direct as a rope, a knife, or a gun. A murderess chooses the indirect weapon, poison or suffocation. But even you must remember I changed my mind! No woman could have hidden in the Norman cabinet; at least, no woman in this house."

"You're always harping on that Norman cabinet!" snapped Sedley impatiently. "What's the big idea, anyway?"

"I'm counting on it," said West, "to get my friend Edward Stacey out of the ridiculous position he's placed himself in. It's dawning on me that he wants to be a martyr, and I shan't let him. Come, Sedley, the whole thing is a farce, and you know it. You might just as well let Stacey go. He made that confession to save the girl. She knows it; so do I. That reconstruction of his supposed crime is just the silly, unimaginative work of a man who knew nothing of the actual circumstances. Don't you remember our first hypothesis, the day we searched the garret together? We read the signs aright that day, and they told us that either the murderer reached the garret first and waited for his victim in the Norman cabinet, or else he came up in her company. Edward Stacey had no more to do with that crime than I had. Followed her? Rubbish!"

"Then why was he trying to get up to the garret when we caught him?"

"Probably just to get himself caught under suspicious circumstances. The dramatic situation would rather appeal to him. But that sneaking crime, no. If Edward wanted to kill anyone he'd walk up in broad daylight and draw a gun and shoot him clean through the head. And Edward would never kill a woman!"

"But the case against him — "

West snapped his fingers.

"Pshaw! The cases against Miss Hyde, and Mrs. Willoughby, and Miss Farbell – so conclusive! Where are they now? Are you dropping all that accumulation of evidence?"

Sedley loosed a shrewd arrow.

"You know how to talk, Mr. West, but I read what was in your mind days ago. You suspected the Major yourself!"

"I did," broke out West. "And I had my reasons for it. But I read the evidence wrongly, thank God!"

He banged his right fist into his left palm. "Sedley! Let Stacey go, now, for your own sake. I'll promise to give you your man – and all the credit!"

Sedley widened his eyes to saucer-like proportions.

"You're not telling me you know who did it?"

"If you care to put it that way – yes!"

"You mean, Mr. West, you've got your case?"

West shook his head.

"That's what I haven't got. I know – and I don't know. It's a situation of this kind: here is a crime *which must have been committed by one of two persons*. The one is proved innocent to my satisfaction. *Ergo*, the other is guilty. But there is no motive! There is no evidence! There is nothing! What can one do? Find a motive! Build up a case! That person is *guilty*; therefore there is somewhere a motive, and a case. You see? I promise you I shall get to work!"

During this speech Sedley's expression of feigned credulity was wearing thinner and thinner, and by the time West had finished he could no longer repress his smiles.

He pulled his ear, and with a shrewd nod said: "It's a queer thing. I've been on dozens of cases in my career, and never one yet but some amateur member of the party has come along and told me he's worked it all out on his own, and will I come at once and arrest the butler or the local Member of Parliament. People read these detective stories. The trouble I've had you wouldn't believe. I've blessed that Doctor Thorndyke and Inspector French! No offence, of course, Mr. West."

West remained calm under the slighting insinuation.

"May I see Major Stacey?"

"If you like. I shall have to come with you."

"I want you to. Can I ask him some questions?"

"You can ask him what you like; only you may do him more harm than good."

"I'll risk that," said West.

Edward Stacey was incarcerated in a cell-like chamber of the keep. The tiny room with its arrow-slits of windows was very dark that morning and the rain came slanting in. Edward was sitting on the bed, his long legs uncomfortably sprawling, and an unlighted cigarette between his lips. He frowned heavily when West and the inspector entered, and mumbled between his teeth, "I say, Inspector! I do complain! Am I not allowed to have matches?"

"While I am here," answered Sedley, "you are allowed to smoke." He tossed a box of matches to the prisoner. "Gentlemen in your position," he explained, "have been known to fire their cells from sheer boredom."

Edward struck a match deliberately.

"How long am I to be kept here?"

"Only a day or two longer," said Sedley meaningly. "Are you thinking you'd like a change?"

Edward dashed out the match and put his foot on it. He turned a stern and frowning countenance on West.

"I suppose Amy is all right? Have you seen to that, Lionel? Is she at liberty?"

"Amy is quite at liberty. I've seen her in the garden this morning."

Edward's granite expression did not relax. "Thank you . . . And thanks also for coming to see me, Lionel. There doesn't seem much to talk about, does there?"

He tipped the ash off his cigarette. West sat down beside his friend upon the bed, which sagged dangerously under the impact.

"Edward, why didn't you remember that that stair creaked?"

The question was so unexpected that Stacey was taken off his guard.

"I – I never thought about it."

"Why didn't Undine hear you coming when you followed her up the creaking stair? And what made you drag out the chest from the rest of the furniture to the middle of the floor? Now, Edward!"

Goaded, Edward said grimly: "To get a better light . . . and I won't discuss it. I tell you, I won't!"

West rose, crossed to the window, and stood with his back turned. He was accustomed to keeping an impassive countenance, but his heart was thumping and he wondered what Sedley had made of Edward's last remark. Of course the chest had never left its original place in the far corner of the garret under the rafters! He swung round.

"Do you persist in asserting that you committed this crime?"

Edward's eyes blazed angrily.

"I do! And I shall answer no more questions! I know you mean well, Lionel, but until I stand in the dock you can curb your kind efforts on my behalf. Then, and then only, I may allow you to defend me on the grounds that I have a good record and suffer occasionally from shell-shock!" He smiled grimly.

With the same impassive face West took out his pocket-book and tore off a sheet, upon which with his Swan pencil he drew a rough rectangle, and placed the sheet before Stacey.

"That, Edward, you will recognise as a rough outline of the garret. Here is the door. I want you to indicate on the diagram, with the pencil, the positions of the chest, where you found it and the place to which you dragged it."

Edward thrust his hands into his pockets.

West said quietly, "You had better do this if you really want them to believe you are guilty. Otherwise someone else may suffer."

"What do you mean?"

"That isn't for me to say. Please do this at once."

Stacey still hesitated, and for a minute West was frightened that he was going to call the bluff; then Stacey took the paper.

"Give me your pencil."

Still he hesitated with the pencil in his hand. West understood why. If, as he believed, Edward was innocent, then he had never been in the garret in his life and had no idea of the position of the chest.

But suddenly with a firm hand he made a cross in the middle of the long left-hand side of the diagram.

"I found the chest here, in the middle of the left-hand wall," he said deliberately.

West was puzzled for a moment, and then light came. Edward was counting on the fact that if the chest was in the middle of the room when the detectives found it, probably no one but himself could have known its original position. It was a weak bluff, but his only chance.

West made no comment.

"Now," he said, "the place to which you dragged the chest."

Stacey flung paper and pencil upon the bed.

"You can't have any proper reason for asking me that. You know as well as I do!"

"Then show us."

"No!"

West passed the sheet to Sedley, across whose saturnine visage weird expressions flitted like bats before the light of day.

"The place where he found the chest, Sedley! Curious!"

The dark blood surged into the prisoner's cheeks.

"Edward Stacey!" said West with awful severity, "you're an uncommonly poor liar. You never committed that crime! And before you confess to another, if you're going to make a habit of it, you had better make yourself more familiar with the details already known. You were never in that garret in your life! And if you had been successful in your attempt to enter it last night I should have found it more difficult to trip you up. You're going to have far more trouble in proving yourself guilty than most people have in supporting their innocence!"

Edward sat still, the forgotten cigarette burning down between his fingers.

"I know you're an excellent talker, Lionel," he said calmly; "I don't doubt but that you can make black white. In this case I don't want to be wangled out of a nasty situation by your forensic zeal. My confession still holds."

"But I'm going to get you out of this in spite of yourself.

Everyone knows you only confessed to save Amy Farbell!"

"And wasn't it time? As if I'd let a girl suffer for my crime!"

"Oh, you young fool!" cried West, suddenly losing his patience. "There isn't any question of Amy suffering for anybody's crime. It isn't your crime, any more than it's her crime! Why will you two persist in trying to be martyrs for one another instead of telling the truth and helping me to find the real murderer?"

It was not often that the calm and controlled West gave way to an outburst of this kind. He felt better for it.

Edward dropped the cigarette and shook his cramped shoulders.

"What do you mean – the real murderer?"

"In kindergarten language, the person who really killed Lady Stacey."

"Do you think you know who killed Lady Stacey?"

"Sedley doesn't!" said West, turning to the bewildered detective with a bright, disarming smile. "He knows it wasn't you, and he knows it wasn't Amy Farbell, but beyond that he only knows that soon I shall hand him his victim, masked and gagged and bound — "

"But I . . . Amy . . . not Amy . . . Are you bluffing me?"

Stacey suddenly dropped his head on his arms and hid his face in his hands.

"So that's it!" murmured West. "You thought all the time that Amy was guilty! And now that you know she isn't, what about a word or two in your own defence? It puts a different complexion on the affair, doesn't it?"

"Do go away!" said Edward suddenly. "I want to think."

West signalled to Sedley.

"We're going, Edward. And remember – neither you *nor* Amy."

Outside in the stone corridor he made an expansive gesture including the inspector, the castle and the whole range of the Welsh mountains.

"You see it all? He's thought all the time that Miss Farbell was guilty!"

"I don't know what to think," confessed Sedley. "But I keep you to your promise. I hold Stacey until you give me a better man."

West went next to find Harry, and discovered him in the garden, oblivious of the drizzling rain, or perhaps finding that preferable to the oppressive atmosphere of the castle.

Beyond the castle walls extended a wall of mist, and the mountains were blotted out. The castle itself might have hung in the clouds for all that could be seen of the outer world. The grass was smeared with silver damp, and the tangled, overgrown plants trailed wet and heavy across the unkempt garden beds. The ornamental trees drooped and dripped. It was as gloomy a spot as one could ever find.

Sir Harry heard West's step on the gravel. He did not greet his friend. It was as though he could not bring himself to ask for news.

"Harry! What would you say if I told you Edward is not guilty?"

He gave a start, and like a man who fears to accept so overwhelming a suggestion, said warily: "I sometimes wonder, Lionel, if what you tell me is true, or merely good for me to know."

West pointed to the tunnel passage of the postern door.

"Let's go there. I refuse to be drenched, even for the sake of good news . . . Well, it's true, and I'm happy. Edward never committed that horrible crime, although appearances have been against him from the first."

"You mean that?" said Harry quietly. "Beyond all shadow of doubt or disproof?"

"Definitely, I mean it."

Sir Harry stood looking out on the garden with unseeing eyes and inscrutable face. There was some relief too great, some joy too tremendous to express itself in extravagant words and smiles and expressions of delight.

At last he said: "How has this been discovered? Are the police convinced? Is he free?"

"Three rather large questions!" West gave a short laugh. "The two first will take some explaining. As for the last, no; but — "

"Then the police aren't convinced!"

"Briefly, this is the position. Sedley knows perfectly well that Edward isn't guilty – tell you all about it in a minute – but as a concession to his professional pride I've promised him that he may keep Edward, for the look of the thing, until I hand him the real murderer."

Sir Harry smiled rather grimly. "I think you encouraged me to hope rather too soon! But tell me how you found out that Edward wasn't the man. What about his confession?"

"It all turned on his confession. It was a most peculiar confession. It contradicted actual facts which we knew to have taken place in connection with the crime; there were glaring omissions; and when we put him to the test he gave away the fact that he had never been in the garret in his life. When they caught him on the stairs he was trying to get up there to remedy the gaps in his knowledge. You see, he wanted to do that confession thoroughly, and he couldn't! And what we all guessed from the first, he did it to save Amy Farbell."

"Need he have taken such desperate measures?"

"Yes. Because he actually thought all the time that Amy was guilty. We have just convinced him that she isn't, and that has put a very different complexion on his frantic efforts to blacken himself for her sake. Harry! I'm more relieved than I can ever tell you! It was black work for me to have to suspect Edward."

"Relief!" Sir Harry's face grew grave. "When this cloud passes there shall never be another between us . . ." He listened for a moment to the hiss of the rain. "But let's face this squarely. You said Edward couldn't be really clear until the real murderer was found. Haven't you set yourself a task?"

"I've found him," said West.

The very rain seemed to hang in the air on that moment of surprise. Then Sir Harry's face grew immobile and dark again.

"But you can't lay hands on him, because . . . oh, for some trifling reason that makes all the difference between conjecture and proof! Am I right? . . . I thought so. There's always a big 'but' in your promises, Lionel."

"I shall prove this."

"Well? What's lacking?"

Through a sudden gust of rain West saw Basil Crown

appear at the door which led to the billiard-room and lift disgruntled eyes to the clouds. The young man's eyes flickered across the wet garden and came to rest upon the two men sheltering by the postern door. Crown looked surprised, ran one long white hand over his glossy hair, and turned to speak to someone behind him. Then he withdrew. The clouds rushed together. The rain pelted down.

"That essential glimpse into the mind of a man before he kills," said West, "which we call motive."

"Edward could have killed Undine," said Sir Harry, his voice suddenly cold, "for what he knew of her past. Could anyone else have had the same motive?"

"No," said West. "No one but Edward knew that secret."

"Then there could be no other motive." A sigh burst from Harry Stacey's throat. In that moment, with his grey, stony face, his short, sturdy figure, suffering and yet defiant before the menace of the old grey walls, the air full of grey rain-clouds and heavy as his words, he seemed to belong to Cleys, to become a part of that sad and ancient house. His fingers curled dryly in his palms. "It's hopeless!" he cried. "You've spoken too soon!"

He turned to go, and as though taking his courage in his hands to hear some shocking name, he blurted: "Who is this . . . new suspect?"

"If I told you," said West, "you would call me mad."

Sir Harry's grey figure went noiselessly over the grass, leaving a wet trail of crushed silver blades.

West stood by the postern door, the same to which Amy Farbell had come wearily back at midnight after her attempt at running away. It was easy to guess how a little earlier the killer had come, and, slipping back the bolts, had stolen out to drink in great breaths of the cool night air under the outer castle wall, where no window could overlook his agitation, as in the bare moonlit garden. Perhaps to his amazement he had seen Amy come panting up the hill, had pressed his body back into the shadow and watched her, happily surprised at her luck, slip in at the postern door, then, when all was safe, to follow her in and shoot the well-oiled bolts . . .

He turned away, and a sudden qualm shot through his heart. Was he indeed mad? Was he imagining too much? . . If he were wrong, the consequences would be too dreadful to face – himself discredited, and Edward lost; for Sedley would have no difficulty in revising his opinions about the Major's actual guilt. He clasped his hands behind his back and walked away through the rain.

Sergeant Ward was waiting to see him, with the old complaint about that stolen silver.

"We've got to do something," he said in an aggrieved tone. "And we're not moving on the obvious line. I know you don't like the idea, but I'm beginning to come round to the notion that Miss Fullerton took the articles away in her trunk. I don't see that we shall get any further until I go up to town and see her."

"I've never suggested that you shouldn't go and see her!"

"No, Mr. West, that is so . . . Oh, it's a petty business at the best! It's really the inspector who's so keen on having it looked into. He thinks that in a mystery case like this you never know when apparently unrelated details don't hang together. I don't see it myself . . . unless there's a plot on. Well, I'd like to suggest to him that he goes up to town himself, and watch his face! I'll have to go; unless you've a better idea, sir?"

"No . . ."

Jack Willoughby suddenly walked into the gate-house in search of letters, and noticing West and the officer, lingered as though he hoped to hear matters of interest. He was probably bored in the billiard-room.

"Horrible weather!" he complained. "This place strikes cold."

West walked away and left him to Ward's gentle entertainment. It struck him as the best expression he had yet heard of the Cleys' atmosphere . . . "This place strikes cold." Cold! On a warm day it could make one shiver, and now, in the rain . . .

Chapter XIII
PETTY LARCENY

A MAID was busy in a pretty room in the small wing as West went by the open door. The paint was white and the hangings pale green. An open cabin trunk stood upon the moss-green carpet, and beside it were a hat-box and a suede handbag. The maid was folding a garment, and presently she laid it in the trunk and took up another from the pile on the divan.

"Is anyone leaving?" asked West.

The maid looked up.

"Yes, sir, Miss Hyde is leaving to-morrow. The police gentleman told her she could. This trunk is going to Cwm Dyffod to-night."

"What is your name?"

"Blodwen, sir."

"Do you usually pack for ladies who have been staying here, Blodwen?"

"Yes, sir, if they don't bring their own maid. I used to be lady's maid at Lady Mervyn's."

West asked thoughtfully: "Did you pack for Miss Fullerton when she left? You remember Miss Fullerton?"

"Oh, yes, sir. I packed for her. She went quite suddenly in the evening. I remember she dragged her trunk out in a great hurry, and she was flinging things out of drawers and I was packing them as fast as I could."

"Had she a large trunk?"

"Oh, no, sir. Just a little cabin trunk. I had hard work to

get all her things in. Patterson came in at the last, and we sat on it and got it fastened and he carried it downstairs."

"Now Blodwen, listen carefully. Did you see that trunk empty and fill it yourself, and never leave it until it was fastened and carried down to the car?"

"Yes, sir, that's quite right."

"Had Miss Fullerton any other luggage?"

"No, sir, except her handbag."

"How large was that?"

The girl opened her eyes.

"Just a little handbag, sir – like this."

She picked up Pandora's, which was of grey suede and could not have held anything more than a purse and a handkerchief.

"Thank you, Blodwen."

West wandered out into the parterre and sent Patterson to fetch Sergeant Ward. He described the conversation he had just had with the maid.

"Those twenty-two stolen articles," he said, "would have filled a fair-sized suit-case. Miss Fullerton took no such case away with her, and I think we can be certain that her trunk contained nothing but her clothes. Patterson carried the trunk down to the car, and Sabelle put it into the luggage container, and off they went!"

"There's a leakage somewhere," said Ward. "I think I'll run up to town and see her. I shall be better satisfied. None of the articles have been disposed of yet – I'm in touch with the pawnbrokers and dealers."

Ward left an hour later for London, and returned in the small hours of the following morning.

West, snug in bed, heard the police car roaring in over the drawbridge, and glancing at his luminous watch saw that it was ten minutes to three. He hesitated, but his curiosity was great. He reached out for his dressing-gown, and five minutes later was watching Ward devouring his belated supper and listening to his story.

"You're right," said Ward tersely. "That girl didn't do it. The butler at her home took in one cabin trunk only from the car, and that was carried to her room and opened at once by a maid. The butler even looked inside the luggage container to see that nothing had been left behind. I asked Miss Fullerton where they stopped for supper, and she told me 'The Nut-Brown Maid' at Witney. I called there on my way back, and they remembered the young couple having supper at about nine o'clock on the Wednesday night; but Miss Fullerton hadn't left any suit-case to be called for. The car had stood right in front of the inn while they were inside, and nothing was taken off it."

"So you're inclined to count Miss Fullerton out?"

"Oh, quite!" The sergeant corrugated his brow. "Now we're up against it again!"

"Then if she didn't steal the things," said West calmly, "Sabelle did."

"Sabelle? . . . Sabelle!"

West shrugged his shoulders. "Process of elimination."

"But why should he?"

"Why should Miss Fullerton?"

Ward bolted a preserved peach whole, and groaned: "It's too much for me! How could Sabelle have got the things away, anyhow?"

"Packed them in a small suit-case. Takes the suit-case to the garage and puts it in the bottom of the luggage container. Drives the car round to the courtyard, takes Rene's trunk from Patterson, and crams it into the luggage container on top of the suit-case. At the inn where they stop for supper, and where inquiry is likely to be made, he does nothing. Half an hour out from London he makes an excuse to stop at a wayside pub – cup of coffee, perhaps – sends Rene inside, runs the car round to the back, deposits suit-case, and books a room for the night, saying he'll return in about an hour. He runs Rene home, returns to the inn, and collects the suit-case wherein the silver reposes wrapped up in his pyjamas. If you test that, Ward, I think it'll hold water."

Ward looked up slowly.

"I've a good mind to. I could put Blackmore on to it. If he starts early he'll be back to-night. But, holy mackerel! has everybody in this house got kleptomania? Sabelle to-day; it'll be Sir Harry himself to-morrow!"

Ward was not a man to sleep while there was work to be done, and before he would consent to retire to his bed he roused Blackmore from his slumbers and primed him for his journey Londonwards. He was to travel by car and make his inquiries at every inn he came to within fifteen miles of the city.

In the chilly dawn Blackmore departed with a grinding of gears, for his skill as a driver was limited, and West went back to bed, where he slept so soundly that breakfast was almost over when he descended. He was greeted by the usual late-comer jokes by Jack Willoughby, who, like the rest, knew nothing of the midnight conference. Pandora and Crown were not in the best of tempers, for in view of the fact that his belief in Major Stacey's guilt was shaken, and the probability of fresh revelations, Sedley had cancelled their leave to depart.

During the morning West was able to pay Edward a visit. He found his friend sitting on his bed, placidly reading a novel and gnawing his finger-ends for lack of the cigarette which he was not allowed when he was alone. Edward was a different man from the tight-lipped, obstinate creature of West's previous visit. The rôle of martyr had not sat well upon him, and it had been a strain on his wits to remember all the time that he was guilty and must act accordingly.

He greeted West with a meaning smile, and after a few minutes' conversation he himself volunteered the explanation which West had been wondering how best to extract.

"I suppose it was a pretty rotten thing," said Edward, gratefully appropriating his friend's cigarette-case, "to suspect Amy at all, and yet from my point of view circumstances were all against her and from the first I've thought her guilty. Mind you, I haven't blamed her. It isn't for me to condemn anyone. I didn't like the way Undine treated that girl, and it seemed to me that the girl had yielded to a temporary madness, a sudden temptation, and committed murder. I didn't know much about her, neither her disposition nor her inherited tendencies. There had been nothing between us, in spite of all this talk, except a kiss or two – you know how it is in an idle moment . . .

"Well, on the night we played hide-and-seek, this is what

happened. I went up to Amy's room to fetch her a little before nine o'clock, and she wasn't there. The fire was burning brightly, so I knew she couldn't have been gone long. I waited a few minutes, and then went to the billiard-room to see if she was there, but the time was getting on, and as it was I was late in sounding the gong. Then when the game was all over and most people had gone to bed – in fact I was on my way to bed myself – I had a sudden impulse to go and explain to Amy and ask her where she had been. I went to her room about ten minutes to twelve. The door was still ajar as I had left it, and the fire was out. She evidently hadn't been back to her room. I wondered at the time, but next morning we were all full of Undine's disappearance and I forgot all about Amy. It was only after the discovery of the murder that I – well, put two and two together! I didn't see how the detectives could possibly get on to her trail, but they did; so I lied and so on, to save her. But when it wasn't any good and they got her . . . poor little kid . . . West, there had been murder in my heart towards Undine! I felt it was my crime rather than that child's. It was easy for me to take the blame!"

Edward drew on his cigarette until it crackled. Suddenly he showed his splendid teeth in a wide smile.

"I took you in, Lionel, didn't I? In fact, I'm not sure yet that I shall ever forgive you for thinking me guilty of a sneaking crime like that. I might have shot Undine before her face . . . but I'd never have smothered her in the dark. And you suspected me from the first, didn't you? Own up!"

"I did," said West, meeting his friend with level gaze.

"You did! And you'd nothing but some wild suspicion to

hang your verdict on, not a shred of evidence. Oh, you lawyers!"

West said slowly, "I had evidence, Edward!"

"What do you mean?"

"Circumstantial evidence, and yet . . . You see, it pointed two ways, and the first time I took the wrong turning and it led me to you. Now I have retraced my steps and taken the other way, and it has led me to the guilty man."

"Tell me."

"The evening I came down here," said West, drawing up his chair, "Inspector Sedley took me to the garret to look over the scene of the crime."

He went on to describe how their attention was drawn to the wiped latch of the Norman cabinet, and how they were able to decide that the murderer had actually hidden there either before or after the crime.

"There were shuffled footmarks on the floor of the cabinet," said West; "there were elbow-marks rubbed in the dust on the sides of the cabinet; and there was a great smudge among the dust and cobwebs on the ceiling of the cabinet where the murderer in standing upright had bumped his head. Now as I stood inside there with the door closed, I suddenly realised that far from bumping my head, the top of my cranium was still a good two inches from the ceiling of the cabinet. I am five feet nine inches tall; and therefore I calculated that the cabinet was six feet, and that the bump had been made by someone six feet or over in height . . . Edward, there were only two people in the castle who fitted that requirement! Yourself, to whom motive and everything pointed – and one who had no motive and to all appearances was blameless to a degree, Cecil Sabelle!"

The Major looked dazed.

"Cecil Sabelle!" he repeated stupidly. "Young Cecil Sabelle!"

"That is what I have been saying to myself, Edward, ever since I knew you weren't guilty."

"But why? How, in the name of Heaven — ? It's absurd on the face of it!"

"I know. But it's true!"

"How can you possibly prove it?"

"By finding that all-important factor, his motive. When you come to think of it, he had the opportunity. He knew the castle as no one else did, except Lady Stacey. He knew the garret; had probably played there as a child. I believe he went there to hide and was actually in the cabinet when she came up and hid in the chest. But why such an apparently harmless, good-natured young ass should take the opportunity to perpetrate a crime of such devilish malice is beyond my power to imagine!"

"And he and Undine were so friendly!" put in Edward, emphasising the words with blows of fist on palm. "He was about the only person who could keep on good terms with her . . . Lionel, it seems all wrong to me!"

"Keep it to yourself!"

"Of course."

West wandered away from that interview with drawn brows. Now that he had actually given expression to his secret conviction he began to find other points to support his theory. Provided that a motive could be found, he could just imagine the horrible Puckishness with which Cecil would race at midnight about the haunted corridors of the castle he knew so well, Undine's mink coat over his arm and the emerald ring, extracted from Pandora's carelessly dangling bag, gleefully clasped in his hand. And, if as Enid's pitiful last letter had said, the letter to Lady Charlotte Wright had been left lying all day on Undine's writing-table, any chance visitor to the room with a bent for mischief could easily have found it and carried it away for future use.

West, fumbling in his pocket, drew out a sheet of paper and discovered the Chart of Comparative Guilt that he had once made. He had awarded Sabelle a total of ten marks only. It just showed how deceptive appearances could be. Motive, none! And there was no prospect of a solution of that mystery. No motive, no evidence; and Sabelle was as safe as houses, even if the whole of Scotland Yard knew, as West knew, that he was guilty!

On a sudden impulse he asked for a packet of sandwiches and, taking a stick and a macintosh, set out to walk. He plunged boldly away from the road towards the mountains, and soon found a wild, delightful valley to tempt his exploring feet. He walked for miles without meeting a soul or seeing any living creature except the timid flocks moving like grey clouds over the olive-green mountains. Finally the valley itself proved disappointing, for it led nowhere but seemed to go on for ever, and at last he had to turn and come back all the way he had gone, which is always an anti-climax to a country walk.

He reached the castle at about five o'clock, and saw that the police car had returned and was standing in the gateway looking very dejected after its exertions. West went to his room, and to his joy was followed by Patterson with a tray of tea.

"Has anything happened?" he asked, watching Patterson light the spirit lamp under the tiny kettle. "Where is everyone?"

"Sir Harry has been in the study most of the day, sir. Mr. Crown and Miss Hyde are in the garden, and I think Mr. Sabelle is in the billiard-room doing something to the wireless . . . Have you everything you want, sir?"

"Yes, thank you, Patterson. That tea is the brightest thought you ever had!"

"Very good, sir."

Patterson withdrew, and collided with Sergeant Ward, who was approaching at high speed.

"Can I come in, Mr. West?"

"Yes, do . . . You don't mind if I drink?"

"Oh, no; you go on and have your tea, Mr. West . . . Blackmore's back!"

"Oh, yes?"

Ward released a look of genuine admiration.

"And it's just as you said! The 'Dog and Hind,' little old-fashioned place just on the other side of Brentford. It took Blackmore a while to find. He tried eight other places and drew blank. Then he got to the 'Dog and Hind,' rather an attractive little place with window-boxes, standing back from the road. The landlord, Alfred Platt, was doing his accounts on Wednesday night when at five minutes to eleven he was knocked up by two people in a dark-blue two-seater saloon car, XB 5496, and admitted a young man and a young woman answering to the descriptions of Sabelle and Miss Fullerton. Besides, that is Sabelle's car number all right. The young man said they had come a long journey and could they have some coffee. Platt was unwilling to serve them at first as his wife and the servant had gone to bed, but the young man was very pressing and offered him ten shillings each for two cups of coffee, so he showed them into the parlour and went to the kitchen to put on the kettle. The young man followed him and asked if he might have some water for his car. He then ran the car round to the back and took the water there. There was a cabin trunk in the luggage container. Sabelle – we may as well give him his name – took this out, and from underneath it a suitcase. He then replaced the cabin trunk, and asked Platt if he might engage a room for the night. He was running the young lady into London, he said, and would return in about an hour. He would leave his suitcase and pay for the room in advance; whereupon he laid down a pound note. Platt said he could only offer him a shakedown, and Sabelle said that would do quite well. He then returned to the lady, and after drinking their coffee very quickly they drove away. Platt carried the suit-case upstairs to an empty bedroom. It was locked, and rather heavy; too heavy to contain only the usual clothing and accessories. He thought the whole affair rather unusual and would not have been surprised if the young man had not appeared again. However, Sabelle returned soon after midnight and went to his room, leaving his car in the garage. Next morning he signed the register as Eric Edwards, Liverpool, and drove away at about nine o'clock with his suit-case. Platt concluded it was some romantic escapade. That's all, but it doesn't leave us with anything lacking, does it? . . . Now do you act, or shall I? You see, I can't charge Sabelle without Sir Harry's consent. Are we to tell Sir Harry what we've found out, or shall we tackle Sabelle and try and get the things back? After all, I didn't come down here to play at petty larceny; I came down to investigate murder, and I must say we don't seem to be getting any farther now that Sedley only half believes the man who says he's guilty!"

Ward hunched his shoulders in an aggrieved fashion.

"I'll see Sabelle myself," said West; "I think he's alone now in the billiard-room."

"Thanks, that's good. You'll have to bluff him a bit, Mr. West."

"I dare say I can manage it," said West coolly.

In the billiard-room a grandfather clock ticked with deliberate solemnity. Cecil Sabelle was perched on the end of a divan with a small battery in one hand and a testing lamp in the other.

"Oh, hallo!" he called cheerfully; "I thought you'd gone out for the day. This battery's a dud. Have you had any tea?"

West lit a cigarette and sat down on the other end of the divan.

"Do you know a man called Eric Edwards?" he asked casually. "He comes from Liverpool."

Sabelle pushed back his forelock and turned a deeply interested eye.

"Yes," he answered calmly; "I was at school with him. Do

you know him too?"

"He ran Miss Fullerton home on Wednesday night in your car," went on West. "And he spent the night at a place called the 'Dog and Hind,' at Brentford, carrying a suit-case which contained twenty-two small articles belonging to the drawing-room cabinets at Cleys Castle."

"There's a comic scenario!" said Sabelle, apparently unmoved.

"It's this way," said West slowly. "The police have got the facts, and I just met Ward on his way to get Sir Harry's formal charge against you. I stopped him, because I wanted to hear what you had to say. I can offer you an alternative. If you persist in bluffing me, then the prosecution will have to go forward, and I assure you you haven't a loophole. But if you'll own up to me now, and promise to return the stolen goods, that shall be the end of the affair and I'll make it right with Sir Harry!"

West waited, his calm face hiding a perfect volcano of suspense. Everything depended on Sabelle's answer, for the last thing West wanted was to see him arrested for theft and placed in custody, safe from self-betrayal.

Sabelle twisted the plugs of his battery.

"I expect you're feeling pretty sick about the Major?" he said in tones artlessly sympathetic.

"Very sick," said West dryly.

"Well, look here, Mr. West" – the older man waited breathlessly – "just between you and me, and because I think you'll be decent about it . . . I did steal those things."

There was a moment's silence. West found an ash-tray and flicked his cigarette.

"I'm glad you owned up," he said as casually as possible. "Why did you let us suspect Rene Fullerton?"

"I didn't . . . At least I did all I could to put you off her. I can't imagine what made you suspect her!"

"Her visit to the drawing-room. Patterson — "

"Oh, that! Well, I'd never have taken the things at all if I'd known old Patterson took such an interest in them. It was easy enough to pinch his keys. I thought the loss would never be noticed!"

The young man was talking easily again in his natural, bantering tone. He might have been discussing a round of golf rather than his own serious misdemeanour.

"But what could have made you steal Sir Harry's silver?"

The pertinent question brought Sabelle up sharply. For a moment he hesitated with guarded eyes, and then replied awkwardly:

"The obvious reason, Mr. West. I wanted money."

"Money? But surely — "

"Oh, you mean Sir Harry's quarter of a million that he paid for the place!" Sabelle said quickly. "You see, the mater got that. She and my three older sisters live in town, and they're frightfully extravagant. You ought to see the place they keep up! I only get what the mater allows me, and she believes in keeping a fellow short. I owe money all over London! I had to get hold of something saleable, and it was a sudden temptation."

"Then have you sold these things?"

"I'm afraid I have. I sold them when I took Rene to town."

"And paid your debts with the money?"

"Yes. I had to get clear. But I'll buy the things back if you'll give me time. I'll get the money out of the mater somehow. I'll write to the dealer and ask him to hold them over for me." Sabelle's face was flushed with his eagerness to oblige. His eyes were as candid as those of a puppy. "And you'll make it all right for me, Mr. West?"

"I think I can promise you that Sir Harry won't prosecute. I must see him, of course."

"And, Mr. West" – the young man grinned artlessly – "don't you think I'd better get back to town? It's rather a delicate situation, me stopping in the house after – this."

"You'll have to see the police about that," said West shortly. "You may even have to put up with the delicate situation."

Sabelle grinned again and wrinkled his nose appreciatively. An icy shudder of disgust ran through West's veins. He hurried away with a violent loathing for this monstrosity whose unclouded eyes and gay, evasive chatter hid the unfounded malice of a demon.

Five minutes later he was closeted with Ward and giving the detective a detailed account of his recent conversation.

"And so," he concluded, "you had better leave the matter with me and make no further move. I will take the responsibility of speaking for Sir Harry. I will make things right with him to-night."

"I see." Ward tapped his teeth thoughtfully. "Well, it's all very tame after all. I didn't think Sabelle would come across so meekly, and I did think the explanation might be more suggestive. Instead of that he tells the obvious story!"

"With two bad lies in it," said West grimly.

"What do you mean?"

"Sabelle is not a man of obvious motives. He told the story that he thought would appeal to obvious and straightforward people like you and me."

"How do you know he was lying?"

"Think the story over. You can see one lie for yourself."

Ward in meditation was an impressive sight. After about five minutes he looked up slowly like a man coming out of chloroform.

"He said he had sold the goods to a dealer. He hasn't; I'm in touch with all the dealers. He's still got them!"

"Quite right," said West. "And here's the other thing. He said that he was heavily in debt and pressed for money, and stole those things to sell and satisfy his creditors. I had a conversation with Sir Harry the other night. Not one of the stolen articles had any intrinsic value! They were not worth twenty pounds!"

"Is that so? Sabelle may have thought they were valuable."

"Sabelle had been brought up with them! He knew to a penny what they were worth!"

And as he thought about the significance of those two lies, West suddenly knew, as though a searchlight had been turned into the obstinate tenebrosity of his brain, why Cecil Sabelle had murdered Lady Stacey.

Chapter XIV
THE BATTLEMENTS OF CLEYS

PATTERSON placed the decanters on the dinner table, with horrified finger removed a crumb from the spotless oak, and withdrew.

"I've got to go up to town in the morning," said Sir Harry. He frowned as he said it, as though the necessity were a distasteful one.

Pandora leaned forward and half opened her lips, but Crown tapped her elbow and she turned a surprised but obedient glance upon her sulky-eyed lover.

Sabelle, like a bad child who has been admitted to table on sufferance, sat rather quietly, trying to steal a glance of approval from anyone who would bestow it.

"I don't think I've mentioned it before," said Sir Harry, "but there's no point in making a secret of it. I'm selling Cleys. Under the circumstances — "

"Quite!" said Crown, inclining his glossy head. "One understands."

West, too, was far from surprised that Sir Harry should wish to be rid for ever of a place of such dreadful memory.

"It seems rather a shame!" said Pandora.

Sabelle flung up his head.

"Shame – nothing!" He glared at Pandora. "Who wants an ugly prison like this? We were glad to be rid of it!"

Pandora subsided meekly.

West, with tingling palms, stared down at his fruit plate.

"I'm afraid you're right, Cecil," said Sir Harry. "It is an ugly prison." He pushed away his glass, and propping his chin on his hand stared unhappily into a gloomy corner of the room.

"I felt like abandoning the place to ruin. But the agents telephoned me yesterday to say that they'd had an offer. It seems that a film director from California is in London, wanting more than anything in the world to buy a real English castle. He's prepared to pay anything, and I don't care if this place goes for an old song. So I shall go up to see him first thing to-morrow morning and fetch him down here, and I propose that the deal shall be through by to-morrow night. He'll find me easy when it comes to the bargain. Cleys is going cheap!"

His fist suddenly dropped with a crash to the table, and it seemed as though the echoes of that sound ran wailing into the dark corners of the room, and shivering through the rafters away along the stone passages of the doomed castle.

"D – does that mean that w – we shall be able to go away?" stammered Pandora.

Crown nudged her savagely, and Sir Harry turned a dull and perplexed gaze upon her.

"I don't know . . . I can't say," he said heavily. He was thinking of his brother under the terrible charge.

"Do you start early?" asked Sabelle in the lightest of conversational tones, as though all he wished were to dispel the atmosphere of gloom and restore a happy calm to the company.

"I ordered the car for nine o'clock."

"Oh, yes?" Sabelle drew out his silver case. "Pan, may I smoke? One has to ask a lady, but her answer is immaterial. Bang goes another Gold Flake! You'll have a good run, Sir

Harry. Rene and I did it nicely in four hours, not counting stops."

He actually had the grace to look embarrassed as he realised the tactlessness of his remark, and added hastily: "What do movie directors look like? Well, to-morrow we shall know. It'll be a change to see a new face!"

West jumped up. "Please excuse me," he said curtly, and went to his room.

He stood staring by the window, wondering what he should do. The scarlet banner drooped against a sea-green sky. There was no movement in the castle bailey, where the grass-grown flags were stained by the lurid light of evening. The old walls waited for another cast of Fate, another owner, another conqueror. The ivy hung like a pall on the gaping windows of the banqueting hall. An atmosphere was diffused, half melancholy, half malignant.

West hastened to Sir Harry's study. His host was there, engrossed in writing a letter under the shaded desk lamp.

"Harry," said West, "don't bring that stranger here to-morrow night."

"Why?"

"Because he won't go away alive."

"What do you mean?"

"I mean the Spirit of Cleys won't like him," said West grimly.

"Lionel, you're mad!"

"Am I? Well, don't do it."

"How can I stop him? He'll have to see the place before he buys it."

"Put him off for a week."

"I could do that, but – I'll have to go up to-morrow and see him. Are you sure you're sane?"

"Quite sure. You must take my word for it."

"Well, tell me if you've changed your mind by breakfast-time. It will upset my plans considerably."

West slept badly that night. It was baffling to watch a man like Sabelle who was so skilled against self-betrayal. West's only strong card was the fact that Sabelle had not the least idea he was suspected. Now that the affair of the stolen silver had apparently blown over he was perfectly secure and at ease.

Would he try to kill the film director? West strongly suspected that he would, and he almost wished that his conscience would allow him to sacrifice this stranger for the sake of capturing his criminal. But that could not be. He must save the man's life, and incidentally Sabelle's neck! He groaned. He still had no evidence against Sabelle, and the story was too fantastic for any police officer, much less a jury.

He fell asleep in the dawn, and woke to broad daylight with a violent jerk into consciousness and the feeling that something was wrong.

He sprang out of bed and ran to the window. The scene was peaceful enough, but he had certainly overslept himself. His bedside clock said five minutes to nine. Under the gateway stood the great, glittering Rolls, with its nose pointed to the drawbridge, and Morton standing at ease beside it, ready for his master's appearance.

West began to fling on his clothes. He must see Harry before he started for London, to remind him that their interview of last night still held good. But almost immediately came the slam of the motor door and the roar of the engine, and West, dropping his second sock, was only in time to see the Rolls glide out of sight. Sir Harry was gone, two minutes before his time!

West sat down on his bed and ran his fingers through his hair. At least, the issue was out of his hands. If the film director came — !

He flung on his dressing-gown and made for the bathroom.

What was that? . . . A crack like a pistol shot, shattering the thick, sun-soaked air!

He waited for ten breathless seconds; and then, sharp and clear out of the distance came the reports . . . one . . . two . . three, four, five! It was the bark of a revolver. And then a desperate silence.

He raced downstairs as he was. Already people were appearing as if from nowhere: the servants, Patterson, Blackmore, Ward, Crown with a slice of toast in his hand, Sedley looking like an offended giraffe.

"Get out there, somebody!" he snapped, "and see what's happened."

There was a rush for the gate-house. Ward was the first to clatter across the drawbridge.

"Ha!" he shouted. "Look there!"

Half a mile away, over the flat, unsheltered road a figure was lurching and stumbling towards the castle.

"Come on!" cried West. "It's Sir Harry!"

As he ran he thought what a fool he'd been to overlook the chance of this. And yet by some miracle Harry was alive!

With the crowd of them streaming after him, he caught his friend in his arms. Sir Harry was gasping for breath, as though he had run a long way.

"The car," he croaked. "A hundred yards back . . . Morton's hit . . . get to him! . . . No, no, I'm all right . . . only a bit . . . winded."

"What happened? . . . Who was it?" everybody was clamouring.

"Ward! You and Robinson get along to the car," ordered Sedley. "Now, Sir Harry, try and tell us what happened."

"I hardly know myself . . . We had just got to that part of the road where the thickets begin when the first shot came. I was sitting at the front next to Morton, and it came clean through the glass on a level with my head. And if you'll believe me, at that very minute I had dropped my paper and stooped down to pick it up! The bullet got Morton in the shoulder and he fell over the wheel. The car lurched. I dragged on the hand brake and shut off the engine, pulling Morton down beside me on the floor of the car. Then five shots crashed in rather wildly. One of them skimmed the top of my head – look! I saw no one. He must have been hiding in the thicket. I believe he made off after firing; I heard the cracking of the bushes. I had to risk it and come for help. Who could he have been? It's a mercy he had no more ammunition!"

"Hallo!" came a cheerful, drawling shout. "What's all this musical comedy?"

Sabelle, in tolerably clean grey flannels, his fair hair as tousled as ever and his face engagingly blank, came lounging, hands in pockets, along the moat side.

West had a second to act. He wheeled round and shouted, "Sedley! Get that man! He's your murderer!"

He sprang as he shouted at Sabelle, with Sedley and Blackmore at his heels. The young man's ingenuous face seemed to crack up in an amazing way. For an instant the eyes of a wolf blazed out of his livid mask; then he dashed for the drawbridge and disappeared in the gloom of the castle gate.

Sedley drew his gun and fired as he ran. The echoes shrieked back at him from the towering walls.

They dashed into the courtyard . . . "That way!" screamed a terrified maid, pointing to the grim, worn stairs of the keep.

There followed a quarter of an hour of desperate chase. The stone passages rang and groaned with the din of the flying hunted man and his pursuers.

"Drive him up!" yelled Sedley. "Up to the roof. Keep that stair. Close in, you men."

They burst on to the roof of the keep. There against the brilliant sky Sabelle had taken his last stand, poised on the boulderous crest of the battlement, astride like a great, grey spread-eagle between the slender rows of rusting pikes which bristled high above the keep.

With a backward spring, he whirled for a second in the sun, and plunged from sight. His body missed the moat, and cracked like an egg against the stanchion of the drawbridge.

Ward was the first to reach him.

"He's alive," he said grimly, staring down at the quivering

thing.

A spasm tore through the body. It opened its eyes and stared at West.

"How did you know?" it whispered; and then, more fiercely, "Yes! And I'd do it again. Kill! Kill!"

With a last desperate effort Sabelle dragged his shoulders from the stones. His right arm shot up. His peaked face seemed to blaze with light between the wet, blood-streaked rags of yellow hair.

The voice of a warrior already dead burst from his throat in a ringing cry: "Cleys is mine! And against all Wales I stand at bay! For I am Sabelle, the Lord of the Marches."

* * *

"There was once a young man," said Lionel West: "the last of a long and dying line of English warrior barons. His ancestors, a magnificent stock, in the old turbulent days when England was carving out its kingdom had held with unwearied valour the King's lands on the Welsh border. Every Sabelle of the past had lived a strenuous life and died bravely. The banner that drooped above their gallant, battered castle was as honoured as it was ancient. But this young man of the twentieth century saw the end of all that glory. His own father lived only for the pleasures of the table, a man of mean spirit and self-indulgence, characteristics which had been horribly repeated with increasing viciousness in the Sabelles of the last three generations. He died, and left behind him for his only son nothing but debts, and that battered, shamed inheritance, the castle of his ancestors' pride. And because that was saleable, at last it must go to provide luxury for and complete the ruin of the family.

"There stood this last young Sabelle, a boy of twenty-three, smitten with horror, recognising in his own idle body and furtive mind the seeds of that same decay of manliness and chivalry. His one passion in life was the castle. He worshipped fiercely every stone of it, every shred of its tradition. No one knew. His own family would have laughed at him and called him a fool.

"So Cleys was sold and strangers came to take possession, and young Sabelle worked feverishly to win their confidence, clinging like a dog to his treasure.

"How would they treat it? Would they revere Cleys and honour its tradition? He watched with jealous eyes. Against one thing his pride revolted, that they should ever guess how fiercely he cared. So he would mock, and disparage the place, and play the empty young fool to perfection. He took every one in; it was a perfect disguise.

"Then there came to Cleys a possessive woman. Her husband had bought her the castle, all it contained, all it stood for.

"Undine, Lady Stacey, had conquered Cleys for herself and her children, and driven out the poor, shivering name of Sabelle. She must be châtelaine now and order the disposal of every room, every chair. This tapestry must be taken down from the place where it had hung for centuries, and be transferred to her own apartments. Those dresses, laid to rest in a quiet garret, rustling plaintively with memories of the dead to whom they had belonged, are to her good for nothing but to amuse her guests and to be ripped and rent by clumsy young hands and dancing feet. Rene Fullerton may go to a London ball tricked out in the pathetic finery of a Sabelle lady, by the kind grace of Undine Stacey. And the last insult of all, her son must stand upon the shamed hearthstone and invoke for himself at her bidding the sacred spirit of all that belonged so passionately and supremely to the Sabelle race.

"Young Sabelle, outraged at his own helplessness, burning with the fierce old blood in him, had doomed her from that moment. And that very night, when he had fled to hide in the garret where he had often played as a child, Fate brought his enemy and delivered her into his hands!"

"Then he had no grudge against Harry," said Edward Stacey, "until — "

"Cleys to be sold again, and to a film producer! Never! Sir Harry was also a vandal; he must die. It was Sabelle's last gesture. I should have foreseen it. I thought it would be the stranger at whom he would strike."

"But when did he lower his guard? When did you suspect his secret?"

"When he formed the plan of carrying away some of those little treasures of his race to feast his eyes upon when he should be compelled to return to London, Sabelle began his own undoing. They were of no intrinsic value, we knew, but their sentimental value to a true Sabelle would be enormous. And if young Cecil would steal for the sake of sentimental values, then our whole conception of his character must be wrong. And if he had deliberately led us astray as to his character, then for what purpose was his deception? Flick aside that carefully assumed mask of Cecil Sabelle, reveal a man who cared too passionately for a past of which he was not worthy, and all our broken pieces came together and the story was complete."

West paused before a flagstone in the ruined banqueting hall, and pointed with his stick to an inscription that was carved too black and deep even for the storms of centuries to destroy.

Est mihi Cleys uni: Galli procul este: Sabellus invocor: hos campos mi paruisse juvat.

... 'Cleys is mine, and against all Wales I stand at bay! For I am Sabelle, the Lord of the Marches.'

* * *

Three months later West was compelled by the ties of loyalty and convention to be present at the wedding of his friend, Major Stacey. Little Amy Farbell had made good use of the mellow moments which followed the release of her chivalrous hero. When it was all over, sated with cold fowl, champagne, tight shoes, and a silk hat, West crept eagerly back to the perfect peace of his comfortable flat.

"Most unsuitable match," he mused gloomily, watching the London sparrows fight on his window-sill. "She's no more the girl for Edward than he's the man for her. But – bah – who dare argue with an infatuated woman?"

And he gave himself a treat that night: his favourite dinner, and a stall at his favourite theatre, three new books from his favourite bookseller, and a very, very good cigar.

9/21